
★

Jake and his associate had Wiley on the stretcher and were bearing him away. Wiley lay still, a model patient, but not for long. His exhibitionist urges soon took over. He sat upright and began clawing at his chest. Then he suddenly pitched backward, arms windmilling wildly in a reprise of his movie death. Jake and the other bearer set the stretcher down. Wiley stopped flailing and lay still again. Jake bent over Wiley's prone form. The next instant, he jumped onto Wiley and started pummeling Wiley's chest with his fists. Linette screamed. Ginny let out an answering howl. She broke away from her father and rushed onto the field where Jake was trying to pound Wiley back to life.

★

Previously published Worldwide Mystery title by
LESLIE WHEELER

MURDER AT PLIMOTH PLANTATION

Leslie Wheeler

MURDER AT GETTYSBURG

WORLDWIDE.

TORONTO • NEW YORK • LONDON
AMSTERDAM • PARIS • SYDNEY • HAMBURG
STOCKHOLM • ATHENS • TOKYO • MILAN
MADRID • WARSAW • BUDAPEST • AUCKLAND

To my parents and their friends,
the late Gilbert Flues and his wife, Anne,
who took me on my first trip to Gettysburg,
and to Bob and Nicholas,
who made the second trip with me

MURDER AT GETTYSBURG

A Worldwide Mystery/February 2007

First published by Five Star Publishing.

ISBN-13: 978-0-373-26590-9
ISBN-10: 0-373-26590-5

Printed in U.S.A.

Acknowledgments

I wish to thank the reenactors I spoke with at the 137th Anniversary of Gettysburg for sharing their experiences with me, and all the others who took part for making the battle come vividly alive. R. Lee Hadden's book, *Reliving the Civil War: A Reenactor's Handbook,* 2nd Edition, also provided me with useful information about various aspects of Civil War reenactment, and *Confederates in the Attic: Dispatches from the Unfinished Civil War,* by Tony Horwitz, introduced me to a colorful cast of die-hard Confederates I would not have met otherwise.

Again I am very grateful to the members of my writers' critique group—Mark Ammons, Kathy Fast, the late Margaret Leibenstein, Cheryl Marceau and Barbara Ross—who saw this book through its different drafts and offered helpful advice and encouragement. Thanks also go to my first editors, Susan Oleksiw and Skye Alexander, and to my second editor, Hugh Abramson, for suggestions that helped make this a better book.

Finally, I would like to thank the late Gilbert Flues for his eloquent reading from Douglas Southall Freeman's biography of Robert E. Lee on my first trip to Gettysburg; my husband, Robert A. Stein, for his continued love and support, especially at times of extreme preoccupation on my part; and my son, Nicholas L. Stein, for the same, including watching all four hours and twenty minutes of the movie *Gettysburg* with me, and providing technical assistance during my various computer crises.

ONE

"Where are the thousands who marched in that proud line from the woods?"

R. E. Lee, A Biography

"GETTYSBURG, EH?"

I turned reluctantly to the man squeezed next to me on the crowded shuttle flight from Boston to Washington, D.C. A businessman, judging from his suit, he obviously wanted to talk, as this was the second time he'd tried to start a conversation. I didn't want to be rude, but after the flurry of my departure, which had included a last-minute trip to the convenience store for cat food and litter and an I'll-show-you escape attempt by my cat, I just wanted to sit back and relax.

"How did you know?"

"Your book." He pointed at the glossy paperback of Michael Shaara's historical novel about Gettysburg, *The Killer Angels,* I'd brought along for light reading. "That, too." His fingertips grazed the top of the folded printout of the Gettysburg Anniversary Committee's schedule of events for the coming weekend I was using for a bookmark.

"One of the worst bloodbaths of the Civil War," he remarked. "All three days of it."

I nodded. "Fortunately, I'm only going to a reenactment."

"Those things can be dangerous, too," he warned. "There was that Frenchman nearly killed someone at a Gettysburg reenactment a couple of years ago."

I felt a quiver of unease. "What happened?"

"Seems he borrowed an antique pistol from a friend, didn't

know it was loaded, got up close and personal with another re-enactor during the battle, fired, and just missed the other guy's jugular. Story was in the papers. Sure you don't remember?"

"I must've missed it. But thanks for telling me," I said politely, wishing he hadn't. I opened my book and made a show of reading. I could feel the businessman's eyes on me, but after a few moments, he gave up and opened his newspaper. When I thought he was absorbed in *The Boston Globe,* I rummaged in my tote bag for the photo I had secretly treasured all these years.

There we stood on Cemetery Ridge at the spot known as the Bloody Angle, where General George Pickett had aimed his fateful charge on July 3, 1863, the final day of the Gettysburg Battle. Teacher and his adoring pupil. We posed beside the huge bronze open book with the names of the Union and Confederate commanders who had taken part in the pivotal battle, which had ended Robert E. Lee's second invasion of the North and ulti-mately cost the Confederates the war. The copse of trees, marking the farthest advance of Pickett's men and the High Water Mark of the Confederacy, offered shade from the summer sun. Dressed in scruffy sneakers, red shorts, and a red T-shirt with a white crab logo, I grinned foolishly at the camera from under a wide-brimmed straw hat. I felt a prick of disappointment at how I looked—so common and Californian next to the distinguished Virginian in his white suit and Panama hat. If only I'd worn a pretty sundress.

At least I was nicely dressed now in a lime green linen pants suit and matching sling sandals. I'd gone out and bought actual clothes for the occasion—real clothes, as opposed to my "fantasy" wardrobe of outfits picked out from catalogs that I never got around to ordering. My outfit was so new I'd forgotten to remove the price tag from the top, I realized, as I felt a scratch of cardboard against my back. I shifted uncomfortably in my seat. The businessman's newspaper crackled against my arm.

"Here's an interesting story," he said.

I quickly slipped the photo between the pages of my book as he handed me the paper. The story was a follow-up piece on a shoot-out between a right-wing survivalist and federal agents. The agents had moved in after a tip that the man had a cache of unregistered guns. An agent had been killed in the crossfire. So had the survivalist's three-year-old daughter. A variation of the Randy Weaver story played out in Brockton, Massachusetts, with this twist: The gun used to kill the federal agent had been traced back to the FBI. It was among the nearly four hundred and fifty guns issued to FBI agents that had been stolen or reported missing over the past several years, along with more than one hundred computers. The article pointed out that some of these weapons had already been recovered by law enforcement personnel after they had been used to commit crimes. But until now no one had been murdered with a stolen gun.

"Frenchmen with pistols, now this—makes you wonder what the country's coming to," the businessman commented.

I didn't see the connection between one Frenchman with a borrowed pistol and hundreds of stolen guns, but I nodded in agreement before opening my book again. The poor guy is just trying to make conversation, I told myself. I pegged him for a frequent flyer, who was bored or lonely or both. At least I didn't have to worry about boredom or loneliness this weekend. My thoughts circled back to the reason I'd wound up on this crowded plane.

The invitation had arrived unexpectedly. Ginny Longford Cross, my old college roommate, and her father, Randall Longford, wanted me to join them on a trip to Gettysburg for the battle reenactments over the Fourth of July weekend. My first reaction was surprise. After all, I hadn't seen Ginny or her father in ages. Next came curiosity. Then, as memories washed over me, I felt a sudden, intense longing. Perhaps I was foolish to believe I could recapture the magic of that long-ago time. But the more I thought about it, the more I realized that the question wasn't whether I should go, but how could I not? I slid the photo from my book and stared at it until the years fell away and I was transported back to that summer.

I was nineteen then, a California Yankee, who hadn't ventured far from my home state, when Ginny invited me to spend the

summer with her and her father in Virginia. She was the first real
Southerner I had ever met, and she made a big impression on me—
her father an even bigger one. Handsome, courtly, well-read, and
silver-tongued, a judge who could make even a life sentence sound
sweet, Randall Longford was the perfect southern gentleman. He
was also a born storyteller, fascinating me with tales of his Virginia
ancestors. They had fought in the Revolutionary War, signed the
Declaration of Independence, served in Congress and the Cabinet,
and in what he delighted in calling "The War of Northern Aggres-
sion" when any Yankees were around. Randall's mementos from
that war included letters written by his great-great-grandfather, a
brigadier-general in the Army of Northern Virginia, his great-
great-grandfather's pistol, and a deck of playing cards tossed aside
by a fleeing Union soldier after the First Battle of Bull Run—all
of which he proudly showed me.

He made regular pilgrimages to Civil War battlefields, and
that summer he invited Ginny and me to accompany him on
these weekend day trips. He took us to Fredericksburg, Antietam,
Manassas, Chancellorsville, Gettysburg. We would set out early
in the morning with a picnic lunch and a large thermos of sweet
tea. In the car Randall would talk about the battlefield we were
going to see. If Ginny or I were driving, he would read from *R.
E. Lee, A Biography* by Douglas Southall Freeman and from his
great-great-grandfather's letters. Then he would walk us around
the field, pointing out the positions of various divisions, explaining strategy, and describing combat in vivid detail. As Randall
spoke, the landscape—empty, green, and monotonous as a golf
course with blue historical markers instead of flags for the
various holes—burst into life with soldiers, horses, cannon,
smoke, and blood.

The plane hit a patch of turbulence, jerking me back to the
present. I was no longer the gangly girl in the picture, but a
woman in her forties, married and divorced, and an author of
American history books like those Randall had encouraged me
to read so many years ago. When the invitation arrived, I quickly
sent him the Civil War chapter I'd written for a forthcoming

textbook, *America: the Republic's Glory and Greatness* (*ARGG* when I was annoyed). He promised to review it and give me his comments while we were at Gettysburg.

I felt a bit anxious on that score and somewhat guilty about the unfinished chapter lying on the desk in my cluttered apartment. But mostly I was eager to see Randall. I knew he had retired from the bench and had granddaughters older than I'd been that summer. I also knew he hadn't remarried since the death of his wife when Ginny was twelve. A widower raising his only daughter on his own, he'd struck me as a romantic figure. I suspected he still would. And so, as the plane began its descent to Reagan National Airport, I felt a keen anticipation.

I SPOTTED HIM IMMEDIATELY in the crowd waiting in the lobby. Like Robert E. Lee, whom he resembled slightly, he had a full head of wavy hair, now turned silver, dark, flashing eyes, and strong features, sharpened rather than blunted by age. From the striped silk Hermes tie at his neck to the highly polished Mephistos on his feet, he was a dapper presence. In his custom-tailored summer suit with a red carnation perched jauntily on the lapel and a white handkerchief peeping out of a pocket, he looked ready for a garden party instead of an airport meeting.

He saw me, smiled, and waved. I hurried over.

"Miranda!" He spoke my name with the slight broadening of the "a" characteristic of Tidewater gentry—the accent, elongated but precise, without the lazy drawl of the Deep South— that was music to my ears. Then, clasping my hand tightly, he said, "You cannot imagine how it warms my heart to see you again. You are every bit as lovely as I remember."

"You, too, Mr. Longford— I mean—"

"Randall, please." He smiled. I blushed. Maybe I wasn't so different from the gawky girl in red shorts after all.

"I hope you were blessed with smooth skies."

"There was some turbulence, but it wasn't too bad. Ginny couldn't make it?"

Randall shook his head. "I am afraid my dear daughter was

detained by the demands of the workplace. An important client wanted a second look at a property. I said I would be delighted to pick you up."

"I could've taken a cab."

"Nonsense. Taxis are for strangers, not honored guests. Is that all your luggage?" He gestured toward my carry-on. I nodded. "Well, aren't you clever! None of the women in my family could ever manage with just one tiny suitcase. Here, let me take it for you. You must be fatigued after your long journey."

Seizing the handle of my bag, he placed his fingertips on my elbow lightly, with a mere suggestion of pressure. It was a small gesture, undoubtedly performed without a moment's thought. But, accustomed to fending for myself in the rude, sometimes downright hostile, environment of the urban Northeast, I found his gallantry enchanting.

As we glided along the George Washington Parkway in his Lincoln Continental, Randall said, "Virginia and I are both so impressed with your achievements as an author, and I was tremendously flattered when you sent me your chapter. I have read it a number of times already and—"

"There's a problem?" I interrupted with Yankee bluntness.

"Quite the contrary. Aside from a few quibbles, I think it's splendid. Absolutely splendid. Mr. Shelby Foote could not have done better himself."

"Thank you." I basked in his praise. "The quibbles have to do with…?"

"Such minor matters that I hope you will forgive me for even mentioning them now. We will have plenty of time to discuss your chapter over the weekend. So tell me, Miranda," he went on, changing the subject, "have you attended other reenactments before Gettysburg?"

"I've visited a couple of Union encampments in the Boston area, but this will be my first full-scale battle."

"Then you have a real treat in store for you."

"I'm looking forward to it. Wiley will be taking part, won't he?" Wiley Cross, Ginny's high school sweetheart and husband, was a Vietnam vet turned Confederate reenactor.

"Well, now, I do not believe he will," Randall replied slowly.

"He's not doing reenacting anymore?"

"Oh, he still does it. In fact, he is more involved in reenacting that ever before, but as a hard-core reenactor rather than a regular one."

"What's the difference?"

"Hardcores strive for the utmost authenticity. They starve themselves to achieve the gaunt look of real Rebel soldiers, go for days without bathing, march for miles in their bare feet, and endure all manner of hardship in the name of experiencing what they call a 'period rush.'"

I had no trouble picturing Wiley as a hardcore reenactor. When I'd first met him, I was attracted by his good looks, tousled and boyish like James Dean's, a certain raffish charm, and the energy evident in his tall, rangy body. But as I got to know him, I became aware of a dangerously manic quality. At times I was afraid he would self-destruct before my eyes.

"But if Wiley's become a hardcore reenactor, why wouldn't he come to Gettysburg?"

"Hardcores do not like to associate with other reenactors whom they consider to be less authentic—'farbs' they call them. People say the word is short for 'far-be-it-from-authentic.'" Randall paused and cleared his throat. "In any case, the last time I spoke with Wiley he told me he was going to South Carolina this weekend for the protest against the removal of the Confederate flag from the statehouse."

I wondered how Randall, as a Southerner, weighed in on the flag issue. Before I could ask, he said, "To tell you the truth, Miranda, we do not see that much of Wiley anymore, he is just so caught up in all his reenactment activities. Why, since the season started in the spring, he has been on the road almost constantly. It tires me even to think of all the traveling he has done."

"I thought he was working as a mechanic."

"Well, now he is, but his boss is such a kind and understanding person—he is a Vietnam veteran, too, you know—that he allows Wiley to take time off in pursuit of his hobby. And when Wiley is in town, his understanding boss even lets him camp out in the garage."

I stared at Randall with astonishment. "Ginny and Wiley are separated?"

This was news. Ginny had dropped out of Stanford in her sophomore year to be with Wiley after he was wounded in Vietnam. They had eloped as soon as he was released from the hospital. The twins, Mandy and Missy, were born a year later. Ginny always managed to put a positive, even humorous, spin on her life, but reading between the lines of her Christmas letters—our chief means of communication since college—I gathered that the early years of marriage had been difficult, with Wiley in pain and unable to hold down a job, the "double trouble" of twins, and her father's disapproval of the path she'd chosen.

Lately, however, she had assured me that things were better. Wiley had found steady employment, she was doing well as a real estate broker, and the twins had finished college and were out on their own. "Wiley and I have become empty nesters, and happily so, though we do miss the girls," she had written in her Christmas letter a few years ago. Now it seemed that the nest she'd worked so hard to build over the years had come unraveled.

"'Separated' is far too strong a word," Randall said mildly. "I prefer to think of Virginia and Wiley as living apart for the time being. I view it as a temporary arrangement that will undoubtedly end when Wiley develops a different, all-consuming interest. But in his current hardcore reenactor phase, camping out in the garage suits Wiley better than living in a house with Virginia and other comforts."

"I see."

Apparently sensing my dismay, he said, "I hope I have not upset you by telling you this. As I said before, it is merely a temporary arrangement, and it certainly will not affect our plans for the weekend. We are going to have a wonderful time. It is so good to have you back with us, Miranda."

He patted my arm the same way he had touched my elbow, and again the gesture, subtle but telling, enchanted me.

A beat-up Dodge Dart was parked in front of Ginny's two-story brick colonial. The car sported Rebel flags and bumper stickers with slogans like "If At First You Don't Secede, Try Try Again" and "Happiness Is A North-Bound Yankee." Every square inch of surface was covered with small plastic horses, cannon, and figures of soldiers in blue and gray arrayed for battle. I'd seen decorated cars before, but never anything quite like this. The vehicle was like a mobile diorama.

"Somebody sure went to a lot of trouble," I remarked.

"Wiley's *pièce de résistance,*" Randall said. "He calls it his Battlemobile. But how unusual to see it parked here in Virginia's driveway." A tense wariness had crept into his voice.

Hot air hit us like a blast from a furnace when we left the Lincoln. A Toyota wagon with a cardboard Coldwell Banker sign propped in the back was parked in the driveway. Ginny's. As we started up the walk toward the house, we heard raised voices within. Randall placed a cautionary hand on my arm. The next instant, a gaunt, wild-eyed man in a ragged Confederate uniform burst from the door. I barely recognized Wiley as the skeletal figure that lurched past us, leaving behind the stench of the long unwashed.

At the end of the walk, he gave the neatly trimmed box hedge a savage kick, sending up a shower of dirt and splintered branches. Then he turned and yelled at Ginny, now standing at the front door, "Over my dead body, you will!" He slammed the Battlemobile's door and drove off with the ear-splitting roar of a broken muffler.

Randall's grip tightened on my arm. His face turned pale. Beads of sweat sprouted blister-like on his forehead. His eyes grew wide and staring. His head lolled. A scratchy "Ahhh" issued from his throat. His body swayed. He looked ready to double over. Ginny rushed to him. "Oh, Daddy, oh, no!"

TWO

"There are moments when the reenactor loses track of the time period. At that moment he has gone beyond fooling others and is fooling himself. Reenactors live for moments like this."
        Reliving the Civil War, A Reenactor's Handbook

"THANK YOU, GENTLEMEN, but I am quite capable of—" Randall protested as the EMTs lifted him from couch to gurney. Tieless, his collar open, the red carnation drooping from his lapel like a blood-soaked bandage, he bore little resemblance to the well-groomed gentleman who had met me at the airport. He was suddenly gray and shrunken, a rumpled bundle in the arms of the EMTs, both tall, blond, and tanned.

Even so, Randall did not go willingly, but tried to rise the instant they laid him on the gurney. "Don't even think about it," the taller and blonder of the EMTs admonished. He placed a hand like a baseball mitt on Randall's shoulder and pushed him down.

Outside, a fire truck and a police car with flashing lights blocked nonexistent traffic on the quiet, residential street. The ambulance doors swung open and a ramp was lowered. Randall lay motionless, except for the fingers of one hand, which drummed a silent melody. Or an SOS?

There was nothing I could do. Not now standing on the sidewalk with Ginny, feeling leaden as the cement underfoot. Nor earlier when Ginny had rushed Randall into the house and called 911. Then I'd followed like a dumb animal, unable to believe this was really happening. I still couldn't believe it. I felt trapped in a nightmare.

The gurney rolled up the ramp. Randall's head twisted

toward Ginny and me. His face registered fear, confusion, and something else—shame that we should see him thus.

A TV BLARED OVERHEAD in the E.R. waiting room, but Ginny wasn't watching. Her gaze was fixed on the door through which the doctor would come with news of her father. Ginny's dark hair was streaked with gray now, and there were telltale lines in her face. Otherwise, she didn't look much different from the girl who had poked her head into my room freshman year and introduced herself as the third occupant of the "Bible suite" in Roble Hall, three adjoining rooms with their own bathroom—Matthew, Mark, Luke, and John. She had the same round face with green cat's eyes and Cupid's bow mouth, and the same fair skin dotted with dark freckles like chocolate sprinkles on a vanilla cone.

"Scarlett O'Hara's in Matthew," Paige Whitney, a cool blonde from San Mateo and the other occupant of the Bible suite, had informed me. "But this Scah-lett has been out in the sun too long without her parasol. She's also helped herself to too many pecan pies."

Despite this unflattering description, I liked Ginny from the start. "Hi, I'm Ginny from Ol' Virginy," she said, stepping into my room. Then she laughed—a wonderful laugh, filled with merriment and mischief that bubbled up from deep within her. It was a big, gutsy laugh for a person only five feet, four inches tall. We quickly became friends and allies against Perfect Paige, queen of the cutting remark.

"Miz Croft?" The arrival of the E.R. doctor, a young man in a white coat with a rabbity face, pulled me from my reminiscences.

Ginny shot up. "How is he?"

"Better," the doctor replied carefully, "although the pulse is still elevated, and the heartbeat somewhat irregular. He appears to have had an attack of angina rather than a heart attack. We won't know for certain until we get the results of his blood work. I'd like to have his cardiologist examine him, too. I put a call in to Dr. Addison."

Ginny nodded. Then she turned and flung her arms around

me. "Thank God, he's all right! And thank God, you're here, Miranda!" We hugged each other. In that long moment of our embrace, I felt that even though we hadn't been in close touch since college, we could still pick up where we had left off, as good friends who'd shared tears, as well as laughter.

When we released each other, I said, "Has your father had trouble like this before?"

Ginny looked at me, chagrined. "I'm sorry I never wrote you about his heart attack. I'm a terrible correspondent—except for Christmas letters, and I don't like to put bad news in them."

So Randall had something else in common with Robert E. Lee, a heart condition. Lee's heart had first begun to trouble him on the eve of Gettysburg. Eventually it killed him.

"Daddy's heart attack occurred about a year ago," Ginny continued. "Fortunately they got him to the hospital in time. He didn't have to have surgery, but he's been on medication ever since. Dr. Addison hopes that the pills, combined with a change in diet and lifestyle, will help him avoid another attack. He's been great about watching his diet and getting proper exercise. But keeping out of stressful situations isn't easy—especially now that..." She frowned and looked away.

I didn't press. Now wasn't the time to ask about her and Wiley. The E.R. doctor returned with the news that Dr. Addison had already left for the weekend, but the cardiologist covering for him would be along soon.

"It's too bad Dr. Addison isn't here," I commented.

"Yes, Daddy will be disappointed. He thinks the world of Dr. Addison, though I sometimes wonder why. He never returns phone calls, he once kept Daddy waiting for nearly three hours, and then there was the time he nearly killed Daddy."

I looked at her with amazement. "What happened?"

"Dr. Addison wrote a prescription for one medication, but because of his illegible handwriting, the pharmacist mistook it for something else. Taken at the dosage indicated for the right medication, this other drug could've killed Daddy if he hadn't caught the mistake in time."

"That was a close call," I said.

"I'll say. I made a big fuss, and Dr. Addison promised to take this special handwriting course they give for doctors, but who knows when he'll get around to it."

After the other cardiologist had examined Randall, he agreed it was a case of angina instead of heart attack. Still, to be on the safe side, he wanted Randall to remain in the hospital overnight for observation.

By the time we were allowed in to see him, Randall was sitting up in bed, joking with a nurse. "Here they are, Miz Sowinski," he said, "my lovely daughter and her lovely friend. I am indeed fortunate to have three such charming young women looking after me. But unlucky to be held up in this hospital when we ought to be on the road to Gettysburg. The doctor even wants to keep me overnight. It is most inconvenient. If Dr. Addison was here, I would be out already."

"Now, Daddy, you know he believes in being cautious," Ginny said.

"Yes, but not this cautious."

After some discussion, Randall agreed to remain at the hospital overnight, provided we left for Gettysburg bright and early the next morning. We stayed with him until Miss Sowinski brought in a tray with his dinner. The covered dishes gave off the unappetizing odor of institutional food. Randall lifted a cover and promptly replaced it. "Now, I will survive one less than superb culinary experience. But only if I know you ladies are out enjoying a gourmet meal. Now go, off with you!" He made a shooing motion.

AT A TEX-MEX RESTAURANT in Old Town Alexandria, Ginny and I attacked corn chips and salsa with the gusto of prisoners on the lam. We guzzled our margaritas with similar abandon. The tequila and the spicy food helped break up the numbness that had come over us after Randall's attack.

"I'd better stop," Ginny said, pushing the bowl of chips away. "I overeat when I'm tense, and it's sure not helping my figure."

She had always worried about her weight. "I wish I were a Modigliani like you," she once confessed. But if she had envied my thinness, I'd envied her Rubenesque voluptuousness.

"At a time like this, I think you're entitled to some self-indulgence," I said.

"It's okay for you to indulge—you're thin as ever. You look great, by the way," she added, surveying me. "I like the way you're wearing your hair."

Thank heaven I'd gotten a long-overdue haircut. "Better a cap of curls than a burning bush," I said. "Burning bush" was how Paige Whitney had described my thick, curly, red hair.

"Paige really knew how to twist the knife," Ginny said. "Still, I wish her well."

Her words reminded me what a big-hearted person Ginny was. When Paige came back drunk from a fraternity party and threw up in our corridor, Ginny was the one who cleaned her up and helped her into bed. If anyone deserved happiness, it was Ginny. But lately she seemed to be having her share of troubles.

"What about you? Your father said you and Wiley are living apart."

Ginny sighed. "That's Daddy's tactful way of putting it. He probably told you it was a temporary arrangement, too. But frankly, Miranda, I don't know if Wiley and I will get back together again. And that's a hard thing to admit after all the effort I've put into making the marriage work. Wiley was pretty messed up when he came back from Vietnam. He was in pain a lot and had awful nightmares and night sweats. I did my best to take care of him, while still trying to be a good mother to the twins. I thought that with my love and support he would eventually heal, but…" She shook her head and tears welled in her eyes.

I reached across the table and gripped her hand. "I'm sure you did everything you could."

Over the years, I had marveled at the love and loyalty that made Ginny drop out of college and elope with Wiley, then stick with him through what must have been very difficult times. Love, loyalty, and defiance of her father, because in marrying Wiley, Ginny had acted against her father's wishes.

"But it just wasn't enough," Ginny went on. "I kept telling myself that things had to get better, that once the girls were grown up and didn't need me as much, I could devote myself to Wiley again and really help him. But instead of getting better, things got worse. Shortly after the girls left home, Wiley went off the deep end with reenacting."

"Your father said he's become a hardcore reenactor."

Ginny nodded. "Reenacting was a good thing we had together that turned bad. It was fun in the beginning. The girls loved it and so did I. It was like going on a camping trip—only back in time and in costume. While Wiley was off at battle, the girls and I would cook and sew and clean and visit with our neighbors. Then in the evening, we'd all sit around the campfire and talk and sing songs. The hardest part was getting in the car at the end of the weekend and returning to the pressures of our lives. But then—" She broke off, as the waitress arrived with our crab enchiladas.

We ate for several minutes in silence, then Ginny asked, "Ever see the movie, *Gettysburg?*"

"No."

"Wiley had a part in that movie. He was so thrilled that he went to see it at least a dozen times—all four hours and twenty minutes of it. When the movie came out on tape, he would sit alone in the den, watching himself get shot in Pickett's Charge over and over again. Everyone praised his performance because it looked so realistic, but I thought it was horrible, just horrible. I didn't realize it at the time, but that's when his attitude toward reenacting changed. He decided he had to be as authentic as possible—to the point of starving himself, while pushing himself to the limits of his endurance. Hardcore reenacting's become his whole life. He's either off doing events or hanging out with other hardcores. And let me tell you, some of those guys are scary. They represent the worst about the old-time Rebels. They're racist and anti-government, guys who'd like nothing better than to turn back the clock by whatever means."

I thought of the far-right-winger in the Brockton shoot-out. If the hardcores Ginny spoke of were anything like him, she was right to be worried.

"When Wiley does come to the house, we end up having scenes like the one you witnessed today," Ginny said. "I don't know, Miranda. When things were tough with Wiley in the past, I told myself he was my cross to bear, my Wiley Cross." She smiled ruefully at the pun.

"I still love him—I always will. But I don't want to spend the rest of my life dealing with his craziness."

She began to cry in earnest. I reached into my tote bag for tissues, but found only used ones. Ginny blew her nose on a paper napkin and hurried off to the restroom. When she returned, her face was washed and her manner composed. "Enough about me and my problems," she said. "I want to hear about you. In your Christmas card, you said you'd started seeing someone. Tell me all about him." She leaned forward with the eagerness and genuine interest I remembered from our college days.

I told her about Nate Barnes, my lover of several months, including the fact that right now we were going through a rocky period. "I'm not sure where the relationship's headed," I said. "We're such different people. I'm a reclusive writer and he's an Indian activist. If we hadn't been thrown together during a murder investigation in Plymouth last fall, our paths probably would have never crossed."

"Well, I hope you two can work things out," Ginny said, "because he sounds like a good person. It could be that it's hard starting up with *anyone* after you've been married a long time, even if…" Her voice trailed off and her expression turned thoughtful.

"What?"

She shook her head. "Let's go back to the hospital and check on Daddy."

IT WAS NEARLY 10:00 p.m. by the time we'd "tucked in" Randall at the hospital and returned to Ginny's house. She gave me a quick tour and showed me the guest room. "I'm going to watch TV or a video in the den," Ginny said. "Since Wiley moved out, I've gotten in the habit of spending my evenings in front of the set. It helps me relax. But if you're tired and want to sleep, feel free."

I was tired—exhausted, in fact—so I hugged Ginny and said good night. I fell asleep almost instantly. I dreamed I was lying on Nate's humongous waterbed, but instead of Nate, Randall was there, curled in a far corner. I reached for him and my arm hit a hard object. It fell to the floor with a crash, the noise waking me up. I opened my eyes. Even in the dimness I could tell I wasn't in Nate's bedroom, or in my own bedroom, either. Where then?

Fumbling in the darkness, I found a lamp on the night table and turned it on. I was in Ginny's guest room. A glance at the clock I'd knocked off the table told me it was 1:00 a.m. Perhaps Ginny was still down in the den watching TV. Now wide awake, I decided to join her. I tiptoed downstairs and through the shadowy, unfamiliar house until I found the door to the basement where the den was located. No light was on in the den, so I knew Ginny had already gone to bed. Still, I flipped on the switch and stepped into the room.

The roses caught my eye immediately, one dozen red roses blooming like a secret garden in a vase on the coffee table between the fold-out couch and the TV. I wondered why they were down here in the den instead of upstairs in the living room. I also wondered where they had come from. I doubted Wiley had brought them. Maybe Randall had sent them to give Ginny's spirits a lift. Or she had bought them herself for the same reason. Their fragrance filled the room, beautiful and mysterious.

I walked over to the TV and examined the stack of videos beside it. They were romantic comedies—just the kind of movie Ginny had enjoyed when we were in college. At the bottom of the pile, I found a two-tape boxed set of Gettysburg. I had no intention of watching the entire four-hour movie tonight, yet I was curious about one part.

Inserting the second tape in the VCR, I fast-forwarded until I came to the start of Pickett's Charge. As the camera panned along the line of Rebel soldiers waiting in the trees for the order to advance, I caught a glimpse of Wiley, his face black-ened with gunpowder, jaw set in a tight line, eyes burning with a fierce determination.

"For the glory of Virginia, form your brigade!" General Lewis Armistead, a brigade commander under Pickett, shouted.

"Virginia! Virginia!" Wiley and the other men yelled, bayonets spiking into the air.

Then, as the camera cut away to provide a panoramic sweep of the charge, I lost sight of Wiley in the gray mass of marching men. I looked for him in the close-ups of soldiers struggling over the wooden fence along the Emmitsburg Road under a hail of enemy fire that blasted away whole sections of the fence and sent men diving to the ground in clouds of dirt and broken wood. But no Wiley. The camera cut to a shot of Lee watching the charge through binoculars, then it moved back to the field. With his hat on the tip of his forward-thrust sword, General Armistead led a small group of men straight into the thicket of Union rifles massed on the other side of the stone wall. Armistead cleared the wall.

So did Wiley. He went over in a crouch, eyes trained ahead, jaw jutting forward, mouth open in a yell of defiance. The next instant, his body collapsed inward onto itself only to explode in a frenzy of backward-falling motion. His head snapped back, as if caught by an invisible wire, his arms flailed wildly, and his legs jerked uncontrollably. The camera zoomed in on Wiley's face as he fell: the burning eyes clouded by approaching death, the defiant yell now a gaping "O" of agony. Then he vanished in a swirl of a gray smoke and tramping feet.

The next close-up showed General Armistead clutching a Union cannon as the life ebbed from him. But to me, Wiley, more than Armistead, stood out as an icon of the desperate bravery of Pickett's Charge—of the entire Lost Cause. I understood why Ginny found his performance horrifying.

I lay in bed for a long time, but sleep wouldn't come. The image of Wiley dying on film kept flickering through my mind. Eventually another image replaced it: in the basement a secret rose garden bloomed.

THREE

"Some things, like wool uniforms, are uncomfortable on hot days. Other things, like courtly manners, are so charming and attractive that they remain with you and become a part of you, even when you take off the clothing of a bygone day."
                    Reliving the Civil War, A Reenactor's Handbook

"IF WE HURRY, we can still catch the end of Howard's Retreat," Randall said as we approached Gettysburg Saturday afternoon. The collapse of the Federal 11th Corps under the command of General Oliver Howard was the first event of the day we had planned to attend.

"It's too late," Ginny replied. "I'm tired from driving and you need to rest."

"I have been disgracefully derelict in my duty," Randall said. "I should have been the one to chauffeur you ladies."

"But then you couldn't have read to us," I pointed out.

"True," he acknowledged, "you always seemed to particularly enjoy that, Miranda."

I glanced over my shoulder at Randall and smiled. Seated straight and tall in the back with the familiar blue tome open on his crossed legs, he looked vigorous and alert, not at all like someone who, only yesterday, had suffered an attack of angina. And he was right about my enjoyment of his reading from Douglas Southall Freeman. Now as then, I thrilled to the sound of Randall's deep, mellifluous voice, as he read about Lee on his way to Gettysburg, the brilliant and beloved commander about to make the worst blunder of his career. Or, as his biographer put it, "On a hill near a little town in Pennsylvania, the bell of a quiet seminary was calling him again to school to learn a new lesson, written red in blood."

"So it's settled," Ginny said. "We'll drive straight to the bed-and-breakfast and rest before dinner."

"You are forgetting our guest," Randall scolded. "It is Miranda's first reenactment, and we must not deprive her of this opportunity. You may be too tired to accompany us, but I feel bound to escort her."

"I'll be fine on my own," I assured him.

I left Randall and Ginny at the B and B with a promise to be back in time for dinner and drove through town toward the reenactment site. Traffic clogged Baltimore Street and pedestrians filled the sidewalks, tourists rubbing shoulders with reenactors in period dress, civilians, as well as soldiers. American flags hung from the windows of the houses and were draped over parking meters. Ahead, a small knot of soldiers in butternut lounged in front of a two-story brick house, their rifles stacked in teepee formation on the sidewalk. They looked hot, but happy—as well they should. This was their moment of glory. Fresh from the rout of Howard's 11th Corps, jubilant Confederate soldiers had swarmed the streets of Gettysburg on this day. "Come see real soldiers fight Mr. Lincoln's conscripts," a reenactor called out as I passed.

I followed Baltimore Street to Steinwehr Avenue, where the National Park Service Visitor Center and a section of the military park were located. The number of souvenir shops and tourist eateries increased exponentially closer to the visitor center. They gave the avenue a honky-tonk atmosphere, culminating in the eyesore of the National Observation Tower. It loomed over the battlefield like the old Parachute Jump at Coney Island. But not for much longer. After a protracted battle between the owner and preservationists to whom it was an anathema, the tower was slated for demolition on July 3, a few hours after the reenactment of Pickett's Charge.

Eventually the last of the tourist traps were behind me, and I came into open countryside. I crossed a sluggish river, then ahead of me I saw the Yingling Farm, the site of this year's reenactment.

On my right, hundreds of parked cars surrounded a large red barn. To the left were more cars, and beyond them on a rise, an encampment of white tents shimmered in the sunlight. I parked by the barn, crossed the road, and climbed a grassy incline to the site. Bypassing the concession stands, I headed for the grand-stands, hoping to see the end of the battle. Only a scattering of soldiers remained on the field. Some still sprawled in the grass where they had been "shot"; others trudged wearily toward camp.

On the field before me, I noticed a civilian reenactor, a woman dressed all in black: black hoopskirt, black bodice, black parasol held over her black-veiled head. She reminded me of a crow picking its way among the gunnysack bodies. I had a grisly thought: if these men were truly dead and she were a real bird on a real Civil War battlefield, she would have pecked their eyes out.

The woman in black suddenly swayed and fell to the ground. I jumped over the rope separating the stands from the field and hurried toward her. A heavyset Rebel soldier got there first. "Are you all right, ma'am?" He knelt beside her.

"My husband—killed at Sharpsburg. Sometimes the grief is more than I can bear."

"If it's any consolation, I'm sure he died a hero's death," the Rebel said.

"No! It was—" The widow broke off, sounding genuinely an-guished.

The Rebel appeared puzzled by her outburst, then, recover-ing, he said, "I'm sorry. Can I give you a hand?"

"I'm all right." She swatted away his outstretched hand and rose with difficulty.

"Buy you a cool one?" he asked.

"You know I'm a temperance woman."

"I meant lemonade."

"No, thanks."

She strode off in the direction of the tent camps. I stared hard at the Rebel's face, which was as round and red as an uncooked hamburger patty.

"Beau?"

He squinted at me, then recognition dawned. "Miranda—Miranda Lewis! I never dreamed I'd see you again." He engulfed me in a sweaty embrace. Releasing me, he said, "You look terrific. Are you here for the reenactments?"

"Yes. I came with Ginny and her father."

"All the way from California?"

"No. I live in the East now, in Cambridge, Massachusetts."

"So you've become a real Yankee. What else you been up to?"

"Oh, writing books and—"

"You marry that fellow you were always talking about?"

"No, someone else. But I'm divorced now."

"Me, too. From Miz New Jersey, my honey back then."

I smiled, remembering. Beau Johnston had been Wiley's best friend. Laurel and Hardy, we'd dubbed the boys because Wiley was thin and nervy, Beau big and affable. The summer I had spent at Ginny's, we often made a foursome together. In the evening we'd drive to Bethesda for spicy Chesapeake Bay crabs. We consumed these by the dozens, washing them down with pitchers of smoky-tasting Stroh's beer. Then we would go to a movie, a party, or a bar. "The Night They Drove Old Dixie Down" blared from the jukebox and peanut shells crunched underfoot as we danced.

Those evenings ended late with us parked at some secluded spot along the Potomac or the old C&O Canal. Beau and I sat awkwardly in the backseat while Ginny and Wiley necked in the front. Eventually they would disappear into the bushes. Then Beau and I would talk, he about his Yankee girlfriend forced to spend the summer working in her father's office in New Jersey, I about the boyfriend I'd left behind in Palo Alto.

Beau grinned at me. "Would *you* like a lemonade?"

I nodded. Beau offered me his arm with a gallantry that reminded me of Randall. He bought our drinks, and we joined the crowd of strollers, tourists mingling with couples in period dress.

"Think your honey'd like a picture of you in that?" Beau pointed at a tent where a man with an old-fashioned, hooded camera was taking a photo of a hoop-skirted woman.

"No, but his son wants one of those." I gestured toward a shop called The Quartermaster that was selling replica Civil War muskets and pistols. "How'd you know I have a honey?"

"I figured you did, and obviously I figured right."

"Yes, but it's complicated."

Beau nodded, then changing the subject, he asked, "How's Ginny doing?"

"Okay," I replied neutrally.

"Too bad about her and Wile. Can't say I blame her, though. Wile can be pretty tough to take sometimes."

"Oh?" I glanced at him questioningly. But Beau's attention had drifted to the widow in black who now stood in line before a Porta-John.

"Who is she?" I asked.

"Linette Peters, Confederate widow, but in real life, a nurse from Long Island."

"She plays the widow part very convincingly. Just now, she seemed truly upset."

"Yeah, though I'm not always sure where she's coming from."

"Hey, soldier, can you spare some change?" A man in a ragged butternut uniform crouched on a blanket on the ground. A slouch hat concealed the upper part of his face, but I made out the tip of a nose like a drain spout with a rusty drip of beard below. His legs appeared to end at the knees. I figured he was sitting on his feet and his shins with the blanket artfully arranged to hide them.

"Lost me legs at Fredericksburg," he said. "Old sawbones of a surgeon cut 'em off an' tossed 'em on a heap. They didn't give me no whiskey to ease the pain neither—just a bullet between my teeth. Bit on it so hard that dammed if I didn't break a tooth." He opened his mouth wide to reveal a black hole where a tooth had been.

I knew it was just an act. Still, I turned away with revulsion. Beau tossed the beggar some coins and guided me away. The beggar's ragged appearance made me think of Wiley. "Is Wiley here?" I asked.

Beau shook his head. "Last I heard, he was heading to South Carolina for the flag protest But even if he doesn't go, I doubt he'll show up here. Too many farbs like me."

"You look pretty authentic."

"Thanks, but as far as hardcores like Wile are concerned, I'm just another fat slob who couldn't hack it in a real battle." I detected an undercurrent of bitterness in his voice. Obviously, he and Wiley weren't the buddies they'd once been.

We had come to the end of the concession area. Ahead lay the camps of the two opposing sides. Beau asked if I'd like to visit the Confederate camp, and I said I would. He led me along a grassy street lined with tents and the occasional fire pit. Soldiers lounged in front of the tents, playing cards, reading period newspapers, smoking pipes, and preparing food. They called out greetings to Beau and tipped their hats to me—all except one particularly scruffy fellow.

A scarecrow in tattered clothing, he lay on his back on the floor of his tent, supporting himself on an elbow, while he clawed at the scalp beneath long, stringy hair. He watched us approach with glassy, red-rimmed eyes, his mouth working a plug of tobacco. Then in one swift, snakelike motion, he rolled onto his belly, grabbed the rifle lying beside him, and aimed it directly at us.

Instinctively I recoiled. Beau stepped quickly between me and the scarecrow with the gun. "Drop it," he growled.

"Jest having a little fun," the scarecrow whined. He put down the gun and let fly with a squirt of brownish spittle. "Ain't nothing wrong with that. It's a free country. Ain't that what we're fighting for? The freedom to do what we want without the government sticking its big butt in and telling us what we can and can't do."

Beau's face turned redder than ever. Anger sizzled from him, as from a side of beef on a hot grill. "That may be what you're fighting for, but I'm—"

"What's going on?" demanded a burly, blond reenactor with red suspenders holding up his gray pants.

"Nothing," Beau said, turning away from the scarecrow. "It's just that Davis really gets to me sometimes."

"Me, too," the blond reenactor agreed. "But this isn't the time for a fight."

"You're right," Beau said. "How about a cool one, Miranda, Paul?"

Paul declined. I followed Beau to his tent, where he lugged out a cooler from behind a rubber gum blanket. He popped the tops of two cans of Stroh's and handed me one. "Like some hardtack with your beer?" He opened a box of Ritz crackers and arranged them on a tin plate. "I've got sowbelly, too." Beau dug in his haversack, producing a can of minced ham. He curled back the lid and used his Swiss army knife to spread ham on crackers. "Welcome to Farby's where the food's at least as good as Arby's. Sometimes even better."

I munched on a cracker and laughed. "What's with the guy who pulled a gun on us?"

Beau shook his head with distaste. "One of Wile's recruits. They connected at a biker bar in Harpers Ferry. Wile thought he had potential as a hardcore, and Dred Davis—well, you heard him—really dug the Confederate thing about resisting tyranny, fighting for freedom. Guess he figured he was already a latter-day Rebel roaring around on his Harley."

"I'm surprised he didn't just join a civilian militia organization," I said.

"Would to God he had instead of signing on with us!" Beau groaned. "He's been trouble from the get-go. When Wile first recruited him, Wile insisted that he, Davis, Paul, and I be 'comrades in arms.' Those are the front-rank and rear-rank men in two adjoining files. Wile wanted us to look after Davis and be sure he was doing his movements safely and correctly. When you're comrades in arms, you gotta trust each other, 'cuz if you're in front, the rear guy is firing right behind you. Should've known better than to let Wile put Davis behind me. Next thing I knew I had a bad burn on the back of my neck. Claimed he aimed over my shoulder, that I moved at the last minute. But dammed if I wasn't right where I was supposed to be, elbow to elbow with Wile, when Davis fired without a word of warning. You won't find it in drill books of the period, but it's customary among reenactors for the rear-rank guy to say, 'coming over,' when he's about to fire. Still gotta scar there."

He showed me the back of his neck. It looked like a tree trunk struck by lightning. My fingers grazed the mark. Beau moaned and caught my hand.

"Sorry," I said. "Did I hurt you?"

"Just the opposite. The back of my neck's a place I especially like to be touched."

Slipping my fingers from his grasp, I said, "No wonder you're not fond of Davis."

Beau faced me with an embarrassed look. "That and all his redneck bullshit."

We ate and drank and chatted. I had always found Beau easy to be with and now was no different. Before I knew it, an hour had passed and it was time to go. Beau walked me to the edge of the encampment.

"How about coming back later this evening? There'll be a campfire, singing, and maybe even dancing. You could bring Ginny and her father, too."

"Thanks, but I don't think we'll make it. It's been a long day for all of us. I'll look for you tomorrow, though."

"Good enough." He grinned and gave me another sweaty hug.

In the parking lot I looked at the license plates. Virginia, Maryland, Pennsylvania, and other neighboring states were well represented, but I also saw plates from as far east as Maine and as far west as California. Some of the cars sported Confederate flags and bumper stickers about secession and southern independence like those on Wiley's Battlemobile. But his Dodge Dart with its distinctive decorations was nowhere to be seen. I noticed a number of motorcycles, including one Harley with enough expletive-bearing slogans to paper a Porta-John.

Dred Davis's machine? Plastic skulls dangling from the handlebars rattled in the breeze. A rustling in the grass made me jump. The beggar scuttled between the cars on bent knees like a crab between rocks. I was relieved that it was only he, a harmless grotesque, instead of the potentially dangerous Dred Davis. Having met him, I understood Ginny's dislike of Wiley's new cronies.

"TREACHERY, THY NAME IS Longstreet!" Randall proclaimed, closing the blue volume with its gilded portrait of Lee. The subversion of Lee's strategy at Gettysburg by his second in command, Lieutenant General James Longstreet, had been Randall's theme during a delicious dinner at an inn in the countryside he had discovered on a previous visit, and now as we sat in the parlor of our B and B, enjoying coffee and cognac.

Ginny smiled indulgently. "Of course, Daddy. After all, you wrote the book on Lee—you and Douglas Southall Freeman."

"Now, Virginia, you know I only spoke with Mr. Freeman on a few occasions. The interpretations in his book are strictly his, though I happen to agree with them," Randall replied. "I thought I would drive out to the military park early tomorrow for my morning constitutional. Would either or both of you charming ladies care to join me?"

"I'm not getting up at six o'clock," Ginny declared.

"I'll come," I said.

"Splendid! Perhaps your example will inspire my lazybones daughter to forsake her bed another time."

"Don't count on it," Ginny said. "But I'm ready for the 'early-to-bed' part of the maxim. How about you, Daddy? Miranda?"

Randall and Ginny said good night and went upstairs. I wasn't sleepy yet, so I stayed in the parlor with my book. As I reached for it, I noticed that Randall had left his copy of the Freeman biography behind. I picked up the blue volume, feeling its weight and substance. The cover was mottled in texture except where it had been gilded. Those places, especially the portrait of Lee in profile, were smooth to the touch. I fingered Lee's gold coat, his beard, his face. Then I stroked the edges of the hand-cut pages, brown and irregular like aging skin, imagining that I was touching the man himself. R. E., Randall Edward.

Should I take the book up to him? No. I didn't want him to think that every time he turned around, there I was, panting for his notice like a puppy. I read awhile, then, feeling restless, I went out for a walk.

Baltimore Street was still packed with strollers, reenactors, as well as tourists, and a festive mood reigned. Even those waiting in line in front of the restaurants didn't look impatient or irritable. Rather they chatted companionably with their neighbors.

Baltimore Street gave way to Steinwehr Avenue with its clutter of tacky tourist shops. I was starting to wish I'd taken Beau up on his invitation to return to camp when I glimpsed him ahead. He was standing in front of a T-shirt shop talking with someone seated in a chair. I called his name. No response. Perhaps it wasn't Beau after all.

Behind me, an engine roared to life. Helmeted and clad in black leather, the rider was unrecognizable, but not his bike. The plastic skulls jiggling from the handlebars identified it as the Harley I'd seen at the Yingling Farm. Although the street was well lit and I was hardly alone, I felt a tingle of apprehension, followed by relief when the motorcycle passed out of view.

I glanced at the T-shirt shop again. Beau and the man in the chair had vanished. Odd. But then again maybe it wasn't so odd. If the biker were Dred Davis, I didn't blame Beau for running for cover. I started back the way I'd come, then, feeling adventurous, I turned off onto a side street.

Twenty minutes later, after various meanderings, including a tour of the Gettysburg College campus I could have done without, I turned a corner and found myself within a block of the B and B. As I approached, I noticed a man and woman seated on the porch. The man was big like my lover, Nate Barnes, the woman short and curvaceous like Ginny.

The man took the woman in his arms and kissed her. The embrace went on and on. Then, like an amoeba dividing, the massed shape split into two separate entities. The man stood up, then the woman. He looked as if he wanted to take her in his arms again. Instead, he bounded from the porch and hurried toward a car parked up the street with the loping gait I remembered from years ago. At the car he turned and made another familiar gesture. His hand flew to his lips, then to his temple in a mock salute.

It couldn't be him. Not here. Not now.

FOUR

"Living historians camping at historic sites mention hearing unexplained gunfire at night, smelling gunpowder fumes, and seeing apparitions."

Reliving the Civil War, A Reenactor's Handbook

"GINNY!" I CAUGHT UP with her just inside the door. "That wasn't Greg Jefferson, was it?" Her face was a kaleidoscope of shifting emotions—guilt, longing, then a burst of happiness that dimmed into sadness.

"Yes, God help me!"

Brief but intense, Ginny's romance with Stanford's star black quarterback and campus hunk, Greg Jefferson, was the one time in college she had been unfaithful to Wiley. Throughout freshman year, she had resisted the advances of plenty of guys. Then in the fall of sophomore year, she met Greg. She agonized over going out with him, but after a certain point the agonizing became acceptance of the strong attraction between them. Wiley had dropped out of community college in Virginia by then and was on his way to Vietnam. Ginny wrote him about Greg, but received no answer. Several months later, she learned that Wiley had been seriously wounded and was coming home. She ended it with Greg, left college, and returned home to be with Wiley.

"You and he are involved?"

"Come upstairs.

"I almost told you last night," Ginny said after we had settled on the canopy bed in her room, "but the whole thing is so crazy. Wiley's always been the child, so I had to be the responsible adult, the Mommy. But now with Greg, I feel like a teenager again—at my age! It's wonderful and awful at the same time."

"The roses in the den came from Greg?"

"Yes, he sends them every week. He's attentive and romantic in ways that Wiley never was." She shook her head. "They're very different men. Greg's a doctor now, specializing in sports medicine, in Cleveland, where he's from originally."

"He never married?"

"His wife died a couple of years ago."

"Ah. How long have you been seeing him?"

"Only a couple of months. He telephoned a few weeks after Wiley moved out. At first all we did was talk. I was feeling lonely and so was he. When he asked if we could meet, I thought I could handle it. But the moment I saw him, all these emotions I didn't know still existed came rushing back."

"Does Wiley know?"

"Greg and I have been careful, and Wiley's so obsessed with reenacting that he barely notices anything else."

"What about your father?"

"Not yet. The scenes between Wiley and me have been upsetting enough without my telling him about Greg." Ginny frowned and worried a nub on the chenille bedspread. "Especially since Daddy's ideas about certain things are rather old-fashioned."

"Meaning race?"

She nodded. "I hope that once he gets to know Greg, he'll accept him. But for the time being, I'd rather keep our relationship a secret."

"In that case, Greg's being in Gettysburg seems kind of risky."

"He wasn't supposed to come. We were going to see each other next weekend, but then his schedule got changed at the last minute. He realized he wouldn't be able to get away again for several weeks. That's why he's here now."

"How long's he staying?"

"He promised to leave tomorrow morning. Oh, Miranda, I know I probably shouldn't have gotten involved with Greg again, but…"

But she had. And knowing how lonely and unloved she'd felt,

I understood why. She was hardly the first woman to seek solace from a difficult marriage by having an affair.

"These things happen," I said, "and if Greg leaves tomorrow morning, everything should be okay—at least for now."

"Yes. Thanks for being so understanding."

DESPITE MY REASSURING WORDS, I was worried. After I had gone back to my room, doubts crept out like night creatures from their burrows. What if Greg didn't leave? What if Wiley showed up and made another awful scene? What if this scene caused Randall to have a real heart attack? These fears kept me awake well into the night.

I had barely dozed off when my alarm went off at 5:30 a.m. I grumped out of bed, into the shower, and then into clothes. Whatever had possessed me to tell Randall I would join him for his constitutional? But when I saw him, my ill humor vanished. His silver hair sleek from the shower, dark eyes alight, tall, trim figure exuding energy, he might have been a racehorse ready for the track, prancing instead of pacing as he waited for me.

"Good morning!" he greeted me. "You are right on time! I know it must seem as if we are up before the birds, but we are actually getting a late start compared to Lee. He arose at 3:30 a.m. on this day. When I brought Ginny's mother to Gettysburg on our honeymoon, I actually made her wake up then, so we could go to Seminary Ridge to inspect the Union position just as Lee did. She was not pleased."

"I can imagine." I smiled at the image of a youthful Randall rousing his bride from bed. His zeal in re-creating Lee's experience at Gettysburg reminded me of Wiley's hardcore reenacting. But getting up at an ungodly hour wasn't the same as starving oneself to achieve the gaunt look of a Confederate solider. That was the difference between the two men. Randall knew where to draw the line; Wiley did not.

"Maybe that is why I never could get her to a battlefield again," Randall continued. "But you don't mind, do you?"

"Not a bit."

On the way to the door, he asked, "Did you happen to borrow the Freeman book?"

"No, isn't it on the table in the parlor?"

"Your paperback is there, but not Freeman."

"Are you sure? The book was there when I went out for a walk last night."

"Well, no matter. One of the guests—"

"But it does matter," I interrupted. "It's your book and we've got to find it."

Randall smiled. "You are kind to be so concerned. But, as I was about to say, one of the other guests probably borrowed the book. I am sure it will be returned in due course. Come along now." He placed his fingertips on my elbow lightly but with a hint of pressure. "I have already been out to fill the thermos with fresh coffee, so we won't have to stop on the way."

We drove west on Route 30 until we reached the red brick Lutheran Seminary that dated back to before the Battle of Gettysburg. During the battle the Seminary had served as an observation post for the Confederate Army. We turned onto West Confederate Avenue, so named because it ran parallel to the Confederate battle line on Seminary Ridge. The avenue was one-way with pull-off parking on the right. Randall parked near the North Carolina monument. Here bronze soldiers, sculpted by Gutzon Borglum of Mount Rushmore fame, strained toward the field in which many of their real-life counterparts had fallen.

"From this point it's about a mile to the Virginia memorial," Randall said. "If we walk there and back, I will have done my two miles. Will that be too tiring for you?"

I shook my head. We strolled along the quiet, tree-lined avenue, mercifully free of cars and tour buses. I understood why buffs like Randall would want to come here at this hour. What better time to "Feel the Presence," as the Gettysburg Web site put it, than now when I could easily picture the ghostly figures of Rebel soldiers crouched behind the stone wall on our left.

After we had walked in silence awhile, Randall turned to me

and said, "This trip brings back such wonderful memories of the time you, I, and Virginia spent at Gettysburg."

I looked at him, askance. "But Ginny wasn't with us at Gettysburg. She had a bad case of poison ivy and decided to stay home."

"I beg to differ. I am positive she was with us."

My better judgment told me not to argue, but I couldn't stop myself. I produced the photo of us at the Bloody Angle from my bag, and showed it to him. "You see, it was just us."

Randall frowned at the picture. *What* had I done? Why remind him of my earlier self, that graceless girl slouching toward womanhood? "I know I look silly," I blurted.

He didn't seem to hear me. "Ah, fugitive time," he murmured. "How much older and grayer I am now. Older, grayer, and saddled with a bad heart." Then turning to me with a flash of his former spirit, he said, "But I am not in my dotage yet, and therefore I must point out that Virginia's absence from this photo doesn't prove she wasn't at Gettysburg. Someone had to take this photo, and in all likelihood it was she."

"You're probably right," I agreed, unwilling to challenge his recollection further. After all, why should he remember? I was only his daughter's friend. He didn't know about my youthful crush on him, had no idea I'd carried a torch for him all these years. The flame had burned strong and bright at first, then flickered and guttered, close to extinction, even in the protection of my cupped hand. But like those trick birthday candles that can't be blown out, it had never completely died. Yet if Randall didn't recall the one entire day we had spent together, I would never forget it.

On the last trip of the summer, Ginny had begged off. The late nights with Wiley were taking their toll, and after one of their forays into the bushes she developed a bad case of poison ivy. I was delighted to have Randall to myself. But that day, as we toured the battlefield, he seemed moody and distracted. Perhaps he was brooding about a case in court, or some personal matter. Then again, maybe he was infected by the atmosphere of death and, to Southerners, defeat. Gettysburg had been the High Water Mark of the Confederacy. After it, the huge gray wave receded, leaving behind the detritus of war: empty cartridges, dry bones, blasted hopes. I could understand why Randall might feel melancholy here.

Still, he was too much of a gentleman to let his low spirits spoil the day for me. He wouldn't leave until he had given me a complete tour. He even posed obligingly when I persuaded another tourist to take a photo of us with my Instamatik. Let it go, Miranda.

"Here we are." His voice brought me out of my reverie. We had reached the Virginia Memorial. Astride his famous horse, Traveler, Lee rose majestically on his pedestal, above a grouping of seven figures representing the various types of soldiers who had fought with him. Randall removed his Panama and held it across his chest. I felt moved myself, not so much by the statue as by the way Randall paid homage to his dead hero.

After a long moment, he cleared his throat and said, "Shall we go out there, as he did?"

We followed a narrow paved path to a historical marker describing Pickett's Charge and how Lee had ridden, hatless, to this spot to console the survivors as they straggled back. Across the open fields, we could see Cemetery Ridge and the copse of trees.

"It was quiet that morning, too," Randall said, "and for the men on both sides, the very silence became oppressive. They knew the enemy was there. But when, they wondered, would he strike?"

An awful keening broke the stillness. The rebel yell from somewhere in the distance. Again I thought of Wiley. He had awakened Ginny, me, and half our freshman dorm with that yell in the middle of the night when he'd come to Stanford for a surprise visit. Wiley, the wolf-man calling to his mate in the moonlight. At first I'd been annoyed at being torn from sleep so unceremoniously. Then the gesture had struck me as romantic and extravagant like Wiley himself, driving straight through from Virginia to California, keeping awake on coffee, cigarettes, and Dexedrine, to be with his sweetheart sooner.

I turned in the direction of the sound, half expecting to see his tall, rangy figure sauntering toward us. Someone was approaching from the monument, but he looked too heavyset to be Wiley.

"I wonder who that is," I said. "The ghost of a Confederate soldier?"

Randall laughed. "It's probably another buff like us."

The figure drew nearer and I saw he wasn't like us. In the landscape of green, punctuated by white stone markers, obelisks, and monuments, he stood out because of his color, a black sphinx in a green-and-white world, where the only other dark objects were the cannon and the occasional bronze statue. Greg! I grasped Randall's arm, as if Greg, like the cannon, was an engine of destruction.

"Don't worry," he whispered, "I doubt he is going to mug us."

Not mug, no; yet Greg was dangerous in another way. How would Randall react if he found out Greg was Ginny's lover? Fortunately, Greg seemed to shy away from the encounter. When he was close enough to see who we were, he stopped and glanced back the way he'd come.

"Good morning!" Randall in his ignorance called to him.

"Hello," Greg answered diffidently.

"It's nice to see someone else out and about at this early hour," Randall remarked. Then to my horror, he walked over to Greg and said, "Was that you who gave the rebel yell?"

Greg regarded him impassively, his handsome face a mask. His arms hung loosely at his sides, but I imagined the right one upraised with a football. The Arm we'd called him in college. His body looked trim and rock-hard beneath the slacks and polo shirt he wore. He hadn't let himself go like some over-the-hill athletes. The beeper on his belt was a new addition. So was the Rolex watch. Successful, strong, and stable, he was the polar opposite of Wiley. No wonder Ginny had fallen for him again.

Greg shook his head. "There's a bunch of Rebel reenactors camped over by the Longstreet Statue, so it was probably one of them."

"The Longstreet Statue?" I repeated. "I thought Lee's was the only statue of a Confederate general in the park."

"That statue was erected a few years ago," Randall explained. "There has not been time to include mention of it in the guidebooks."

"Yes, and looks like they're still paying for it," Greg said. "I noticed a heap of coins on the upraised hoof of the statue's horse. Somebody also put a real cigar on Longstreet's arm and there's a bouquet of red roses, along with a piece of hardtack, on the ground by the horse's hooves. Interesting how that one stands smack on the ground, while this one's way up high." He gestured at the statue of Lee.

The difference between a god and a mere mortal, I thought.

"Reenactor I was talking to," Greg continued, "said the reason it took so long to get a statue of Longstreet into the park was because he disagreed with Lee." He looked at Randall, as if he expected a response.

Changing the subject, Randall inquired, "Is this your first time at Gettysburg?"

"Yes. I was in Hershey visiting the chocolate factory, and figured I might as well come over here." His brown eyes slid guiltily in my direction.

"I've never been there myself," Randall said. "Is it interesting?"

"Sure—if you like chocolate."

"I am fond of it, but I'm afraid it's too rich for my blood now."

"Too bad."

An awkward silence followed. If Greg had been a white man from the South or the North, they could've swapped stories about their great-great-grandfathers who'd fought in the war. Instead, when Randall asked, "Did you travel far to get here?" The question seemed forced.

"Cleveland," Greg replied. "And you're from—" he hesitated slightly "—Virginia?"

The game's up, I thought with a sinking feeling. He's going to spill the beans.

Randall looked surprised. "How did you guess?"

"This is the Virginia Memorial, isn't it? The place where all good sons of Ol' Virginy come to pay their respects."

I thought I heard a trace of mockery in his tone, but I wasn't sure.

"What did Pickett say when he led his charge?" Greg went on.

"Up, men, and to your posts. Don't forget today that you are from old Virginia." Randall spoke flatly without the exclamation points Pickett would have used to exhort his men.

Was Greg doing this on purpose, deliberately reminding Randall of the moment when everything was about to be lost? Again I wasn't sure.

"I thought it was something like that," Greg said.

"You've read about Gettysburg?" Randall asked eagerly.

Greg shook his head. "I only saw the movie."

If Greg had seen the movie, then he'd watched his long-time rival die, assuming that Greg knew Wiley had a part in Pickett's Charge. Wiley had become obsessed with his performance. And Greg? Was he sorry it was just that, a performance instead of the real thing? A tremor went through me.

"Are you cold? Would you like my jacket?" Randall asked solicitously.

"No, thanks, but I think we should start back."

"It has been a pleasure speaking with you," Randall said to Greg. "I hope you enjoy your visit to Gettysburg."

"You, too"

"Odd," Randall remarked as we walked away from the memorial.

"What?" I practically snapped. The unexpected meeting with Greg had left me on edge.

"That fellow back there. One does not often see blacks at the battlefields. But then I suppose it is not surprising more don't come."

"Why?"

"Well, now, you know, it was not *their* fight."

I assumed he meant that relatively few blacks had fought in the Civil War. Yet as a struggle to end slavery, the war had been very much their fight. Surely Randall, for all his interest in the conduct of the war, understood this. As for Greg, I wondered what had brought him to the battlefield this morning. Did he, like us, want to "Feel the Presence, Share the Experience"? Or did he, as a descendant of slaves, want to remind us of a major cause of the conflict? I had never gotten to know Greg well. His intentions were a mystery to me.

"YOU SEE, I was right!" Randall crowed, seizing the Freeman biography from the table in the parlor. "One of the guests borrowed my book, and now they have returned it. They even left my bookmark in." He opened the book to the place marked by a schedule of reenactment events, scanned it, and frowned.

"What's the matter?" I asked.

"Nothing." He closed the book and glanced at his watch. "My goodness, it's nearly eight o'clock. We had better have breakfast and drive to the reenactment site. They advise arriving at least two hours before the battles to avoid being held up in traffic. Could you check on Sleeping Beauty and see if she is up? If not, it's probably a good idea to wake her."

I knocked on Ginny's door and she told me to come in. Still in her bathrobe, she was seated in front of a mirror, brushing her hair. She turned to me with a smile. "I hope you enjoyed your walk as much as I enjoyed the extra sleep."

I cut to the chase. "We ran into Greg on the battlefield."

"What!" Her face registered shock and alarm. "Did you—did he—?"

"He played the stranger and so did I."

"That's a relief. I'll be even more relieved when he's back in—"

A knock at the door interrupted her. It was Randall bearing a breakfast tray with enough food for an army. "Rise and shine, my dear!" he said. "I hope you ladies will partake of a hearty breakfast, because you are going to need your strength for this morning's battle: The Wheatfield, 'The Valley of Death.'"

FIVE

"No hand-to-hand fighting except that specifically designated by the scenarios and rehearsed."
                              Gettysburg Reenactment Regulations, 1988

THE PENNSYLVANIA BRASS BAND was playing a rousing march in the living history tent to a large audience seated on bales of hay. Randall hurried us on to the grandstands, eager to get a good seat for The Wheatfield, "The Valley of Death." Although the battle wouldn't begin for another half hour, the stands were already filled with spectators equipped with sun umbrellas, sun visors, binoculars, cameras, and camcorders. The air reeked of sun block, sweat, and fried grease from hot dogs, hamburgers, and French fries. Randall spotted a small opening near the top in the middle section of the stands and gestured toward it.

"We'll never get all the way up there," Ginny protested.

"Nothing ventured, nothing gained," Randall replied. "Allow me to blaze a trail for you ladies." Then like Moses parting the waters, he did just that. In response to his polite "Pardon me's," the sea of humanity made room for him, and he ascended, sure-footed as a Sherpa guide despite the fact he was overloaded with a bulky camera bag, heavy old-fashioned binoculars, and a large thermos of lemonade. Reaching the summit, he turned back to us with an outstretched hand, eager to provide the help he would never have accepted from Ginny and me.

A cannon boomed, drawing our attention to the field. Directly in front of the stands, a small group of Union officers on horseback stood ready. The two battle lines were arrayed on either side, Confederates on the left, Federals on the right. I scanned the Confederate line for Beau, but even with binoculars the men were too far away to distinguish individuals. The cannonading sent grayish clouds and the occasional perfect smoke ring into the air, obscuring the lines. Explosions erupted in the tall grass. Small children screamed and covered their ears.

After a barrage of artillery fire, the two lines advanced toward each other, blue uniforms blending with gray and brown in the middle of the field. Like a sportscaster at a game, the announcer tried to work us up with frenzied descriptions of the battle. In real time it had begun in the late afternoon of July 2 and lasted for three hours. During that time the Wheatfield changed hands as many as six times. The battle we saw lasted about a half hour, and in the melee I could hardly tell who was winning, who losing. Although the announcer informed us that this was one of the single bloodiest days of the entire war, with approximately 16,500 casualties, we saw few men fall.

The most dramatic moment came when a Union horse, spooked by the firing, reared into the air, dislodging his rider. A ripple of excitement ran through the crowd. Was the rider hurt? Interest gave way to disappointment when the officer got up, brushed himself off, and remounted. I didn't share the crowd's sense of letdown. After the shocks and surprises of the past few days, I was content to watch a carefully scripted event, where little, if anything, was likely to go wrong. The near-fatal incident with the Frenchman had to be the exception rather than the rule.

The battle ended with Union and Confederate officers riding over to one another and shaking hands while the announcer led us in a "Hip, Hip, Hooray!" People began to stir. Binoculars and cameras were lowered, coolers inspected. It was almost noon and lunchtime.

"They do a fine job," Randall commented. "But it is impossible to portray the real horror of what happened in the Wheatfield. That tangle of chest-high grain has been compared to a whirlpool because of the way regiment after regiment vanished into its bloody, swirling vortex. But forgive me for speaking of such unpleasant matters. Why don't we have a look around the camps now and replenish our supply of cold lemonade?"

While Randall and Ginny waited in line at a refreshment stand, I went over to The Quartermaster to buy Nate's son a replica Civil War musket. I picked up one of the muskets and examined it. With a wooden stock and heavy metal barrel and trigger, it looked like a real gun and felt like one, too. I began to have qualms about buying such a realistic replica for an eight-year-old. But I doubted Sam would be content with a plastic model. His father was a hunter, and he'd been around guns all his young life. I, on the other hand, would feel uncomfortable carrying around a near-authentic weapon. And I couldn't walk onto the plane with it. I'd get it wrapped and send it to Sam when we returned to Alexandria. After I'd paid for the musket, I asked the salesclerk to wrap and hold it for me, promising to return before the end of the day. She seemed annoyed by the request, but took the gun to the rear of the tent.

I rejoined Ginny and Randall, and we started toward the camps when a voice from behind said, "You're not in costume." It was Linette Peters, yesterday's Confederate widow.

"I'm here as a tourist," Ginny replied. "But I see you're still doing your widow bit."

"Men really died here," Linette said stiffly. "I want people to remember that. In the Wheatfield alone, five hundred Confederate soldiers perished horribly. Their blood soaked the ground and turned the brooks crimson."

Ginny moved away deliberately, but Randall stepped into the breach. "I'm Randall Longford, Virginia's father, and this is Miranda Lewis," he said, extending a hand.

"You were here yesterday," Linette said to me.

"Yes, I saw you faint."

"You fainted?" Randall addressed Linette with polite concern.

"Almost. The heat made me light-headed."

"My dear, you must exercise the utmost caution in weather like this," he said. "Be sure you have plenty to drink and do not become dehydrated. Would you like some of my lemonade?"

"No, thank you. I was just about to get one myself." Her pinched features softened, and for a moment she almost looked pretty. I felt a flash of jealousy. Randall's solicitude toward a total stranger di-minished the special regard I liked to believe he had for me.

"Where are your manners, Virginia?" Randall demanded when Linette was out of earshot. "You should have introduced Miranda and me to your friend."

"She's not my friend," Ginny snapped.

"Your acquaintance then. I am glad she has chosen the role of a Civil War widow, because it is important to remind people of the war's impact on women and society as a whole."

"Okay, but that doesn't mean I have to like her. There's some-thing strange about Linette. Strange and very off-putting."

"Virginia! I have never understood how you women can tear each other apart. You are worse than a pack of hyenas."

"Better a hyena than a ghoul like Linette," Ginny quipped.

"Now that's ghoulish!" I pointed toward a tent where a man wearing a bloody apron wielded a scalpel over the prone figure of a wounded soldier.

"Civil War medicine at its finest," Ginny said. "This time I will introduce you," she added with a playful glance at Randall.

The tent had a sign identifying it as a field hospital. Tables had been set up in front and along the sides. On them lay a variety of sharp instruments including a saw, vials and bottles of different sorts, basins containing blood, blood-soaked sponges, a few fake body parts, and in one corner, a neat pile of well-bleached bones. The man in the blood-spattered apron glanced up at our approach. "Miz Ginny, long time no see!" He waved his scalpel at her.

"Hi, Jake. I'd like you to meet my father, Randall Longford, and my roommate from college, Miranda Lewis. Jake Euell."

"Sir, ma'am."

I noticed that the surgeon resembled yesterday's beggar. "You've got your legs back."

He squinted at me through tiny, round spectacles. "Begging your pardon, ma'am?"

"Aren't you the same person who said he'd had his legs am-putated at Fredericksburg and was asking for spare change?"

"No, ma'am, I prefer to remain on this side of the knife. And if any of you needs my services, I'll be happy to oblige soon's I finish up with this one. I'll just use my finger to probe for the bullet, then we're on our way." He wiggled his index finger like a worm. "Only takes me about ten to fifteen minutes to do an amputation, and you won't feel the pain because we just got a fresh shipment of chloroform in from Richmond."

"What is the survival rate from amputations?" Randall inquired.

"Depends on the kind. If we're talking a finger, about ninety percent, arms and legs fifty percent. But lots of men are gonna die from infections and from being left on the field a day or more before we can even get to them."

"The survival rate was much higher once *we* got involved—at least on the Union side." A woman in a pink gingham dress with a navy blue apron strolled over from a nearby tent. She had the face of a bulldog with gray-streaked hair pulled severely back in a net, but her voice was warm and friendly. She introduced herself to Randall and me as Dorcas Nutley from the United States Sanitary Commission. Ginny she greeted like a long-lost friend: "Hey, Ginny, great to see you again! We've missed you. Camp life hasn't been the same since you and the girls stopped coming. If you feel like switching sides awhile, we could use your help at our tent. Give us a chance to catch up."

Leaving Ginny with Dorcas, Randall and I continued on toward the Confederate camp. "Strange," I remarked. "I could have sworn that army surgeon was the period panhandler I saw the other day."

"It is easy to make mistakes like that," Randall said. "I, myself, have often been mistaken for—but look, there is General Lee."

A man resembling the general stood in front of a tent with a sign indicating that it was the headquarters of the Army of Northern Virginia. Handsome and white-bearded, he looked so much like Lee that I found myself tongue-tied in the presence of greatness, albeit simulated.

"General Lee, my compliments, sir," Randall said. "Your men fought bravely today."

"Thank you, sir," Lee replied. "We came very close to winning the field, and would, I believe, have done so if the attack had been better coordinated. But tomorrow we will do better."

"I am sure you will," Randall said without a trace of irony.

At the tent of the 3rd Virginia, Beau sprawled on a blanket on the ground, the soles of his bare feet pointing upward, pink as underdone pork. With him was Paul, the burly, blond soldier from the day before, and a few others including Dred Davis. Davis also sprawled on the ground, though at a distance from Beau and the others. A hat covered his face and he appeared to be asleep.

Beau got up to greet us. "Didn't we whip those Yanks but good? Gonna give 'em hell this afternoon, too. Hope you're planning to be around for the attack on Cemetery Hill."

"We will try to," Randall replied. He studied a patch of well-trampled grass at his feet. "You haven't seen Wiley, have you?"

"No," Beau said. "Don't think he's coming."

"He'll be here all right." The voice rose from underneath Dred Davis's hat like a noxious vapor from a manhole cover.

"What d'you know about it?" Beau growled.

"I just know," came the answer.

"Would you care to join us for lunch in town?" Randall asked Beau.

"Thanks, but I'd better stick around. We've got a meeting and a safety check a half hour before the battle, and if I miss it, I don't fight. If you'd like to lunch with me at my tent, I've got plenty of food. Can't promise gourmet fare, but it's better than anything you'll get at the stands."

"I am afraid my lunchtime medications make me so drowsy that I will need a nap afterward," Randall said. "But why don't you stay, Miranda? You will have more time at the camps, and better company than I can offer you this afternoon."

Age deferring to youth, I thought with a pang. Didn't he realize I'd rather be with him than almost anyone else? But staying would give me a chance to "do" the reenactment more fully. I was a relentless tourist, never satisfied until I'd seen everything there was to see, read every scrap of printed material, and drained the experience to the last drop. I gave in to their combined appeals. Randall left to fetch Ginny, and Beau and I started toward his tent. Happening to glance back, I noticed that Dred Davis had removed his hat and was sitting up, glassy-eyed, with an evil grin on his face. His head and upper body bobbed like a cobra teased from its basket by a tune he alone heard.

"MMMM." I YAWNED and stretched. After a beer and an over-stuffed deli sandwich, I was feeling no pain. In fact, I felt more relaxed than I had all weekend.

"Tired?" Beau asked.

"A little. I didn't get much sleep last night.

"Late night on the town?"

"Not really. What about you—were you in town last night?"

His grin vanished behind a paper napkin as he wiped his mouth. "Why do you ask?"

"I saw someone who looked like you in front of a T-shirt shop on Steinwehr Avenue around ten."

"Must've been my doppelganger," Beau said. "What was he doing?"

"Talking with someone in a chair. You're probably right about the doppelganger part, because the next thing I knew, both men vanished."

"Too bad. I would've enjoyed running into you. Things were pretty dull here in camp. But if you're tired, why not take a nap?" He spread out his bedroll and I settled down thankfully.

From nearby tents came the sounds of people performing domestic tasks. These blended with snatches of conversation, laughter, and clicks from the triggers of replica muskets, forming the white noise of camp. A horse's high, shrill whinny broke into the drone. Then the cry died away and the white noise returned, lulling me to sleep like the lap of waves against the shore.

When I woke up, it was time for Beau's meeting and for me to go to the stands for the Rebel assault on Cemetery Hill. I found a seat next to a dad with a young boy about Nate's son's age. The boy toted a replica rifle like the one I'd bought for Sam. I looked around for Ginny and Randall, but didn't see them. Most likely they'd decided to stay in town for the afternoon.

While music I thought I recognized from the movie, *Gettysburg,* blared from speakers set up on the field, the Union line assembled directly in front of the stands. At a signal, they advanced a short distance forward on the high ground meant to represent Cemetery Hill. They squatted or sat with their hats stuck onto their bayonets, as skirmishers darted into the tall grass in an effort to draw out the enemy. Shots were exchanged and the skirmishers withdrew. Cannon boomed, coating the landscape with a smoky haze. When the haze finally lifted, a gray line could be seen sweeping toward the blue one.

"For the Rebs, that was seven hundred yards of bloody hell," the dad next to me muttered, then, "Look at that! Lady out there's right in the line of fire."

A figure clothed all in black hovered in a patch of grass slightly to the left of the two lines, but still within range of a stray missile. Linette, or the Suicide Lady, as my neighbor dubbed her. "Wonder what she's doing in the field?" I said.

"Could be filming the battle," the dad suggested. "Was a Japanese film crew here this morning dressed up like Union soldiers and shooting away with their cameras."

I peered at Linette through my binoculars, but saw no camera. She just stood there watching the soldiers like a crow on the lookout for carrion. Ginny was right: Linette was strange.

The two lines closed in on each other, Confederates pushing Federals up the slope toward the grandstand. More soldiers took hits than in the morning's battle. They either lay motionless on the ground, or struggled to crawl back to safety. The "dead" and "wounded" included several young drummer boys at the rear of the Union line. They fell to the ground with frenzied flailing. No doubt, they were having great fun. But seeing these youngsters "die" in battle reminded me of the grim fact that in the Union army, two hundred thousand soldiers were under age sixteen, and three hundred were under thirteen.

In the hand-to-hand combat that followed, two soldiers played

"Capture the Flag." The Rebel grabbed at the Stars and Stripes held by the Federal. This tug of war ended in a tussle on the ground. The men formed a human barrel, each roll bringing them closer to the stands. They exchanged real blows until soldiers from both sides yanked them apart and led them grunting and protesting away. The Union soldier had a nasty bruise under his eye; the Rebel sported a bloody, possibly broken, nose.

"Serves 'im right," my neighbor commented.

"Who?"

"Guy with the bloody nose. I've been to enough reenactments to know that you never, but never, try to capture the enemy's flag. You're supposed to take the flag bearer prisoner."

"How come?"

"Money and love. Regimental flags are expensive, and there's an emotional attachment to them. You want to start a fight, you go for the flag."

I should have known; the Rebel now clutching a bloody hand-kerchief to his nose was none other than Dred Davis.

For a brief while, it appeared that the Rebels had won. Then, with a fresh burst of musket fire, a Union brigade forced them from the hill. The announcer informed us that the battle was over. The commanders shook hands and we gave them a rousing cheer. The Union General, George Gordon Meade, galloped back and forth in front of the stands to further applause.

"We saved the Union!" he shouted, waving his hat in the air.

"Again," a large woman wearing a T-shirt that identified her as the wife of a Civil War Bore remarked wearily.

Men began moving off the field, singly and in small groups. A detachment of a half-dozen victorious Union soldiers stopped to pose for a photo opportunity near where I sat. While we snapped them, they studied us.

"You in Nam?" a sunburned soldier called to someone behind me.

"Yeah" came the reply.

The Union soldier stepped forward with an outstretched hand. The other man climbed down to meet him. Dressed in shorts and an "I Survived Pickett's Charge" T-shirt, he looked like any other tourist except for the flag and insignia on his cap identifying him as a Vietnam veteran. The two men shook hands and swapped war stories. I stared at the vet, struck by something familiar about him. He was tall and rail-thin with a scraggly beard.

"Wiley?" I hazarded. He twisted around like bent barbed wire springing back into position. Bill-shaded eyes bore into me.

"Miranda. You by yourself?" The voice was wary, without any of the instant camaraderie with which he'd responded to the Union reenactor.

"Yes. Ginny and her father went back into town after the morning's battle."

"That's good. Real good. I don't want them to know I'm here. Least not yet."

Join the club, I thought. Ginny had her secret, and so apparently did Wiley. "How come?"

He put a finger to his lips and pulled me toward him until I was under the awning of his cap. Then he laughed his bad boy laugh. I caught a whiff of spearmint breath saver masking the rank odor of acid indigestion. But thankfully, he no longer gave off an unwashed stench, the switch from reenactor to tourist having included a stint in the shower. I smelled only sweat mingled with a faint, sweet odor that wasn't readily identifiable. It probably came from soap, shampoo, or aftershave. If so, he'd made an unfortunate choice. The scent had the sickly sweetness of rotting papaya, not repellant, but still cloying.

"Who's your friend, Miranda?" Beau's voice interrupted my olfactory analysis.

"Why, Beauregard Johnston," Wiley simpered with a limp-wristed wave, "you mean to tell me you don't recognize your old buddy, Wile?"

"What the hell're you doing in that tourist getup?" Beau demanded.

"As I was just explaining to Miranda, my being here is supposed to be a secret—at least for the time being."

"What's up? You on the wrong side of the law?"

"More like in-law."

"Your boy Dred's been acting up again," Beau said tightly.

"You mean that scuffle he had with the Yank? He was just giving the folks in the stands a little fun for their money."

"Feds don't see it that way. They don't like it that one of theirs got beaten up. Or that their flag got wrecked."

"Pansy-asses. They ain't seen nothing yet."

"Wile." Beau drew himself up into a stern stance. "Your boy's pushing the envelope too far. One more incident like today's and he's out."

Wiley scowled and seemed ready to argue. Instead, backing down, he said, "Okay, I'll speak to him, give him some advice about the proper way to treat a Yank." His gaze shifted to the field. "Hey, Linette, c'mon over here."

Linette approached in fits and starts like a sailboat tacking against the wind to reach shore. "This is Miranda," Wiley introduced us. "Gin-gin's old roommate from the Farm. Funny nickname for a university, ain't it? Makes it sound like they was raising chickens or hogs instead of world-class scholars."

"We've met," Linette informed him curtly.

"Now that we're a foursome, why not go for a drink at Herr Tavern?" Wiley suggested.

"I need to take Miranda back to town," Beau said.

"What's the rush? The evening's young, it's not even dark yet. You'll only get stuck in traffic if you go back now. What d'you say, Miranda?" he asked, turning to me. "The Dancing Crab it ain't," he said, referring to our favorite hangout of twenty years ago. "But Herr Tavern's still a fine place for a few pops."

I hesitated, pulled in different directions. On the one hand, I was anxious to get back to Randall and Ginny. But on the other, I was curious about Wiley's game—why he'd shown up disguised as a tourist and wanted his presence kept a secret from Ginny and Randall. Going for a drink with him would give me a chance to find out. "All right."

"That's my girl!" Wiley lassoed me with his arm. "You coming, too, Linette?" He held out his other arm to her.

"I guess." She sounded resigned rather than pleased.

"We'll need to take your wheels," Wiley told Beau. "I had to leave the Battlemobile at the garage and borrow a friend's wreck. It's not very reliable, either. And we sure as hell don't want Linette driving."

Linette gave a cry like that of a wounded animal. "Wiley— how could you?"

"Sorry, I shouldn't have said that," Wiley apologized. "Linette's kinda touchy about her driving ability," he explained to Beau and me.

More than just touchy, I thought, as we left the grandstand. There was something between Wiley and Linette, but I hadn't a clue what—unless it had to do with the fact that they were both unstable, and therefore, kindred spirits.

On the way to the parking area, we stopped at The Quartermaster, so I could pick up the replica musket I had purchased earlier. A teenager with a pimply face and spiked bleached-blond hair manned the stand. He started to hand me a rifle from the counter, but I explained that the one I'd bought had been wrapped. "Don't know nothin' 'bout that," he said in a surly voice.

"The woman who was here this morning said she'd take care of it for me," I persisted. "Maybe she left it in the back. Could you please check?"

The teenager picked at a pimple and held his ground.

"Don't just stand there, punk," Wiley growled. "Get the lady her rifle."

The boy shuffled to the back, returning a few minutes later with a long, narrow package wrapped in newspaper. He gave it to me with a strange look. I grasped the package awkwardly, feeling slightly foolish. Beau must have sensed my discomfort because he offered to carry it for me. I smiled my thanks, and we continued on to the parking area.

Scraps of paper and food wrappers littered the back of Beau's Ford Crown Victoria. He made a clean sweep before letting us in. I got into the back with Wiley, who immediately began rooting around in the space between the seat and the backrest. "Finder's keepers!" he crowed, brandishing a small packet of what looked like pills.

"Gimme that!" Beau swiped at the packet.

"Nuh-uh." Wiley whipped his hand away. "Doctors get 'em for free, so why not me?"

I looked at him inquiringly.

"Guess Beau hasn't told you what he does for a living," Wiley said. "He's a sales rep for a pharmaceutical company. Peddles pills. Uppers, downers, in-betweeners, you name it, he's got it in these nice little 'sample only' packets." He dangled the packet in front of Beau, prompting another abortive strike.

"Give me the pills, Wiley." Linette held her hand like a dog trainer ordering a stubborn pup to relinquish a shoe. Like a pup, Wiley didn't comply immediately. "Give them to me," Linette repeated.

A cunning look came over Wiley's face. "Only if you say, 'Pretty please.'"

"Pretty please." Linette's voice remained harsh, but her eyes pleaded. Wiley dropped the packet into her outstretched hand. Her fingers snapped shut like a trap.

"Thank you, darlin'," he murmured.

What was going on between them? I suspected they'd acted out similar scenes before. Wiley had played the role of the bad boy looking to be saved by the love of a good woman often enough with Ginny. And for all her erratic behavior, Linette seemed genuinely bent on rescuing him.

"So, sweetheart," Wiley drawled into my ear, "you having yourself a good ol' time here in Gettysburg?"

SIX

"Most nurses were male during this period; women generally took care of convalescents by writing letters, keeping bed linens clean, and conversing with soldiers."
Reliving the Civil War, A Reenactor's Handbook

A TWO-STORY BRICK building dating back to the early 1800s, Herr Tavern had served as a hospital during the Battle of Gettysburg. Even now, a doctor was in attendance. Clad in his blood-spattered apron, Jake Euell nursed a beer at the bar.

"Yo, Jake," Beau greeted him. "Why aren't you at the site looking after the injured?"

"Wasn't much work for me, only those two that got into a fight, and I let one of the other EMTs take care of them."

"You're an EMT?" I took a seat next to him.

Jake turned to me with a slow smile. "In my other life, yeah."

Beau asked, "Did Davis get his nose broken in the fight?"

"Just bloodied," Jake replied.

"Too bad. Might've taught him a lesson."

"Now, now," Wiley said. "Beau doesn't like Dred on account of a little accident that happened a while back," he explained to me.

"He told me about it," I said quickly, not anxious to hear the story again.

"Accidents happen." Wiley straddled the seat on my right. "But we're in good company 'cuz if anything goes wrong, Jake's an EMT, Linette's a nurse, and there's always Beau with his pills. So let's eat, drink, and be merry, 'cuz tomorrow who knows?"

The bartender brought beers and a soda for Linette, and we followed this advice—all except Wiley, who merely licked at the foam. "You should eat something." Jake pushed a bowl of pretzels toward him.

"Think I'm too thin? As my mama used to say, you can never be too rich or too thin," Wiley said in the mincing tones that went with his limp-wrist act.

"There's thin and there's anorexic," Jake replied. "And you're—" He broke off at a warning head shake from Linette. "You look better cleaned-up, though," he finished.

Wiley groaned. "I feel like such a farb. I can't take part in Pickett's Charge tomorrow looking like this." He sounded like Cinderella lamenting the lack of a ball gown. "Wonder if they've got some grease in the kitchen I can smear into my beard." He glanced toward the rear, where an entryway led to another dining room and presumably the kitchen and restrooms.

"Think there's a pay phone?" I figured I'd call the B and B and let Randall and Ginny know where I was.

"Allow me to escort you, ma'am." Wiley stood up, clicked his heels together—no easy feat considering he wore flip-flops—and offered me his arm. In spite of myself, I was charmed by the gesture. Wiley the eternal child, maddening in his refusal to grow up and assume the responsibilities of adulthood, but in his more playful moments, fun to be with. Though egocentric as any child, he could be surprisingly empathetic.

One evening during the summer I had spent with Ginny, I was particularly upset. I couldn't remember why. What I remembered were Wiley's efforts to cheer me up. "Hey, sweetheart, you seem awful sad tonight," he said, draping an arm around me as we sat at the bar. "C'mon now, let's have a smile." He made funny faces until he got what he wanted. Then sensing a residual melancholy, he put a song on the jukebox. We danced together, belting out the chorus of "It's My Party and I'll Cry If I Want To" while Beau and Ginny looked on in bewilderment.

Recalling that evening helped me understand why Ginny had put up with Wiley's shenanigans for so many years. If marriage to him had been a wild ride, at least it had had its fun moments. I took his arm with a smile.

A couple sat at a small table just inside the entry to the rear dining room. Heads bent close and hands clasped next to a bud vase with a single blossom, they formed a Hallmark picture of romance—except that Hallmark cards didn't usually feature interracial couples. Wiley spoke Ginny's name in a strangled voice. She looked at him, dumbstruck. Greg stood up as if in response to an emergency summons. I half expected him to grab his black bag and rush out the door. Instead, he gave Wiley a look that was cool and clinical, but in which I detected a glimmer of compassion. Greg put out a hand and Wiley reacted as to an actual blow, wobbling on the balls of his feet like a bowling pin about to go down. If he had wanted to, Greg with his massive build and machine-honed muscles could have flattened Wiley with the ease of a tank rolling over a reed. The realization of Wiley's vulnerability made me feel protective. I pulled him from that room I wished he'd never entered.

"What the—" We backed up against Jake Euell, who had come to see what was the matter. "Omigod," Jake muttered, as Ginny and Greg swept past. At the door Ginny wavered. Her free arm fluttered back like a streamer. Wiley would have grabbed it if Jake and I hadn't held him fast. A tug from Greg, and Ginny cleared the door and vanished.

Wiley went limp in Jake's and my supporting arms. "C'mon, man, let's get you a drink." Jake steered Wiley toward the bar.

I wanted to console him myself. But under the pressure of the moment, the wrong words bubbled out: "I'm so sorry, Wiley. I had no idea they'd be here."

Everything in the room stopped. In the silence I imagined I could hear the click-clack of circuits being activated, as the full meaning of what I'd just said registered on Wiley's brain. But it was Beau rather than Wiley who spoke. "You knew Ginny was seeing someone?" he asked.

"Yes, but…" I glanced helplessly around, aware of the accusation in Beau's eyes, Linette's, and even Jake's. They seemed to withdraw from me, the traitor in their midst. Only Wiley still clung to me, perhaps because he was still too shocked to do otherwise.

"Who's the guy?" Beau demanded. Whatever animosity he had felt toward Wiley was gone; he'd resumed the role of old buddy.

"Not now," Jake said with a nod toward the door where the dinner crowd was beginning to arrive.

"Let's go back to camp," Linette suggested.

"All right, but first I need to drop Miranda in town," Beau said.

In the car Beau shook his head and said, "I'm amazed at Ginny. Bringing a lover to Gettysburg is like shitting in your own backyard. She must've known she'd run into Wiley or one of his old buddies."

"Maybe she doesn't care who she hurts anymore," Linette piped up from the backseat.

"It was his idea, not hers, to come here," I retorted, rising to Ginny's defense.

"I'll bet! That must be why the old man—Christ! Fix him but good," Wiley muttered.

"Wiley! You mustn't let the devil—" Linette began.

The devil? She was really wacky.

"Don't you worry 'bout me, darlin'," Wiley said. "You got enough to do with your grieving," he paused ever so slightly, "for all the Confederate dead. Besides, I ain't gonna hurt the guy—just rip out his black balls an' toss 'em in the trash. As for Gingin and her Daddy—"

"Randall doesn't know they're involved yet. I didn't find out myself until last night."

"Ever the loyal friend, ain't you?" Wiley mocked. "But I seen what I seen."

The rest of the ride passed in ominous silence. I wished I could count on Linette and Beau to prevent Wiley from going after Ginny and Greg. But Linette was no friend of Ginny's. And I wasn't certain any more whose side Beau was on.

Beau pulled up at the B and B and waited for me to get out. The light was on in the parlor. I thought I saw Randall. He was probably waiting for Ginny and me, waiting and worrying. I said good night and got out. I was almost to the front door when a sharp prod in the back sent me stumbling.

"Too bad this ain't a real gun, or I'd be tempted to use it," Wiley said. "But not on you, sweetheart." He held out the replica musket in its newspaper swaddling. I grasped it with shaky hands. Wiley rocked on the balls of his feet like a skeleton in the wind. A skeleton in flip-flops and a Pickett's Charge T-shirt with the burning eyes of an unquiet soul.

I turned to go, fleeing the sight of him, at once comical and terrifying. He caught me by the elbow. "I ain't finished." He pulled a crumpled envelope from the pocket of his shorts. "Give this to Gin-gin. I love her, y'know." Again I smelled the sickly sweet odor of rotting fruit. "And I'd do anything to get her back."

SEVEN

"Women visiting the camp alone were considered 'loose women.'
A lady was generally escorted by a male relative or military
escort, or stayed with a group of women."

> *Reliving the Civil War, A Reenactor's Handbook*

DINNER THAT EVENING was excruciating. Ginny had told her father she was going to visit a reenactor friend who was ill. When she returned, clearly upset, Randall thought she was concerned about her friend. He tried to cheer her up by regaling us with anecdotes about the battles of today and tomorrow. I listened as politely as I could, wishing the meal would end and I could speak with Ginny alone.

That moment finally came when Ginny, pleading a splitting headache, went upstairs to her room. She was lying face down on the bed when I entered. I went over and sat beside her. "What happened? Why didn't Greg leave when he said he would?"

Ginny raised a blotchy, tear-streaked face. "My fault," she replied miserably. "Last night when Greg asked about our plans for today, I told him we'd go to the reenactment in the morning, then probably come back to town for lunch, so Daddy could take his nap. Greg saw a window of opportunity and left a message for me at the B and B, begging me to meet him. Fool that I am, I went to him as soon as Daddy'd gone up to his room. This is my worst nightmare come true. I never meant for Wiley to find out about me and Greg this way. When I think of the look on his face—it was as if I'd stuck a knife in his heart. I've got to find Wiley and explain about me and Greg, and that I didn't bring Greg here to throw our affair in his face."

"No," I protested. "That's the worst possible thing you could do. Wiley was in a state of shock when he saw you and Greg, but later in the car he started talking about getting back at Greg—you and your father, too. Hopefully, the others have managed to calm him down, but if you go to him now, you'll only add fuel to the fire. Promise you won't."

Ginny looked at me with her green feline eyes. In them, I saw the same stubborn independence that was in my cat, Love's, eyes when I ordered her off the kitchen counter.

My cat held her ground until the last possible moment. Then, as soon as my back was turned, she was up on the counter again.

"Ginny, please. I don't want you to get hurt." Green eyes stared at me without blinking. "There's your father, too. Think of how he'd feel if anything happened to you."

Ginny's gaze slipped sideways, then back. "Okay, I promise."

"Good. Now why don't you try and get some rest? I've got Tylenol PM if you want something to help you sleep."

Ginny smiled weakly. "I don't need anything. You get some rest, too. It's been a long day, with more excitement than either of us bargained for."

Back in my room, I noticed Wiley's letter for Ginny lying on the dresser where I'd left it before we went out to dinner. I decided not to give it to Ginny tonight. She was upset enough.

I settled into a chair with *The Killer Angels,* reading with an ear cocked in case Ginny reneged on her promise. But after an hour or so with no telltale noises from the hallway or the street, I figured I could let down my guard. I'd slept poorly the night before, and the evening's events had left me emotionally drained. I felt like an empty husk nodding in the breeze. My eyelids fluttered. The print before me blurred, then blacked out altogether.

I woke with a start from a nightmare of Wiley attacking Ginny and Randall. A glance at my watch told me it was past 11:00 p.m. Filled with a premonition of danger, I went to the window and peered out. There was an empty space where Randall's Lincoln had been parked. Dammit! I should have known better than to trust her. I hurried downstairs. No one was around in the alcove that served as an office for the B and B. I used the phone there to call a taxi.

It was nearly midnight and all quiet on the combined Union and Confederate front when I reached the Yingling Farm. I paid the cabdriver and rushed off to find Beau, figuring he would know where Wiley and Ginny were. Guided by the moonlight and the occasional flicker of a candle, lantern, or flashlight, I made my way to his tent. Empty. I prowled the rows of tents, looking for someone to ask if they'd seen him or the others.

Ahead, I spotted the field hospital tent. If this had been a real army camp at the time of the Gettysburg Battle, this tent would have presented a hideous scene of blood, gore, screaming men, and severed limbs. Instead, the place was dark and deserted, the sharp instruments, basins of bloody water, and bogus body parts having been put away. Jake Euell had closed up shop for night. But someone was about, judging from a faint glow at the rear of the closed tent. I was about to whisper Jake's name when the light moved, and a silhouette appeared on the tent wall.

The shadow was seated in a chair with one leg stretched out on a stool, presumably resting from the day's exertions. Then to my surprise, the shadow reached for an implement that resembled a hand saw. He sliced the air over his leg, as if performing a mock amputation. With each slice the distance between saw and leg grew narrower. *Jesus.* What was happening here? He looked as if he really intended to cut himself. "Stop!" I cried.

The shadow saw dropped from view. I heard a muttered curse within. Outside, footsteps approached. A light shone on me. "What's going on?" Dorcas Nutley thrust her bulldog face into mine. "Don't you realize people are trying to sleep?"

"Sorry. I thought I saw…" I didn't know what to say. If I said Jake had been about to cut off his leg, she'd think I was crazy. Perhaps it had only been shadow play.

"A ghost?" Dorcas Nutley prodded sarcastically.

"Something like that."

"My shadow." Jake Euell emerged from the tent *sans* saw.

"What're you doing here, anyway?" Dorcas Nutley demanded. "Camp's closed to the public."

"Beau Johnston invited me back," I fibbed. "When I got here, I couldn't find him. Have either of you seen him?"

"Not since he and the others left Herr Tavern," Jake said.

"I saw Beau at camp earlier in the evening," Dorcas volunteered. "But then I think he went out again. You must've gotten your signals crossed."

"What about Wiley—is he here?"

Dorcas nodded. "Camped by himself on the other side of those trees." She gestured toward a line of trees on the far side of the field.

"Ah. Think I'll pay him a visit. He might know where Beau is."

"I'd leave him be, if I were you." She laid a hand on my arm, detaining me.

"Why? He's okay, isn't he?"

Dorcas's stern expression softened into a smile. "Better than he's been in a long time."

"What do you mean?"

"She's with him," Dorcas replied.

"Ginny?"

"Yes, and they don't want to be disturbed."

"Are you certain everything's all right?"

"Yes. She came here all upset looking for him. Told her where he was, but then I started thinking maybe I shouldn't have. Wiley was pretty steamed up when I saw him earlier. They must've worked things out, though. When I checked back on them, they were lying in each other's arms spooning, as we call it." She sounded like a doting mother speaking of her children.

I felt relief, but also amazement at the vagaries of love. Wiley and Ginny were back together again—for better or for worse. Their reconciliation might prove temporary, but for tonight at least I could rest easy. I said good night to Dorcas and Jake and walked to the road, hoping to hitch a ride with a passing motorist.

I'd been walking about ten minutes when I heard the roar of an engine behind me. Good. I didn't relish the idea of going the whole way on foot and had begun to regret not asking Dorcas or Jake to drive me. Glancing over my shoulder, I saw that a motorcycle rather than a car was streaking toward me. Damn.

A chill went down my spine, as the precariousness of my situation dawned on me. A lone woman on a dark, deserted road at night, I was an easy prey. But not if I made myself scarce. Hopping to the side of the road, I crouched in a tangle of low-lying bushes. The motorcycle slowed down. I crouched lower. A few feet away, the bike came to a halt. Moonlight glinted on the plastic skulls dangling from the handlebar. My heart thumped wildly. A black leather-clad figure dismounted and raked the roadside with a flashlight. I flattened myself into the ground, shutting my eyes in the childish hope that if I couldn't see him, he couldn't see me, either. Light trapped me within its glare.

"It's me, Jake Euell. What're you doing in the bushes? You okay?"

I opened my eyes, letting my gaze travel upward to the rusty drip of his beard. "I was just taking a closer look at the local flora." I rose slowly and faced him.

"Why didn't you ask for a ride back at camp?"

"I wanted to walk."

"It's a long way into town."

"I need the exercise."

"If you get tired, there isn't a lot of traffic this time of night. Come along with me."

Sure, I thought. So you can take me to an even darker and more deserted place where nobody will hear my screams when you start hacking me to pieces. My gaze flicked from one end of the road to the other, seeking the distant glow of headlights and help. No vehicle was in sight. "That your bike, or did you borrow it?" I stalled.

"Mine."

"Soldier, sailor, biker, beggar," I murmured.

He shrugged. "Maybe I did want to see what it was like on the other side of the knife."

"Is that what you were doing tonight?"

I'd gone too far. He drew himself up, as if in readiness for an attack. I scanned the road desperately. No dice. Jake stood between me and his bike. He would pull me off before I got the damn thing going. I could run but doubted I'd get far.

"Ever play with matches when you were a kid?" Jake surprised me by asking.

I shook my head. "You did?"

"Yeah. Wanted to see how long I could keep my finger in the fire before the pain became unbearable. I found out all right. Since then I've known different kinds of pain. And in my work as an EMT, I've seen plenty of people who were hurting bad. Still, it's hard to imagine how those soldiers stood it when their limbs were being sawed off. I've read descriptions of the butchery that went on in field hospitals during the war. But reading about something's not the same as experiencing it yourself. Tonight I thought I'd…think I'm crazy?"

I took my time answering. Probably he was a bit crazy. But all the same, as an historian I understood the urge to replicate an experience from the past, however ghastly. It was the same impulse that drew people into reenacting, and for purists like Wiley into hardcore reenacting. "I guess I understand your curiosity," I said finally.

"Fair enough. Now will you let me give you a ride?"

"I'd rather—"

"You're safe with me, you know," he broke in. "Despite what you saw earlier and what I've just told you, I'm in the business of helping people. I'm an EMT, remember."

"I'd still rather walk."

"Suit yourself." He stalked to his bike. I felt relieved as he mounted the bike, revved the engine, and looped around in the direction of camp. I started walking toward town again.

I'd been walking about five minutes when a pickup, filled with drunken reenactors, pulled up alongside me. "Need a ride?" one of them yelled.

"No, thanks." I continued walking, but the pickup rumbled next to me, the men calling out and even making grabs at me. I was beginning to regret not having accepted Jake's offer of a ride when the motorcycle appeared.

"Leave the lady alone, or I'll arrest you all for disorderly conduct!" Jake shouted. I caught a flash of silver as he gestured at the men in the pickup.

"Didn't mean no harm, officer," one of the men protested.

"Then get the hell outta here!" Jake shot back.

The pickup took off. Jake dismounted and came over to me. "You're not really a cop," I challenged.

He thrust his face into mine. "Shut up and get on the bike!"

This time, I obeyed. I put on the helmet he handed me and climbed onto the bike behind him. Speeding along in the darkness with the wind whipping in my face, and my arms wrapped around my companion's hard, leather middle, I felt young and reckless, a biker's moll with her man. "Whew!" I gasped when Jake deposited me, flushed and breathless, in front of the B and B.

"Liked it, huh?" He grinned.

Before I could answer, Jake stepped on the gas and roared off into the night. My heart still racing from the ride, I went upstairs to my room. As I fumbled in the semidarkness for the light switch, I bumped into a hard object propped against the wall. It clattered to the ground. I flicked on the switch. The package with the present for Nate's son lay partially unwrapped on the floor. I didn't know much about guns, but even I could see that this was no replica of a Civil War musket but a modern-day assault rifle.

EIGHT

"Soon Pickett galloped up, as debonair as if he had been riding through the streets of Richmond under the eye of his affianced. 'Up, men,' he called, 'and to your posts! Don't forget today that you are from old Virginia!'"

R. E. Lee, *A Biography*

"WHY, MIRANDA, WHAT a wonderful surprise! I was just thinking about you." The words spilled out of him like the coffee that sloshed from the container in his hand, as he swerved to avoid colliding with me. His dark eyes flashed and his face was flushed with excitement. Ordinarily, such a greeting from Randall would have brought an answering flush to my cheeks. Not this morning. Not when he had caught me sneaking from the B and B with an assault rifle wrapped in newspaper. He was on his way in with a newspaper in one hand and coffee in the other.

"I thought you took your constitutional at 6:00 a.m.," I babbled. When I had made my plans last night, I had never dreamed he'd be up and about a whole hour earlier than usual. Otherwise, I would've set my alarm for 3:30 a.m. instead of 4:30.

Tucking his newspaper under his arm, Randall wiped away the trail of muddy brown liquid from his coffee container with a pocket handkerchief. "Alas, I rarely sleep through the night anymore. This morning, when I realized that further slumber was impossible, I decided I might as well start the day. What about you?"

"I'm a light sleeper, too."

In fact, I had lain awake most of the night wondering what to do about the gun. At my most paranoid, I was ready to believe that someone had deliberately set me up. More likely, the assault rifle had come into my possession by accident. The teenager at the shop could have picked up the wrong package, an easy enough mistake as the assault rifle's high-tech lightness made it difficult to distinguish from the replica. But what was an assault rifle doing at a shop like The Quartermaster, which was hardly a serious gun store? I'd best turn the gun over to the police. But I didn't want to go to the station in the middle of the night. I'd wait until the following morning.

Now, face to face with Randall, I wondered how to respond when he asked the inevitable question about the package in my hands. I could say I had discovered a defect in the replica musket and wanted to exchange it. But he would want to know why I was doing this at 5:00 a.m. when the shop wasn't even open yet. Like a rabbit seeking a hole, my brain scrambled frantically for a believable excuse. Instinctively I lowered my gaze until I was staring at Randall's well-polished shoes. Wet grass had darkened the leather uppers and a few blades still clung there.

"I have already taken my constitutional, or I would ask you to join me," he said. "But I would welcome the pleasure of your company. Perhaps this would be an opportune time to discuss your Civil War chapter—over coffee, of course."

"Yes, I just need to go back upstairs for a minute." I returned the package to my room, relieved he hadn't inquired about it. I'd get the gun to the police later.

"Remember when I mentioned having a few small quibbles about your chapter?" Randall said after we had settled ourselves in the parlor with our take-out coffees. "This morning on my walk I realized what was bothering me."

"Bothering you?" I echoed, already feeling defensive.

"Forgive me. That is much too strong a word," Randall back-pedaled. "It is more a sense I had of something not being quite right, but I could not put my finger on it until now. All the important information is there and the chapter is beautifully written, so it is really a matter of organization and emphasis. You do a marvelous job of describing the early battles of the war and the relative strengths and weaknesses of each side, but then comes a long section about Emancipation."

"What's the problem there?"

"As I said before, it is a matter of organization and emphasis. You get your readers, eighth graders if I am not mistaken, caught up in the battles; then you interrupt the narrative flow with a discussion of Emancipation."

"But it's too important a subject not to be included," I protested. "And where else should it go other than after the Battle of Antietam, which gave Lincoln the victory he needed to issue the Emancipation Proclamation?"

"I am not saying Emancipation should not be mentioned," Randall demurred, "but perhaps you could do it in a few lines rather than devoting an entire section to it. The Thirteenth Amendment was not passed until after the war, so why not put a comprehensive treatment of the subject in the chapter on Reconstruction?"

"Because my editors want it where it is," I blurted.

"Ah. Your hands are tied?"

"Not entirely. If I wanted to, I could make a case for postponing a full discussion of Emancipation until a later chapter, but I agree with them that it belongs in the Civil War chapter."

"Well, then," Randall said mildly, "you asked my opinion and I have given it to you. I am probably old-fashioned in thinking all children want is an exciting story."

They want an exciting story, I thought, but they deserve a true one, and that's why Emancipation needs to be not only touched on, but discussed at length. I was disappointed that Randall couldn't see this, but also disappointed in myself. I hadn't really wanted his opinion, I'd wanted his unqualified praise. I felt like a petulant child who doesn't find the one gift she truly desires under the Christmas tree.

"Writing textbooks must be terribly difficult these days," Randall remarked, moving from the specific to the comfortable realm of generality, "with the all different constituencies you have to take into consideration."

"You can say that again. Despite your best efforts, there's always someone you end up offending. And if they have a loud enough voice, they can play a major role in determining how history gets written."

With Randall's encouragement, I launched into a discussion of the politics of textbook publishing. He was a good listener and asked probing questions. Before I knew it more than an hour had passed. We were still going strong when Ginny wandered into the parlor in her bathrobe a little after 7:00 a.m. Her eyes were red and puffy, and her hair was uncombed. She looked the worse for wear after a night of sleeping in the open with her hardcore husband. I wondered if she regretted the return to his difficult embrace.

Randall gave her a look that was at once fond and filled with parental concern, but did not remark on her disheveled appearance. "I am so glad you are up, Virginia," he said. "I have some notions about how we should spend today, and I would like to discuss them with you and Miranda."

Randall's "notion" was that we visit the Angle on Cemetery Ridge before going to the reenactment site. He thought that if we saw the field from the vantage point of the Union troops, we could better appreciate the valor of Pickett's and Pettigrew's men, as they charged across a mile of open ground toward the enemy. Ginny stayed in the car while Randall and I prowled the area around the copse of trees, reading historical markers, examining the various monuments, and gazing out at the hazy expanse of field over which the Rebels had struggled.

"There is the Virginia Memorial, where we were yesterday." Randall pointed to a spot in the distance where Lee sat astride his great bronze horse. His face assumed the reverent expression of the day before, reverent and regretful. He walked over to the stone wall behind which Federal infantrymen had launched their deadly fire. Kneeling in the grass, he placed an object from his pocket in between the stones. I was standing several yards behind him, so couldn't see what the object was. I assumed it was some sort of memento left to mark the spot where a Rebel might have fallen, as others placed flags, flowers, coins, and even pieces of hardtack beside the various monuments throughout the military park. Randall rose and turned back to me with an apologetic look. "Would you mind awfully if we went over to Little Round Top? I would like to revisit that place, too."

From Little Round Top, we drove to Devil's Den, the Wheatfield, and the Peach Orchard—all scenes of bloody combat on the second day of battle—then out the Chambersburg Pike to the sites of the first day's battle. Only then did I realize that Randall was taking us on a tour of the battlefield in reverse, moving backward in time to the moment when the conflict was just beginning and victory remained within tantalizing reach of Lee's army.

It was after 1:00 p.m. by the time we got on the road to the Yingling Farm. Staring at the line of cars stretching ahead of us, I became increasingly antsy. Instead of going to the police station, I'd decided I would turn the assault rifle over to the first police officer I found at the reenactment site. Not wanting to alarm Ginny and Randall unnecessarily, I hadn't told them about finding the weapon, only that the replica musket had turned out to be defective and I needed to exchange it. But now, as the minutes ticked away and we remained stuck in a gridlock, I was afraid I wouldn't be able to dispose of the gun before Pickett's Charge at 2:00 p.m. I was tempted to leave the car and run the rest of the way. Good manners kept me in my seat but didn't prevent me from drumming nervously on the door handle. A glance from Randall and I stopped.

At last the Yingling Farm came in view. The parking area across the street from the reenactment site was full. We were diverted to another lot on the same side, but farther away, with a hill between it and the tent encampment.

"I'll go ahead and make my exchange," I said, springing from the car. "Meet you in the stands."

Randall and Ginny seemed surprised by my haste, but I couldn't afford to lose another minute. I sprinted up the hill, stopping briefly at the top to catch my breath. Although the sky was overcast, the absence of sun brought no coolness but rather a sticky heat. The polo shirt I was wearing clung to my skin. My hand was grimy with a mixture of sweat and newsprint from the package. Pulling out my shirttails, I fanned my shirt like a bellows to let in air. Then, heedless of the gray marks it would leave, I wedged the newspaper-wrapped gun under my arm with the barrel pointing safely downward. Best to make it appear as unobtrusive as possible.

I reached the far end of the concession area. A few people still stood in lines at the refreshment stands, but the other shops were largely deserted. Most of the crowd already occupied prime viewing spots on the ground in front of the field, or in the grandstand. I quickened my pace as I approached The Quartermaster. No one staffed the table in the front, but I spied a figure moving among the boxes of merchandise in the rear. I had no reason to believe anyone connected with the shop even knew what I'd been given, but I wasn't taking any chances. I bolted past the shop, nearly colliding with a woman carrying a cardboard drink tray. After a muttered apology, I hurried on.

I didn't see any police, but perhaps I'd find an officer at the entrance to the grandstands. Ahead lay the first of the reenactor tents open to the public. Most of the tents were empty, the reenactors having left to prepare for battle. At the field hospital tent, a man dressed in black was displaying a glass jar filled with amber-colored liquid to a small knot of tourists. Because of his stovepipe hat, I thought at first he was an Abraham Lincoln impersonator. On closer examination, I realized he was an undertaker and that the liquid in the jar was supposed to be embalming fluid. The undertaker faced away from me. When he turned in my direction, our eyes locked and he gave me a look as if to say, "Fooled you again, didn't I?"

In that long moment of recognition, I was dimly aware of movement around me. "Pardon me, ma'am." The voice belonged to a teenage boy who was walking toward me. An explosion had erupted on the left side of the boy's face. Where before there had been pink, pimply skin, now an ugly purplish bruise ran all the way from his jaw line to one swollen, slitted eye. Despite his appalling appearance, the boy smiled, revealing metal braces. "We all make mistakes," he said softly. "But this one's easily fixed if you'll just…"

He held out his hand. I backed away. Someone grabbed me from behind and pulled me into a nearby tent. He yanked hard on the stock of the gun. Metal and wood ground into my ribs, as he tried to pull the gun out from under my arm. I seized the barrel with my other hand and opened my mouth to cry out. A hand clamped over my mouth. The teenager had followed us into the tent. He worked to pry my fingers from the barrel.

All this happened very quickly, but I experienced it in the slow motion of a nightmare. One minute I was on a grassy concourse with other people around; the next, I was enclosed in a narrow canyon by my captors. Their bodies pressed against me, forming steep walls that shut out more and more of the light until all I could see were the dark roots of the battered boy's bleached hair. Then I heard a cracking noise, followed by a yelp of pain. Hands stopped pulling and prying. My attackers vanished in separate blurs of color.

I stood there, dazed and blinking like a rabbit pulled from a magician's hat. The tall, black hat itself lay on the ground near my feet. Jake Euell picked it up and dusted it off. He hustled me out of the tent and over to the field hospital.

"I don't usually rescue my clients," he told the knot of startled tourists. "Just bury 'em. Now if you'll excuse me, I need to administer first aid to this lady here." He whisked me into the hospital tent before the people watching realized what the tattered package under my arm really contained.

"Where the hell did you get that?" Jake demanded after he'd closed the flaps of the tent behind us.

"I thought I was buying a replica musket, but they gave me the wrong package at The Quartermaster yesterday."

Jake's eyes narrowed. "The Quartermaster, huh?"

"Yes. I didn't realize the mistake until late last night. I was on my way to turn the rifle over to the first policeman I saw when those two guys jumped me."

"Should've brought it to me the minute you found out what you had," Jake said.

"Then you really are a cop?"

Before he could reply, Dorcas Nutley called, "You in there, Jake?"

"Yeah. What d'you want?" he called back after a muttered curse.

"The battle's about to begin. I thought you'd be down on the field with the stretcher. Aren't you supposed to bring out the dead and wounded?"

"Be with you in a minute." He stashed the gun in a long, narrow instrument case. "We'll talk later."

While Jake and another medic in period dress bore the stretcher to the field, I hurried to the grandstands. They were jam-packed with people. I scooted along the pathway, scanning row after row without seeing Ginny and Randall. The sun pierced the clouds, producing an unwelcome glare that made me squint and shade my eyes. Hot, tired, and still shaken from the encounter with the teenager and his accomplice, I wanted to cry in sheer frustration. Then, miraculously, I heard a voice call, "Miranda, over here!"

Randall stood and waved from a perch in the middle section. I scurried over and squeezed in beside him and Ginny. With practically no legroom, my knees scrunched uncomfortably against my chest, but I didn't care. Now that I was reunited with them, especially with Randall, I felt that everything was going to be all right.

"Were you able to accomplish your errand?" he asked.

"There was no one at the shop when I got there. I waited, thinking someone would come. Finally I gave up and left the package."

"What a pity! Would you like me to go back and see if anyone is there now?"

"No, thanks. The battle's about to begin and I'd hate to have you miss it."

"It is no trouble really."

"Look, they're starting." I pointed toward the field where the soldiers were getting into position.

As in yesterday morning's battle, the two forces were arrayed on opposite sides with the Union troops occupying the high ground to the right, as they had in the real battle. Randall trained his binoculars on the Confederate line. Ginny did, too. I focused in that direction also, scouring the line for a glimpse of Beau or Wiley without seeing either of them. Beau was probably there, but I had my doubts about Wiley. He had been in such rotten shape last night that I hoped he'd decided not to take part. Maybe Ginny had talked him out of it.

The artillery barrage began, obscuring the line in smoke. At the first concussion, a baby in the stands nearby started shrieking. The baby's young father did his best to quiet it, but finally left with the squalling infant in his arms.

The real bombardment on the third day of battle had lasted for nearly two hours; the one we witnessed went on for about twenty minutes. But twenty minutes of cannonading was long enough, even for someone like me whose misspent youth had included hours of listening to loud rock music. I wished I'd thought to bring earplugs. The firing stopped on the Union side first, because in the real battle the Federals wanted to save ammunition for the coming attack. Mistakenly believing that the Federal guns had been destroyed, the Confederates called a cease-fire and made ready to advance. The moment we had all been waiting for had arrived.

The air was charged with excitement as the long gray lines moved forward: drums rolling, flags snapping, and raised bayonets gleaming in the sunlight. I felt a brush against me as Randall craned to get a better view. I wondered what he was thinking. Was he hoping that this once it would be different, that the Rebels would actually win their desperate gamble? For a short while, a Confederate victory almost seemed possible.

As if paralyzed by the sight of the mighty foe marching toward them in perfect formation, the Federal artillerists held their fire. The gray lines drew closer with still no resistance from the Federals. Then just as the Confederates approached a wooden fence representing the real post-and-rail structure along the Emmitsburg Road, the Union artillery roared to life again.

The gray line wavered and shook like a clothesline in a heavy wind. Men flapped to the ground like errant sheets, as first cannon, then musket fire ripped holes in the line. Binoculars pressed against his face, Randall was leaning so far forward I was afraid he would lose his balance and fall. He shook the clenched fist of his free hand, as if urging the Rebels on. Ginny was likewise intent on the Confederate line, which grew more ragged with each passing moment. I zeroed in on the men dashing toward the stone wall behind which the Federals were massed, and saw Wiley running alongside three others. Like a marathoner near the end of a race, he broke away from his companions and surged ahead. A thrill shot through me as he neared the finish. His feet left the ground. He hurled himself at the pile of rocks in his path, only to crumple against it like a twig snapped over a stone.

I knew my reaction was inappropriate; still, I couldn't help feeling a bit let down. Wiley's performance now wasn't as dramatic as the one I had watched in the movie. But maybe that was because he was weakened from malnourishment. Not so the soldier who raced past Wiley. Clearing the wall, he dodged the Union soldiers on the other side, unstoppable in his headlong charge.

Other Rebels leaped over the wall and smashed into the Union line in a frenzy of fisticuffs and point-blank-range gunfire. They were either "shot" down or taken prisoner. Then it was over. Bodies littered the field and slumped against the stone wall. I focused on Wiley, waiting for him to "resurrect." Randall and Ginny had their binoculars trained on Wiley also. Ginny couldn't be pleased by the sight of crow-woman picking her way toward him.

In the field behind Wiley, Jake Euell and his medic colleague were lifting a man onto the stretcher. Linette reached Wiley and turned him over like a rag doll. With his head cradled in her lap, she pressed his canteen to his mouth. Then abruptly she began waving her arms. Jake and his companion unceremoniously dumped the man they'd been carrying and came running over. Linette was still waving and pointing at Wiley. Was he faking, or was he really hurt? The display was convincing enough for Ginny. She gasped and lurched forward, held back by Randall's

restraining arm. "It's all right," he soothed. "Everything is going
to be all right."

Jake and his associate had Wiley on the stretcher and were
bearing him away. Linette scurried alongside. Wiley lay still, a
model patient, but not for long. His exhibitionist urges soon took
over. He sat upright and began clawing at his chest. Then he
suddenly pitched backward, arms windmilling wildly in a reprise
of his movie death. Jake and the other bearer set the stretcher
down. Wiley stopped flailing and lay still again. Jake bent over
Wiley's prone form. The next instant, he jumped onto Wiley and
started pummeling Wiley's chest with his fists. Linette screamed.
Ginny let out an answering howl. She broke away from her father
and rushed onto the field where Jake was trying to pound Wiley
back to life.

NINE

"Another pause, brief this time, and then he exclaimed in a voice that echoed loudly and grimly through the night, 'Too bad! Too bad! Oh, too bad!'"

R. E. Lee, A Biography

"BUT ISN'T THERE ANYTHING you can do?" Ginny's eyes bore into Dr. Aram Vertulian's bald, egg-shaped head, as if willing him to hatch into a being who could give her hope. Only a few days ago her father's apparent heart attack had turned out to be a false alarm, so why, she probably wondered, couldn't this prove true in her husband's case? Though not in the best of health, Wiley was, after all, a much younger man and had no previous history of heart trouble, at least as far as I knew.

Dr. Vertulian's head began to shake. Ginny grabbed his arm. "What about the bullet? He was shot, too, you know. Can't you operate?"

Dr. Vertulian's gaze flicked nervously from Ginny to her father and back, as if trying to gauge whether a malpractice suit was in the making. "So he was, Mrs. Cross," he said carefully. "But in the leg. And yes, your husband would be in surgery this very moment if he hadn't already succumbed to sudden cardiac death. Everything possible was done to revive him. CPR was performed in the field and they had him on a defibrillator in the ambulance. I'm afraid that when he arrived here, he was already—"

"No!" Ginny screamed. "He can't be dead. This shouldn't have happened!"

In a sense she was right. Randall was the one who had appeared at risk, not Wiley. Yet in another sense, the wonder was that Wiley hadn't died sooner. He'd always lived on the edge, tempting fate to deal him the final blow. How fitting then that he should have died in such a doubly violent manner.

"This is indeed a tragedy. I am so sorry, Punkin, so sorry." Randall enfolded Ginny in his arms.

An infinitesimal change in the atmosphere told me that someone had come into the E.R. waiting room. Jake Euell stood just inside the door, still dressed in his undertaker's black suit. Was it purely a coincidence he had picked today to switch from army surgeon to undertaker? Or did he possess a sixth sense about death? "I don't usually rescue my clients, just bury 'em," he'd said. Yet he had rescued me twice already, on the road last night and this afternoon in camp. As a trained EMT, he'd surely done his best to resuscitate Wiley. Why then did I shrink from him as if he meant harm instead of help?

I felt the same about Linette. Like Jake, she belonged to the healing profession. She had demonstrated her concern for Wiley in last night's episode with the pills and again this afternoon on the battlefield. Still, if I'd been Wiley, lying on the field, bleeding from a real wound, I would have tried to drag myself away before Linette's crowlike figure cast a shadow over me.

Randall's low, murmurous voice drew me out of these thoughts. He was patting Ginny's hair and speaking softly to her. She raised a tear-stained face from his chest. "I want to spend some time alone with Wiley, to say good-bye."

"By all means, Punkin. Take as long as you like. Miranda and I will wait here for you."

"No hurry," Dr. Vertulian added magnanimously. "I have a call in to the medical examiner, also the police. They should be along shortly."

"The police?" Ginny stumbled over the word.

"Standard procedure when the patient arrives DOA," Dr. Vertulian explained.

An emotion I couldn't name flickered across Ginny's face. "Oh." She disappeared through a set of doors into the E.R. Randall sank into a chair. I followed suit. Dr. Vertulian excused himself.

When the doctor had gone, Randall said, "Virginia is right. This never should have happened. Poor Wiley never should have taken part in the charge in the condition he was in. He was not a well man. No wonder his heart gave out on him."

"He didn't look very good when—" I broke off, remembering that I wasn't supposed to have seen Wiley yesterday because that might lead to telling about Ginny and Greg, as well. How long would the pretense continue? Perhaps now that Wiley was dead, Ginny would feel she could be open with her father. "When I saw him leaving Ginny's house the other day," I finished. "Over my dead body!" he had yelled with what now seemed remarkable prescience.

As if on cue, Jake Euell left his post by the door and walked over to us. Randall stood up and shook hands with him. "I want to thank you again for everything you did for my son-in-law. As a heart patient myself, I appreciate the importance of a speedy response."

"I'm just sorry I didn't get him on the defibrillator sooner," Jake said. "Then maybe he'd still be alive." He sounded so genuinely troubled that I half regretted my earlier reservations about him.

"You mustn't blame yourself," Randall said. "Wiley was such a consummate performer that it was often difficult to tell when he was acting and when he was really in pain."

For a few moments neither man spoke. Then addressing me, Jake said, "They've put a fresh pot of coffee on in the cafeteria if you'd like to join me."

He made it sound like an invitation, but his eyes told me otherwise. He didn't really care that Wiley was dead; he just wanted to question me further about the gun. Once again I revised my opinion of him.

"Go ahead," Randall said, sensing my hesitation. "Virginia may be quite a while."

"Can I get you anything?" I asked.

Randall smiled wanly. "No, thank you, my dear."

"Persistent, aren't we?" I said to Jake when we were out of earshot.

"Look," he bristled, "I meant what I said about Wiley. I liked the guy and I'm sorry he didn't make it. But I also have a job to do."

The cafeteria was located in another part of the hospital from the E.R. As Jake steered me down one Lysol-scented corridor after another, a voice behind us called, "Yo, Jake! Taking a break?"

"Uh-huh. How about you, Pete?" Jake was all friendliness, but I could tell from the way his grip tightened on my elbow that he resented the intrusion.

"Yeah," Pete said. He had long hair pulled back into a ponytail and wore a T-shirt and jeans with a beeper at his waist. "Figured I'd grab a quick coffee before I get another call. Tower won't be blown up for a couple of hours, and it's already a zoo out there. Traffic's a mess, backed up for miles, and what does this bozo biker do? Cuts in and out of line until one time he doesn't make it and runs smack into an oncoming truck. Like this."

Pete jammed the heel of one hand into the palm of the other for emphasis. I winced, envisioning the motorcycle splatted against the truck like an insect against a windshield.

"Guy wasn't even wearing a helmet," Pete went on with disgust. "Not that it would have helped him. Looked like one of your boys from what was left of his clothing."

"A reenactor?"

Pete nodded.

Jake squeezed my elbow so hard it hurt. "Where is he now?"

"Morgue I'd guess. Sure as hell wasn't anything we could do for him."

Jake didn't wait for Pete to finish. He was already sprinting down the corridor toward a set of elevators. "Jeez, hope it isn't someone he knows," Pete muttered.

Dear God, don't let it be someone I know and care about, I thought as I ran after Jake. Don't let it be Beau. By the time I reached the elevator, the doors had shut on Jake. I jabbed the button furiously, but to no avail. The damn thing had begun its descent. While I waited for its return, I tried to remember the last time I had seen Beau. He'd come running over while Jake was performing CPR on Wiley, but in the confusion I'd lost sight of him. I'd figured he'd show up at the hospital eventually. He could've gotten stuck in traffic. But then again, in his haste to get here, he might've borrowed Jake's or someone else's bike and—dammit! Why didn't the elevator come? I jabbed the button again. And waited. I was about to head for the stairs when the elevator returned.

I pressed the button for the basement and was soon deposited in the bowels of the hospital. A long, winding corridor brought me to the hospital's power plant. I retraced my steps to the elevator and tried another corridor, only to arrive at another set of locked doors with a sign, "Authorized Personnel Only." This could be the morgue, or it could be some other part of the hospital. No one answered when I pounded on the doors. Even if someone had, it seemed unlikely I'd be let in without the appropriate ID. I waited outside for several minutes, hoping Jake would appear. When he didn't, I decided I might as well go back to the E.R. waiting room. If the victim of the motorcycle crash were Beau, surely Jake would let us know.

Randall was seated by himself in the waiting room. A magazine lay open on his lap, but he wasn't reading. His melancholy gaze was fixed on a point in space while his lips moved soundlessly. The next instant, he realized I was there and turned to me. "Are you back already, Miranda?"

"Jake ran into a fellow EMT. It looks like another reenactor was killed today in a motorcycle crash."

"Why, that is terrible! I hope it wasn't anyone we know."

"Me, too." We sat in gloomy silence for a while. Then, my anxiety making me restless, I went to look in on Ginny.

Seated in a chair next to the gurney where Wiley lay, she appeared old and tired, her complexion so dulled by grief that her freckles looked like specks of dirt on a gray surface. In contrast, Wiley appeared young and untroubled, his face shiny as a freshly waxed floor. His eyes were half-open. I could easily imagine he was still alive, and that at any moment he might sit up and fling off the sheet covering his body except for his head and his feet. "Fooled you, didn't I?" he would declare with a roguish grin. I stared at the soles of his boots, watching for a telltale twitch. His feet remained splayed and stiff. They would never again execute a heel-click in flip-flops as they had only the night before. Sadness welled in my chest. I couldn't begin to imagine the enormity of Ginny's grief, how the weight of words left unsaid, actions left undone, would press upon her, how in death perhaps even more than in life, Wiley would be her cross to bear. I would miss him, too.

Ginny turned and stared bleakly at me. I felt suddenly like an intruder. Giving her shoulder a quick squeeze, I closed the curtain on her mournful face, Wiley's motionless feet. Feet that would no longer move with mine as we danced together, belting out the words, "It's my party and I'll cry if I want to."

The sadness in my chest grew until it was ready to burst forth. *Cry if I want to.* I might have held myself together if it hadn't been for Beau. He stood beside Randall with a hand on Randall's shoulder in a gesture of manly support. Thank God, he was alive! Tears of relief sprang to my eyes. At the sight of me, Beau's composure gave way. His features wavered and shook like a reflection in a pool of disturbed water. Like a Narcissus of sorrow, I was drawn to him as to the mirror image of what I felt. *Cry if I want to.* He opened his arms and I rushed into them, the two of us blubbering like babies.

At least that's how we must have appeared to Jake when he came into the room a few minutes later. He stood by the door with his arms folded across his chest and his head cocked slightly to one side, watching Beau and me impassively. The question formed in my brain before my voice was steady enough to utter it. "Who was the crash victim?"

"Dred Davis."

"Serves the bastard right," Beau muttered.

I hadn't liked the man myself; nevertheless, Beau's reaction came as a shock. I wouldn't wish that sudden windshield splat of a death on anyone, even someone like Davis.

"He shot Wile, Miranda," Beau said.

"What?!" Randall and I cried in unison. He stood up. I spun around to face Beau.

"We're pretty sure he was the shooter," Beau continued. "Paul was close to him, saw him fire, and Wile go down. Then Davis dropped his gun and lit out like a bat from hell. He ran straight through the Union line and just kept on going. Paul and me and a few others went after him, but he was too fast for us."

"Too fast for his own good." Randall remarked. "Who was this Davis person?"

"One of Wile's recruits and trouble from the start," Beau replied. "He got into a fight with a Union reenactor yesterday. I told Wile that if it happened again, Davis was out. Wile said he'd talk to him. If he did, the dressing-down might've turned Davis against Wile." Beau frowned and shook his head. Obviously he didn't put much credence in his own theory. "What happens now?" he asked after a pause.

Randall told him that we were waiting for the arrival of the medical examiner and the police—and for Ginny who was with Wiley. "Guess I'll look in on my old buddy, too," Beau said. He disappeared behind the set of doors.

Jake hung around awhile longer. I thought he might suggest another trip to the cafeteria, but after telling Randall again how sorry he was, he left. Randall and I sat quietly, neither of us inclined to make small talk. Randall kept his eyes downcast, as if in prayer, though every now and then he would glance at the doors through which Ginny and Beau had gone. I gazed idly at the waiting room's TV, and an image caught my attention.

A blonde woman with an overly bright smile and a hyped-up manner was interviewing a man seated in a wheelchair in the midst of a large crowd. The soon-to-be-demolished National Observation Tower loomed in the background. Another woman stood just behind the man in the wheelchair; I recognized Dorcas Nutley's bulldog face. The man in the chair had a huge torso that was out of proportion to the legs dangling from it, crumpled and spindly like those of a discarded marionette. He wore pink-tinted glasses and a white plastic sun visor that made him look like a casino croupier, an impression reinforced by the hands moving restlessly in his lap, as if shuffling and reshuffling a deck of cards. If a gambler, he was not a happy one. While his hands moved restlessly, his mouth worked angrily. Curious, I rose and turned up the TV's volume.

"So you're against the tower coming down?" the blond woman asked, her exaggerated smile contrasting with the man's surly expression.

"'Course I am. Feds and the National Park Service got no business doing this. First they seize the property, now they're about to destroy the poor owner's livelihood."

"But what about the preservationists who say the battlefield ought to be returned to its original state?" the blonde woman countered.

"They're a bunch of rich people who never did a honest day's work. Act like this battlefield is their exclusive club. They don't like the way something looks, they've got to get rid of it. It's the big guys against the little guys all over again, the same kind of tyranny our forefathers fought against, 'cept now it's coming from our own government." He bit off the words like a snapping dog.

As if fearful he'd chomp down on the microphone, or even worse, the hand holding it, the blonde woman moved the device out of range. "Thank you for your opinion," she chirped.

"I'm not finished." The man grabbed the microphone back. "Far as I'm concerned, the NPS can take their explosives and shove 'em up—"

"Thank you!" the blonde woman shrilled, wrenching the microphone from him and moving quickly away. "As you can see, the demolition of the tower is controversial in some quarters. Now let's talk to someone else. Where are you folks from?" She held the microphone out to a patriotically attired couple dressed in matching Stars and Stripes T-shirts.

I turned the volume down low again. Randall shook his head.

"The implosion of the tower seems to have brought out the lunatic fringe," he remarked.

I nodded. Living in the rarefied atmosphere of Cambridge, Massachusetts, where almost everyone subscribed to the same liberal creed, I was often amazed by the views I encountered in the wider world. The man in the wheelchair's virulent anti-government stance reminded me of the now-dead Dred Davis. I wondered if Dorcas Nutley shared her companion's beliefs; her stolid expression throughout his diatribe gave no clue.

IT WAS NEARLY 5:00 P.M. before we were ready to leave the E.R. The medical examiner and a police detective had come, done their work, and gone. Ginny had been persuaded to say her final good-bye, and Wiley's body was on its way to the morgue. Given the circumstances surrounding his death, the ME had requested an autopsy. All that remained was to finish the necessary paperwork. This completed, Ginny and I started glumly toward the door.

"I would like to watch this, if you ladies don't mind." Randall stopped in front of the TV screen, where the countdown for the destruction of the National Observation Tower had begun. It took two countdowns before a group of reenactors, Confederate, as well as Union, fired dummy charges from cannon aimed toward the tower. Seconds later, real explosives were detonated. The steel supports holding the observation booth to the tower ripped apart. The entire structure veered to one side, then vanished in a cloud of smoke behind the trees.

Randall's face wore the triumphant smile of a general who has annihilated a long-time foe. He flicked his fingers. "Poof!"

TEN

"One of the most touching, although seldom done, scenes is that of the women coming together to watch their men march off to battle. Spectators love it, and to be honest, so do the men. It's nice to be missed by people who care, even when it's pretend."
Reliving the Civil War, A Reenactor's Handbook

"IF THAT IS BEAU, he must have gotten his signals crossed," Randall remarked, observing a heavy-set man seated in the shadows of the porch as we drove up to the B and B. "I thought he was going to meet us at the restaurant." Earlier, Randall had invited Beau to join us for what looked to be a lugubrious meal.

While Randall parked, the man on the porch rose and stepped out of the shadows. Greg. What on earth? He was supposed to be back in Cleveland. Maybe he had heard about Wiley's death and come to offer his sympathy. Still, there was no way he could have gotten here so quickly—unless he'd never left.

Ginny left the car in a flash. As she hurried up the stairs to the porch, Greg held out his hand. Ginny swatted it away and swept past him into the B and B. For a moment, Greg looked as if he would go after her. Then he bounded down the steps, got into his car, and drove away.

"Isn't that the man we met at the Virginia Memorial?" Randall asked, mystified.

I nodded.

"What is he doing here?"

I shrugged. "Beats me." Ginny could tell her father about Greg in her own good time.

THROUGHOUT DINNER with Beau, Randall skillfully steered the conversation away from anything likely to upset Ginny and bring on a fresh burst of tears. He and Beau made small talk about the food, the weather, and the destruction of the National Observation Tower. Randall also made a few polite inquiries about Beau's family. Besides an ex-wife, Beau had three children, two of whom were still in college. Beau complained about the exorbitant costs of a college education and Randall concurred. "It'll be a big relief to me when they're finished and can get jobs," Beau said. "My middle son's making noises about graduate school but—"

"Did you call the girls?" Ginny broke in.

"No, I—" Randall looked perturbed. "Would you like me to try them now, or shall I wait until we get back to the B and B?" he asked gently.

"I'll do it now." Ginny removed her cell phone from her purse and left the table to make the calls in private.

Randall watched her go with a worried expression. He turned back to Beau. "You were saying?"

"It's not important," Beau said quickly. "This is a difficult time for Ginny, for the whole family. If there's anything I can do, just let me know."

The compassion in his round, red face touched me deeply. What a good person he was. He had been a loyal friend to Wiley and now he would be there for the dead man's family.

"Your very presence now is a source of consolation to Virginia and me," Randall said. "Yours, too, Miranda," he added with an affectionate glance at me.

"I can stay a few more days," I volunteered, wanting to be helpful, but also to have him think well of me, though I was behind in my work and needed to get back to it soon.

"Can you, Miranda? That would be wonderful because what Virginia needs more than anything is the support of her family and close friends."

The smile he gave me momentarily lifted me out of the gloom that had settled around me like a noxious cloud since Wiley's death.

"I reached Mandy, but not Missy," Ginny informed us when

she returned to the table. "She's flying into D.C. tomorrow, and she's going to keep trying Missy."

"She is such a fine girl; they both are," Randall said with grandfatherly pride.

"Yes," Ginny murmured. She was silent during the rest of the meal. We tiptoed around her, as around a squalling infant that has cried itself to sleep, keeping our voices low and careful about what we said lest she awaken and show us what we had suspected all along, that we were incapable of consoling her.

Back at the B and B, the habit of tiptoeing had become so ingrained that Randall and I went on whispering even after Ginny had gone upstairs to her room. He thanked me again for offering to stay. We said good night soon afterward.

To my surprise I found Ginny slumped on the bed in my room. Her face was wet and red from a fresh burst of tears. Wiley's letter, which I had neglected to give her, lay open on her lap.

"I came in here to wait for you and discovered this. When did you get it?"

"Wiley handed it to me last night. I didn't give it to you then because I figured it would only upset you more."

"It is very upsetting, but I still wish you'd given it to me last night. Then maybe…"

"What?"

"I don't know," she replied miserably. "Here, read it for yourself." She thrust a piece of blue paper at me. It was covered with old-fashioned script, penned in India ink.

My dearest wife,
Tomorrow we shall meet the enemy in battle once again. I pray we shall prevail and that I may return to you shortly. But my heart is heavy. I know I have not been all you hoped for in a husband—indeed, all that you deserved. And this knowledge of my shortcomings weighs upon me, especially in light of certain premonitions I have had of late. A few nights ago, I heard a dog howling in the distance, and the next morning I awoke to find a crow alighted on

*the ground beside me. Try as I might I could not shoo it
away. It stood there staring at me with bright, black eyes.
Finally it flew off, only to perch on a branch nearby. This
bird has shadowed me ever since.*

*Perhaps I am foolish to put stock in such signs, but I
cannot rid myself of the fear that I am to die without seeing your lovely face again, without holding you in my arms,
without having the chance to make amends for at least
some of the neglects and hurts you have suffered at my
hands. If these omens prove true, if tomorrow I should fall
in battle, never to rise again in the flesh, know that my spirit
will be with you always. It will be in the sun that warms
your face, the breeze that ruffles your hair, watching over
you with tender love and care, waiting for the day when
we shall be joined in spirit as once we were in the flesh.
Your loving husband,
Wiley*

"What do you think?" Ginny looked at me expectantly.

I hesitated. Though well-written, there was a certain generic
quality to the letter. It sounded as if it could have been written
by any Civil War soldier to his wife. The part about Wiley's
spirit being in the sun that warmed his wife's face even
reminded me of a letter that had been read in Ken Burns's docu-
mentary of the Civil War. But of course, I didn't want to tell
Ginny this.

"And I thought all that mattered to him was hardcore reenacting and hanging out with other hardcores," Ginny moaned,
"when, in fact, he still cared about me. If only I'd known, I
might not have gotten involved with Greg. It was wrong—so
wrong! I can see that now. I should have stuck with Wiley and
tried harder to make our marriage work. Instead, he went into
that battle so devastated by the hurt I inflicted on him that he
wanted to die."

"But that's not what it says here," I countered. "He writes that he's sorry about the pain he's caused you, not the other way around. And you two patched things up."

Ginny sat up straighter. "What're you talking about?"

"You spent last night with him, didn't you?"

"I most certainly did not."

"Then *who* was with him?"

"Linette," Ginny hissed. "She saw her chance and took it."

"Huh?"

"Last night I drove to the reenactment site to look for Wiley. I know I promised I wouldn't, but I had to. You saw Wiley's face when he discovered me with Greg. I couldn't leave things like that. Dorcas Nutley told me he was camped by himself behind the trees. When I went there, I saw them lying asleep in each other's arms. I guess I should've expected it. He'd caught me with Greg, so why shouldn't he turn to Linette? But it meant I never had a chance to tell him how sorry I was, how I still loved him. He died brokenhearted—because of me!"

"Ginny, please!" I pleaded. "You've got it wrong. Wiley gave me the letter after we came back from Herr Tavern, but he had to have written it beforehand—before he saw you with Greg."

"Maybe," Ginny said glumly, pulling at the nubs on the chenille spread as if they were weeds that had invaded her garden. "But if he'd written a second letter, it would have been even more desperate."

"You don't know that," I protested.

Yet I wondered. I remembered Wiley's burning eyes when he'd handed me the letter, the sickly sweet smell that had reminded me of rotting fruit, but could just as well have been the stench of despair. *I'd do anything to get her back,* he'd said. Did *anything* mean deliberately thrusting himself in harm's way? But how could he have known that Dred Davis's gun held a real bullet, or that he'd suffer a fatal heart attack after he was shot?

"Did Wiley have any history of heart trouble?" I asked.

"Not that I know of," Ginny replied. "They wouldn't have let him go to Vietnam if he'd had so much as a heart murmur."

"He could've developed a problem later on," I speculated.

"If he did, he never mentioned it."

"Was he seeing a doctor on a regular basis?"

"From time to time he checked in with a doctor at the VA hospital who treated him when he came back from Nam."

"It might be a good idea to talk to his doctor."

"You're right. I'll give him a call when we get back to Alexandria."

The mention of Wiley's doctor made me think of Ginny's M.D. lover. "I was surprised to see Greg here this evening. I thought he'd gone back to Cleveland."

"Me, too. But…" Ginny paused, looked thoughtful.

"What?" I prompted.

"Yesterday evening before he left, Greg said something that really disturbed me."

"Yes?"

Ginny heaved a sigh. "This is hard. You have to understand that both Greg and I were very upset. He was afraid I was going to ditch him for Wiley just like I did nearly thirty years ago. He accused Wiley of playing the pity card again and begged me not to fall for it."

"The pity card?"

"He said that just because Wiley looked like he didn't have much longer to live, I shouldn't feel I had to go back to him."

"What do you think Greg meant?"

"That Wiley looked ill, I suppose," Ginny said.

"In Greg's professional opinion as a doctor?" Or as a jealous, once-again-jilted lover, I wondered. I also wondered about Greg's whereabouts from the time Ginny had left him until he'd showed up at the B and B earlier this evening.

"He didn't elaborate and I didn't press for details. We were both too upset."

"All the more reason for you to speak with Wiley's doctor," I said.

Ginny nodded.

"Where do things stand with you and Greg?" I asked.

"I honestly don't know. I've got a lot of things to work through before I can even begin to think about Greg and the future."

"I understand." Another question nagged at the edge of my consciousness. "What did you do after you found Wiley with Linette?"

"Well, I—I—" Ginny seemed taken aback.

"I ask only because I was out at the reenactment site myself and didn't see you," I said. "And when I arrived back at the B and B, the Lincoln was still gone."

"Oh... Yes... Now I remember," Ginny replied with the halting manner of a recovering amnesiac. "After I left the site, I didn't know what to do, where to go. So I just drove around until I was exhausted and came back here."

"You must be really exhausted now," I said gently. "I certainly am. I didn't get much sleep last night, either, and now I feel like I'm coming off a string of all-nighters." I paused. Maybe a little excursion into the past would help take Ginny's mind off her present sorrow. "Remember what that was like?"

"I remember you doing it," Ginny said. "I never could myself, and to this day I don't understand how you managed to write such brilliant papers on no sleep."

"I'm not sure how brilliant they were," I said.

"You got A's, didn't you?"

"True, but I was a wreck afterward."

"You'd be so tired you'd sleep the rest of the day," Ginny recalled. "Through lunch and dinner even. That was another thing I never understood, how you could miss meals."

"I didn't go hungry. You saw to that by sneaking food from the dining hall for me. When I finally woke up, there was a care package you'd left me."

A ghost of a smile flickered across Ginny's face. "Someone had to look after you, Miz Miranda, and who better than your roomie, Ginny from Ol' Virginy?"

"Also known as Scah-lett," I teased.

We spent the next hour or so quietly talking. Ginny seemed calmer when she went back to her room. I hoped she'd be able to get some sleep. I felt ready to sink into oblivion myself. I'd no sooner turned off the light and gotten into bed than the roar of a motorcycle in the street below roused me. I put a pillow over my ears, hoping against hope it wasn't who I thought. The noise wouldn't go away. Each growl of the circling machine became a summons to a rendezvous I would have gladly avoided.

ELEVEN

"People often do unwise things with weapons."
Reliving the Civil War, A Reenactor's Handbook

"ONE THING I DON'T GET." Jake—whose real name was Carlton James, agent of the Bureau of Alcohol, Tobacco, and Firearms—tugged at his beard as if trying to squeeze the last remaining drop of moisture from it into his empty beer glass.

I felt squeezed dry myself. During the half hour we had sat in this barroom booth, he'd made me repeat my story about the assault rifle so many times and questioned me so thoroughly I couldn't believe there was anything I could possibly add. Yet he still wasn't satisfied. I shifted impatiently in my seat.

"Now what?"

"How about a refill first?"

"No, but you go ahead."

I was determined to nurse my one beer as long as possible. Although I'd done nothing wrong, the cat-and-mouse intensity of the interrogation made me feel that I needed to keep my wits about me lest I said the wrong thing. Jake rose and strolled to the bar with his glass. Taking his time, giving me a breather. While he waited for the bartender to fill his glass, he glanced back at me. The casualness of the gesture didn't fool me. He wanted to be sure I hadn't flown the coop.

Jake was smiling as he returned with his glass and a bowl of Goldfish crackers. "I brought these in case you're hungry." He put the bowl on the table between us, chucked a handful into his mouth, chewed, swallowed, took a drink of beer, and wiped his mouth, all in a leisurely manner. Then, cushioning his head in his hands and leaning against the back of the booth, he said, "An assault rifle's a lot heavier than those toy guns they sell at the souvenir shops. I'm surprised you didn't notice the difference."

So that was the monkey wrench he'd decided to throw into my story. It wouldn't work; my account would hold despite this challenge to its credibility.

"Actually, the replica musket I bought weighed more than I expected. That's why I didn't want to carry it around. And, as I've already told you, I didn't go back to the shop until the end of the day. By then I was with Wiley, Beau, and Linette. They were in a hurry to get going. The teenager handed me the package and I didn't think twice about it. It wasn't even in my hands very long."

Jake's head sprang from its hammock and craned toward me. "What d'you mean? You didn't mention that before."

"Beau offered to carry the package for me and I let him."

"Beau, huh? He carried the package all the way to the car without remarking how heavy it was?"

"He may have been aware of a difference in weight," I replied defensively, "but didn't want to mention it, because it would sound like he was complaining. Beau's too much of a gentleman for that. Besides, he had other things on his mind."

"Such as?"

"Wiley's surprise appearance threw us for a loop. At least it did me."

"What was the big deal about his being there? He *is,* or rather *was,* a reenactor."

"Yes, but nobody seemed to know he was coming—not even his best friend Beau. He showed up in the stands disguised as a tourist. I wouldn't have noticed him myself if a fellow Vietnam vet hadn't greeted him. When I approached him, he acted jumpy, wanted to know if I was alone, and was relieved when I said I was."

Jake was silent for a moment, digesting this. Then he said, "Back to the package. After Beau carried it to the car for you, what happened?"

"He put it on the floor in the back, and that's where it stayed until he dropped me off at the B and B. Wiley realized I'd forgotten the package and brought it to me."

"I'm surprised Beau didn't bring it, him being such a gentleman and all."

I detected a mocking note in this last, but decided to ignore it. "Wiley happened to be in the backseat with the package, both on the way to Herr Tavern, and then when we drove to the B and B. So it was more obvious to him. Also, Wiley had a letter he wanted me to give Ginny."

"Did *he* indicate there was anything unusual about the package?"

"Are you kidding?" I flared. "You saw how upset Wiley was at the tavern. I don't think he was aware of much else after that."

"Maybe not," Jake conceded. "I still need to ask."

"Why? You must've seen the teenager and the other person who tried to get the assault rifle away from me. They're the people you should be questioning instead of me."

"I wish I could, but the teenager's disappeared and the other guy's dead."

I stared at him in bewilderment. "Wiley?"

"No. Dred Davis."

Of course. I'd momentarily forgotten that he, too, had died today. "The assault rifle belonged to Davis?"

"Not exactly. We think he was part of a ring that—"

"A ring?" Without realizing it, I'd raised my voice.

"No ring," Jake replied loudly. "I'm not ready for that yet. I like you fine, but we've only just met."

The abrupt shift confused me. Then I noticed the bartender staring at us and understood. Jake wanted him to think we were discussing an entirely different matter.

"What kind of ring?" I asked quietly.

Jake leaned forward, pale, rainwater eyes boring into mine. "Gunrunners, Miranda."

I shook my head with disbelief. "Here in Gettysburg?"

"I'm afraid so. These guys provide illegal weapons to people who'd have a hard time getting them otherwise."

"Criminals, you mean."

Jake steepled his hands, took his time replying. "Some guns do go to garden-variety crooks, but the ring's main clients are the real bad guys."

"For example?"

Jake's chin crashed onto the steeple of his hands. He leaned forward again, this time so close that his narrow weasel's face filled my line of vision. His fingers clenched, then flew apart in a speeded-up version of the old childhood rhyme, "Here's the steeple, here's the church, open it up and here are all the people."

He said, "Like the guy who blew up an office building filled with innocent men, women, and little children without a moment's remorse."

I shuddered as Jake's face became Timothy McVeigh's, boy-next-door ordinariness masking the mass killer instincts of a terrorist. I looked away, but another image had already superimposed itself on my consciousness.

"Or the Brockton man who killed a Feebie with another Feebie's gun?"

"Whaddya know about that?" Jake asked sharply.

"Only what I read in the papers."

"Yeah, well, in fact, we have reason to believe he was one of the ring's clients. He'd attended a reenactment shortly before we got the tip about his cache of guns."

"This ring operates at reenactments?"

"Yes. When you think about it, it's the perfect setup for them. People come from all over the country to these events, from all over the world. Now most of these people are just plain gung-ho about the Civil War, but some hold extremist views like the guy from Brockton. So Brockton comes to a reenactment and hooks up with other like-minded guys like our friend, the late Mister Davis, and one thing leading to another, they start talking guns, and Davis happens to mention that if Brockton's interested in building up his own personal arsenal, he knows someone who can help him—for a price, of course. And so it goes.

"The other thing about reenactments is that you've got guns everywhere—the reenactors have 'em, dealers are selling 'em, and plenty of people are looking to buy, most of them legit, but some not. With all these guns around, and all these guns changing hands, who's gonna notice if the wrong kinds of weapons end up in the wrong hands—especially if the guns are wrapped up."

"This ring actually sells illegal weapons at reenactments?"

"We think at least some of their business is cash and carry, but they probably also make deliveries to interested parties they connect with at these events. They may also have a Web site we don't know about."

"The assault rifle I got by mistake was intended for…?"

Jake sighed. "Some bozo with a grudge who would've used it to blow away family, friends, coworkers, or a random bunch of strangers."

My stomach turned at the thought of what might have happened if the rifle had wound up in other hands than mine. "If only I'd found out sooner what was really in that package, maybe…"

"We could've nailed them," Jake finished. "But you didn't and we'll just have to live with that. At least now you understand why I've been asking all these questions. I was hoping you could give us something more than Davis, whom we already suspected."

"If you suspected him, why didn't you bring him in for questioning while you still could?"

"Because until today when I saw him having a tug of war with you over that rifle, we didn't have any hard evidence." Jake scooped up a handful of Goldfish and shoved them into his mouth. "Besides, we're after bigger guys than him."

"The leader of the ring?"

Jake nodded.

I had an unpleasant thought. "Davis was one of Wiley's recruits—do you think Wiley was involved in this?"

Jake traced a dent in the wooden tabletop. "It's certainly crossed my mind. Wiley did some crazy, risky things. Still, he was basically a one-man show. I have trouble imagining him being connected with anything as organized as a gunrunning ring."

"It could explain why Davis shot him, though. Maybe the

other members of the ring decided that Wiley was expendable and ordered Davis to shoot him."

"It's possible, but Davis was such a loose cannon that he and Wiley could've had a falling-out over something entirely different. Or maybe Davis was aiming at another guy and hit Wiley by mistake. Or he just felt like shooting someone and Wiley happened to be there—I don't know."

"And you don't much care."

"Give me a break! I already told you I liked Wiley and I'm sorry he's dead. But I've got other things to worry about. Speaking of that, what did you want with a toy gun in the first place?"

"It was a present for my boyfriend's son."

"The Indian activist?"

"How do you know about him?" If I'd caught him rooting around in my underwear drawer, I couldn't have felt more violated.

Jake shrugged. "Should've stayed married to the professor. Then you might've kept out of trouble."

"You have no business—"

"I'm only doing my job, and part of that job is knowing who I'm dealing with."

I'd had enough. Being with Jake was like riding a seesaw with a maniac; just when I had gotten comfortable in the "up" position, he would jerk me down, and vice versa.

"Are we done?" I asked impatiently.

"I suppose so," he said with a trace of regret. "Though I, for one, have enjoyed our little talk. It's given us a chance to get better acquainted, and it's been productive in other ways, as well."

"Really?"

I had a hard time believing he had extracted slivers of meaningful information from the thicket of words that had been spoken tonight. I hoped he hadn't misconstrued something I'd said.

"What have I told you that you didn't already know?"

"Nothing definite, but you've raised some interesting possibilities."

"Such as?"

Jake wasn't telling. He yawned, opening his jaws so wide that I could see his tonsils dangling like fleshy fangs in the dark cavern of his mouth. "Let's go."

The return trip on his motorcycle passed more quickly than the trip out, partly because I knew where we were headed, but also because Jake drove much faster than before. He careened around curves and risked skidding on a roadway still slick from the thundershower that had occurred in the late afternoon while we were at the hospital. At least there was little traffic at this time of night, and therefore less chance of a collision like the one that had proved fatal to Dred Davis.

I wondered if the difference in Jake's driving reflected a change in his attitude toward me. Now that he'd gotten what he could from me, I was no longer precious cargo to be brought safely to the interrogation booth, but someone he had no further use for and was eager to be rid of. Or maybe he was simply tired and anxious to get home himself. Whatever the reason for his recklessness, it made me throw my arms around him on a particularly sharp curve, and keep them there until our wild ride was over.

"Well, that was…" I left the sentence unfinished while I dismounted, unfastened my helmet, and thrust it at him.

Jake pressed a piece of paper into my palm. "This is where I can be reached in case you suddenly remember some detail I should know about. Or if—"

"Don't hold your breath waiting for my call," I interrupted.

His grip tightened on my wrist. "This is important," he hissed. "There's a chance someone may contact you about the rifle. If so—"

A vision of the teenager with the battered face rose up in my mind. "Oh, no," I said quickly. "I'm out of it. I don't even have the rifle anymore."

Jake pulled me so close that the rim of his helmet jabbed into my forehead. "You get in touch with me pronto. Because, like it or not, you're involved in this."

He let go of my wrist and gave me a little shove backwards,

clearing the way for his thunderous departure. I glanced nervously around, half expecting to see sinister, bad-guy shapes emerge from the shadows and surround me. The street was empty. My gaze traveled upward. A light was on in one of the B and B's second-story rooms. Ginny's? No, Randall's. That was his room, not hers. I felt a rush of relief mixed with gratitude. Jake Euell might be ready to throw me to the wolves, but not Randall. He wanted to be sure his "ladies" got home safely. As I approached the entrance of the B and B, the light winked off.

TWELVE

"Keep marching to a comfortable cadence. A slower pace is sometimes annoying to twentieth-century reenactors, but it is more authentic."

Reliving the Civil War, A Reenactor's Handbook

THE NEXT MORNING I was sitting at the breakfast table with Randall and Ginny, about to pour myself a third cup of coffee, when a police detective, a different one from the day before, entered the room. A short, somewhat paunchy man with graying hair, he introduced himself as Detective Fred Seeger-No-Relation-To-The-Folk-Singer-Pete. "Mind if I join you?"

He dragged a chair over from another table and sat down backwards, resting folded arms on the rim like someone leaning against a fence to have a friendly chat with his neighbors. But if this was meant to put us at ease, it had the opposite effect on me—he was on one side of the fence, we on the other.

"First let me say how sorry I am about your loss, Mrs. Cross."

I winced at the unintentional rhyme. Seeger-No-Relation's gaze flicked from Ginny to me and back again, fixing on her after her muted, "Thank you."

"I want to bring you up to date on the progress of our investigation into your husband's death," he continued. "According to the medical examiner, he died of a heart attack. But he was also shot in the leg, and it's the shooting part that concerns us. We have a witness, Paul Newberger, who swears he saw the suspect, Dred Davis, fire at Mr. Cross. Also the fact that Davis fled the scene suggests he's our man. We'll need to match the bullet removed from Mr. Cross's body with Davis's gun before we know for sure, of course. But the bottom line is that both the victim and the prime suspect are dead."

Seeger clapped a hand palm-down on the table, rattling cups and tableware. His hand lay on the white cloth, flat and immobile, fingers splayed. We stared at it as we might have a corpse that had suddenly landed in our midst. Randall appeared slightly repelled, as if the hand were an intruder that had no business being there. Ginny looked horrified. The sight seemed to have brought home not only the finality of Wiley's death, but also the futility of understanding why it had happened.

Seeger surprised us again by raising his hand a half-inch or so above the table. We stared at the space in-between, curious about what lay beneath the bottom line, what worms would be revealed when the rock was removed. Seeger didn't keep us in suspense for long.

"There is one thing, though. The suspect, Davis, had a lot of cash on him. So either he'd just won the lottery, robbed a bank, or someone paid him to shoot Mr. Cross. You know of anyone who'd want to have Mr. Cross shot?"

His gaze circled the table. I could think of at least one person. Still, I added my headshake to Ginny's and Randall's.

"That's it for now then." Seeger rose and returned his chair to the adjoining table. "I'll be in touch if anything else turns up, and you do likewise."

MORNING DRIZZLE had given way to a full-fledged downpour by the time we got on the road. Rain lashed Randall's Lincoln, rendering visibility almost nil, as waves of water from passing cars washed over us. I gripped the wheel, craning my upper body forward like the prow of a ship pushing through choppy seas. I probably resembled a myopic old lady crawling along the highway at well under the speed limit. But Ginny and Randall didn't complain. Ginny had accepted my offer to drive without a word. Although I'd sensed a protest forming inside Randall, he left it unspoken. There was no suggestion of his reading from Freeman's biography of Lee as he had on the drive to Gettysburg.

Instead, he and Ginny sat in the back, each as silent and lost in thought as if they had occupied separate isolation booths.

Driving under such hazardous conditions took all my concentration. But when the rain had abated somewhat, I let my mind explore what lay beneath Detective Seeger's bottom line—the possibility that someone had paid Davis to shoot Wiley. Davis, I now knew, had belonged to a gunrunning ring, so it seemed all the more likely that the ring was behind the shooting. If Wiley hadn't actually been involved in the ring, he could have found out about the operation and been shot before he could blow the whistle on it.

But then again, the person who paid Davis could be someone from one of two love triangles—Greg, Ginny, Wiley; or Ginny, Wiley, Linette. Although Ginny figured in both triangles, I couldn't imagine her hiring a hit man to get rid of Wiley. She had loved him in a can't-live-with-him/can't-live-without-him way. So that left Greg from the first triangle, Linette from the second. Which was it, the ring or one of the triangles?

By the time we reached Ginny's house in Alexandria, I had batted these two shapes back and forth in my mind so much I was ready to focus on a different geometric form: parallel lines.

The parallel lines were the twins. They were identical, each having inherited their mother's dark-haired beauty coupled with their father's tall, slim build. When they were little, Ginny had dressed them alike. But now in young womanhood, they had decided to emphasize their otherness in both appearance and manner.

Mandy was an investment advisor for Merrill Lynch in New York. Having taken the shuttle, she was already there when we arrived. Sleek and well-groomed in a tailored pants suit with dark hair pulled back from her face, she had a crisp and businesslike manner. She embraced her mother briefly before shooing her upstairs.

"Terrible about Dad. You go lie down, Mom. I'll take care of the arrangements and whatever else needs to be done."

I sensed that Mandy was someone who stepped around

emotions, as around messy puddles, rather than wading through. She paid a price for her avoidance. It was evident in the tight line of her jaw and the sharpness that came into her voice as she called funeral homes, comparison-shopping for a coffin and the best overall package.

Missy, now a potter living in Venice, California, was just the opposite. Arty verging on unkempt in flip-flops, an oversized, tie-dyed T-shirt, baggy shorts, and a Medusa-like mass of permed and dyed red hair, she blew in a few hours later with the force of a Santa Ana wind.

"Omigod! I can't believe it. I just spoke to Dad on the phone a couple of days ago, and now he's dead! This is horrible, just horrible!"

She collapsed into her sister's reluctant arms, sobbing noisily. When her sister gently but firmly extricated herself, Missy fell upon Randall with similar abandon. After a long moment, she raised a red, ravaged face to demand, "Where's Mom? She must be totally freaked out."

"Virginia is upstairs lying down."

Randall's words were lost in a clatter of flip-flops as Missy hurled herself upstairs to her mother's room. Missy's desperate keening found a ready response in Ginny. She seemed to have been waiting for her daughter's arrival to unleash an outpouring that, combined with Missy's wails, was terrifying in its intensity. Randall and Mandy exchanged alarmed glances. I was shaken myself by the sound of so much raw emotion.

"I'd better finish my calls in the den." Mandy retreated to the basement.

Randall remained with me by the phone in the entrance hall. He glanced after Mandy, then upstairs, as if trying to decide which way to turn. Then, picking up a pen from the table by the phone, he said, "Mandy appears to have forgotten her pen. I will bring it down to her. Perhaps you could take this upstairs? I think Virginia and Missy—poor dears—will be needing it." He handed me a flowered box of Kleenex puffs.

So it was settled: I would tend to the weeping women while

Randall and Mandy handled the business end of death. When I went into Ginny's room, mother and daughter were locked in each other's arms, swaying back and forth on the bed, their eyes open but unseeing. I put the tissue box on the night table and quietly closed the door.

When the five of us came together briefly for a take-out Chinese dinner, the twins engaged in a curious kind of dance. Mandy sat down at one end of the table, Missy at the other. During the course of the meal, they gradually edged closer until they were practically on top of one another, jumbled together like kittens in a litter. Mandy rose to get something from the kitchen. When she returned, she positioned herself at a distance from her twin, and the tango of separation and union started again.

I realized then that the twins were parallel lines determined to meet. I imagined how this dynamic would play out over time and space. Each twin would subtly alter her appearance so she looked more like the other. While Mandy moved a few miles west each year, Missy would move a few miles east. Eventually they'd meet in the middle: two elderly women, virtually indistinguishable from each other, occupying the same house in Kansas.

After dinner we withdrew to our different stations, Ginny and Missy to Ginny's bedroom, Randall and Mandy to the den in the basement. I settled in the living room with a magazine, keeping my ears open in case either party needed me. Thirty minutes passed without a request from bedroom or den. Then an hour. Randall, Mandy, and Missy seemed to have the situation well under control.

Except for the hum of the air conditioner, the house was quiet. Above me, Ginny and Missy comforted each other, while below me, Randall and Mandy made the necessary arrangements. The disruption caused by Wiley's death would be smoothed over, order restored. Already I felt that the process of healing had begun.

The phone's ringing jolted me from my complacency. I went into the hall and picked up, only to get a dial tone. The ringing persisted. I moved quickly from room to room, searching for the offending instrument. Mandy had left her cell phone in the dining room. A client was on the line.

The den door was closed. I hesitated a moment or two before knocking. Inside I heard their voices. "Of course, I want to do whatever I can to help," Randall said. "But I'm afraid I am somewhat short on funds just now."

"If I don't get my numbers, I'll be canned." Mandy sounded panicked.

Numbers? What was she talking about? None of your business, I scolded myself, rapping determinedly on the door.

"What is it?" Mandy's voice was edgy and impatient.

"Telephone for you." I handed her the cell phone, mouthing the word "client."

The transformation from disgruntled granddaughter to eager-to-please saleswoman was instantaneous. "I'm so glad you called back, Mrs. McVeedy," she cooed. "Because I really think that amount you have in a CD would be much better invested in…"

Randall and I left the room discreetly. "Poor Mandy has been under a great deal of pressure at work lately," he remarked as we headed upstairs. "Unfortunately, she has to go back to New York first thing tomorrow. I know you must have pressing commitments of your own, so I hesitate to ask this. But it would be wonderful if you could remain with us a few more days."

Worries about the unfinished chapter awaiting me in Cambridge and doubts about the importance of my role as Kleenex carrier and phone answerer vanished before the appeal in his dark eyes. I couldn't disappoint him.

"Of course," I said.

Randall patted my shoulder, sending a flush up my neck into my face. "Thank you, Miranda. Virginia is indeed fortunate to have a friend like you."

Later that evening, after Randall had returned to his own house and Mandy had gone to bed, Missy rather than Ginny sought me out.

"Whew!" she exclaimed, plopping down in a chair opposite me in the living room. Beneath her, the cushion let out a sympathetic sigh.

"How's your mom doing?" I asked.

"Asleep. Finally. Mandy gave her a pill and took one herself."

"You must be worn out, too."

"I am, but I won't be able to sleep till I've decompressed."

"Feel free," I urged.

I hadn't seen much of the twins since they were little, so didn't feel I knew either young woman well. But already I felt more at home with Missy than Mandy. She had an openness I found appealing, whereas Mandy was more tightly wrapped. Missy kicked off her flip-flops and stretched bare feet onto the coffee table. The flip-flops reminded me of her father. Three nights ago, he had been alive and cavorting around in similar sandals. The soles of Missy's feet were grimy with a mixture of dirt, sand, and tar from the beach where she'd walked before coming here. The California beach. I felt a nostalgic pang for my home state.

"It's all so weird, I still can't believe it," Missy began. "First Dad gets shot by another reenactor, then he has a heart attack and dies. I never even knew he had heart trouble."

"He might've had a problem he didn't tell anyone about. Your mom's going to check with his doctor."

"I hope she does, because I sure as hell would like to understand how this happened. There's another thing, too. Mom told me she's been having an affair. She said you know about it, but Granddaddy doesn't yet. And that Daddy found out the night before he died. She thinks his discovering them together was the final blow."

"He was very upset," I agreed.

"I'll bet he was!" Missy flared. "I mean, how could she do that to him?"

I took a deep breath and let it out slowly. Explaining wasn't going to be easy, but I felt Missy needed to understand the why and wherefore of her mother's affair.

"Your mother's been very unhappy," I said. "She saw your father through some pretty difficult times, especially right after he returned from Vietnam. Then, when she hoped things would finally be better, he went overboard with hardcore reenacting.

She thought it was all that mattered to him. So, after years of being the one to hold the marriage together, she went off the deep end herself by having an affair.

"Also, this man she's involved with isn't just a guy she met at the supermarket. He's a person from her past, someone she cared deeply about when they were in college together."

"She looked him up?"

"No, it was the other way around. And since they started seeing each other, she's felt very conflicted."

"She should. It was the worst thing that could have happened from Dad's point of view. Just when he thought they were going to get back together again, he found out she'd hooked up with someone else."

"Why did he think he and your mother would reconcile?"

"Apparently he'd come up with a surefire plan to win her back. At least that's what he said when we spoke on the phone a few days ago."

Missy's mention of Wiley's interest in a reconciliation corresponded with the apologetic tone of the letter he'd written Ginny. The letter was probably part of his campaign to win her back. I wondered if there was more to it.

"What was this plan?"

"He wouldn't tell me. Dad was like that. Full of secrets and surprises." A wistful smile played at Missy's lips.

"It made him lots of fun to be with when we were kids. But then…" Her face clouded over. Reaching beneath her T-shirt, she pulled out a gold chain and fiddled with it while she continued. "By the time Mandy and I were teenagers, we didn't think Dad was so funny anymore. He embarrassed us. We wanted a father who acted like a grownup instead of a crazy kid. Someone who got up and went to work every day. Like our friends' fathers. Not just when he felt like it. We were ashamed by the kind of work he did, too. I mean, there we were at our expensive private school with a grease monkey for a dad! God, we were snippy little brats!" She shook her head with disgust at her own youthful intolerance.

"Of course, we'd never have gone to private school if it hadn't been for Granddaddy. He was the one who saw that we wore nice clothes, lived in a nice home, and went to good schools."

Randall's keeping the family afloat financially didn't surprise me. It was a testimony to his generous, forgiving nature. Although he had disapproved of Ginny's marriage to Wiley, he wasn't about to cut his daughter off. Instead, he had made sure she and his granddaughters had the best money could buy. But where money was involved, there were usually strings attached, too.

"I guess we all betrayed Dad in our different ways," Missy said gloomily.

"What do you mean?"

"Mandy and I betrayed him by wishing we had someone else for a dad."

"I wouldn't call that a betrayal. Most kids wish they had different parents at one time or another."

"Maybe. But we took it a step further."

"How so?"

"Freshman year at Madeira, Dad decided to surprise us by picking us up at school in his Battlemobile. That's his car decorated with plastic figures of Civil War soldiers."

"I've seen it."

"Then maybe you can imagine how we felt. We were leaving school with these girls we wanted to impress, when who shows up but our weirdo dad in his weirdo car. He waved to us, but we just walked right on past like he was some crazy instead of our father. I'll never forget the look on his face." Tears came into her eyes, and her voice quavered. "He was so-o-o hurt."

Missy tugged at her gold chain so violently, I was afraid it would break. Which would be a pity, because the chain was anything but commonplace. Rather it was an intricately woven band of dark gold, exquisite and, no doubt, expensive.

"That was a long time ago," I soothed. "He forgave you and moved on. If he hadn't, you wouldn't have had the close relationship you obviously did."

"What makes you think we were close?"

"You talked on the phone, he confided in you."

"Yeah, but he was the one who called me, and I wasn't always that thrilled to hear from him. Friday when he telephoned, I was about to leave to meet some friends. We were going roller-blading along the Venice speedway; then we planned to have a drink at one of the beachfront bars. While Dad was carrying on about getting back together with Mom, all I could think about was that he was keeping me from a good time with my friends. He must've sensed my lack of interest because after a few minutes he said, 'Are you there, Missy?' 'Of course, I'm here,' I said. 'It's just that I'm getting ready to go out.' 'Well, you go ahead then, sweetheart,' he said. 'We'll talk another time.'" She paused to gulp air.

"But now there's not going to be another time. I'll never be able to tell him that in spite of all the bullshit I really did love him." Her face contorted with anguish.

Instinctively, I reached out and patted the part of her that was closest to me, her bare foot. "I know you did, Missy. And I'm sure your dad knew it, too."

"Do you really think so?" She looked at me hopefully.

I nodded.

She was silent for a long moment, as if debating whether to believe me or not. Then she burst out, "Dad was like Peter Pan—he wasn't supposed to die. Ever."

"I know, honey, I know." Again I patted the sole of her tar-and-grit-encrusted foot.

Missy started to go into another emotional meltdown. Then abruptly, her features reconstituted themselves. "Okay," she muttered, "better stop before…" She swung her legs off the table and stood up. "I'm going to make some herbal tea. Would you like some?"

"No, thanks."

As she was leaving the room, the lamplight caught the gold chain lying against her collarbone like a crescent moon. I couldn't resist remarking on it.

"That's a beautiful necklace you're wearing. I've never seen anything quite like it. Did one of your artist friends make it?"

"Oh, no. It came from Tiffany's." She paused, fingering the chain thoughtfully. "I may be an artist, but I'm hardly a starving one. Thanks to Granddaddy."

So he had been with us all along: Randall appearing like Zeus in a shower of gold on his granddaughter's neck.

THIRTEEN

"Whatever the beliefs, reenactors cling to their units and uniforms in mystical ways. A surprising number have been buried in their uniforms, and even more have been married in uniform."
Reliving the Civil War, A Reenactor's Handbook

"OMIGOD!" MISSY GASPED. It was the next morning and we were in the kitchen together. Missy stood at the sink filling a teakettle while I rummaged in the refrigerator for breakfast makings.

"What is it?" I asked, turning from the fridge.

Missy looked as if she had seen a ghost. "Somebody just drove up in the Battlemobile."

I joined her at the window. The Battlemobile was parked in front of the house, along with an older model Oldsmobile. A woman wearing a buttery yellow sundress and sandals got out of the Oldsmobile and walked to the driver's side of the Battlemobile. Bending next to the window, she appeared to be speaking with someone inside. Moments later, Randall's Lincoln pulled up. He joined the woman standing by the Battlemobile. After they had exchanged a few words, a man in coveralls unfolded himself from the Battlemobile. He was tall and lanky like Wiley. For an instant, I imagined he was Wiley. Missy recognized him as someone else.

"It's Chad and Peg!" she cried, dashing from the kitchen. I followed. Missy threw herself into Peg's outstretched arms with staggering force. Peg did not waver, but kept her feet firmly planted on the ground, holding herself as erect as the nearby utility pole.

"Oh, baby, I'm so sorry," she murmured.

She wore her gray hair in a single, thick braid, and had a round, kindly face. She gave the impression of being solid and substantial. Were a tornado to sweep through, she would probably be the only one left standing.

In contrast, Chad had a tentative air. Head bowed, shoulders stooped, as if he were about to enter a low-ceilinged room, his long, bent body clothed in faded blue coveralls, he reminded me of a curl of smoke that might at any moment vanish into the hazy air. He kept his eyes on the sidewalk, as though embarrassed by the women's emotional display. Then, with his gaze still averted, he patted Missy's shoulder shyly.

"The Yagers are the kind and understanding people I told you about earlier," Randall explained. "They own the garage where Wiley worked and where he was living before his untimely death. He left his car with them to be repaired and now they have brought it back."

Peg Yager slowly released Missy. "There's something else, too," she said. She withdrew a sealed envelope from her pocketbook. "Chad found this in the glove compartment of the Battlemobile when he was looking for old service receipts. It's addressed to Ginny and says it's to be opened in the event of Wiley's death."

Wiley speaking to us from beyond the grave, I thought with a jolt. Randall's forehead creased; Missy's eyes opened wide.

"How fortunate that you happened to look there," Randall said. "Otherwise, the letter might have gone unnoticed for heaven only knows how long. I myself keep my important papers in a safe deposit box. But I will see that Virginia gets it."

He held out his hand for the envelope. Peg Yager's face lost its warm, compassionate look. She regarded him coldly for a moment, then deliberately handed the envelope to Missy. I felt a prick of annoyance at the slight to Randall, but he accepted it without a word.

"Won't you come in and join us for a cup of coffee?" Missy urged. "Mom's still asleep, but I'm sure she'll want to see you once she knows you're here."

"Oh, no, we don't want to disturb her," Peg said quickly with a glance at Randall. "We'll stop by another time. But please tell your mom how sorry we are, and if there's anything we can do, to call us." She hugged Missy again and started toward the Oldsmobile. The keys to the Battlemobile jangled as Chad silently handed them to Missy.

The noise made Peg turn around. "I almost forgot about the money," she said.

"Money?" Missy repeated.

Opening her purse again, Peg removed a wad of crisp bills from her wallet and extended it to Missy. "Your dad insisted on paying us in cash in advance for the work on his car. In fact, he overpaid us. You give this to your mom. I'm sure she can use it."

When we went back into the house, Ginny was just coming down the stairs in a robe and slippers. Her hair was uncombed, her eyes were puffy, and her face bore the striations of sleep.

"Up already, Punkin?" Randall greeted her. "I had so hoped you would have a longer rest."

"I heard voices outside. Who was it?"

"The Yagers," Missy volunteered. "They brought Dad's Battlemobile from the garage, along with an overpayment he made in cash for the work they did on it, and—"

"Cash—really?" Ginny interrupted.

"Yeah. Here." Missy gave her mother the wad of bills.

Ginny plopped down on a stair, counted the money, and looked up with a startled expression. "There's eight hundred dollars here."

"Wow." It was Missy's turn to be surprised. "Dad must've won the lottery."

Ginny frowned. "Did the Yagers mention where your dad got a hold of so much cash?"

Missy shook her head. "No, but Peg—" She broke off at a warning headshake from Randall.

"What about Peg?" Ginny demanded.

"It's nothing that cannot wait until a more suitable time," Randall said quickly. "Why don't we all—"

"No," Ginny interrupted stubbornly. "I want to know. Now."

Randall sat down on the stair next to her. "Punkin, Punkin," he murmured, putting his arm around her, "you have been through enough already without—"

"It's something to do with Wiley, isn't it?"

Randall sighed. "I'm afraid so. The Yagers found a letter addressed to you in the glove compartment of the Battlemobile. It's to be opened in the event of Wiley's death."

"Let me have it," Ginny said.

Randall nodded at Missy, who handed her mother the letter. Ginny's fingers shook as she tore open the envelope. My neck and shoulders tightened with tension. I hoped that the contents wouldn't plunge Ginny into another round of self-recrimination. On the other hand, if the letter shed light on activities of Wiley's that might have landed him on someone's hit list, it would help clear up some of the mystery surrounding his death.

Randall hovered protectively over Ginny. She blinked and seemed to have trouble focusing, either because Randall's shadow was in the way, or because her eyes were filling with tears.

Randall fumbled in his shirt pocket for his reading glasses. "Would you like me to...?"

"Here, Miranda, you read it."

Her arm shot out. I stared at her with disbelief. Why me instead of Randall, whose half-opened glasses dangled in the air like a bird with a broken wing? Or Missy, her daughter? Maybe she'd turned to me because I wasn't part of the family and could be trusted to give her the truth unsparingly. Or maybe it was simply that the music had stopped and there I was.

I took the letter gingerly, self-conscious as an actress auditioning for a part she hasn't had a chance to prepare for. Clearing my throat, I began: "Hey, Gin-gin." This was obviously Wiley speaking and not some generic Civil War soldier, as in the other letter.

I went to a funeral the other day and it got me thinking. Remember how I've always said I wanted to go out with a bang? I mean it. Literally. When I die, don't go and give

*me a regular funeral with flowers, a coffin, a preacher say-
ing words, and all that shit. I want my body to be cremated,
and my ashes loaded into cartridges, and fired into the sky.
I'd like this to be done on the Gettysburg Battlefield at the
site of Pickett's Charge because, as you know, my role in
that movie was a big high for me. I've often thought that if
I'd died then, I would've died happy. But that would've
meant leaving you and the girls before I was ready.*

*If those bastards at the National Park Service give you
a hard time about doing it on their land, maybe you could
try one of the reenactment sites. Beau and our other friends
in the reenactment community can help. I want them to
wear their uniforms and play the soundtrack from the
movie before and after they blast me into the atmosphere.*

*Please do this for me, Gin-gin. It's the last thing I'll ever
ask of you . Except that when I'm up there blowin' in the
wind, I hope you'll think of me now and then and remember the good times we had—and if you can—forgive the
bad. Because I've always loved you and I always will.*
Wiley

Not what you thought it was gonna be, was it, sweetheart? I
imagined him saying. I even glanced over my shoulder, half expecting to see Wiley standing there, I'd had such a strong sense
of his presence while I read. I had spoken his words, yet it was
his voice I'd heard in my mind as if I'd merely lip-synched his
speech. I wondered how Ginny felt about what I had just read.
Her features worked convulsively; she looked as if she wasn't
sure whether to laugh or cry. Missy's expression registered a
similar confusion. Randall looked mildly disapproving. He
closed his reading glasses and put them back in their case.

"Well," he said carefully, "it appears that Wiley had other plans
for his funeral than the ones Mandy and I arranged yesterday."

Defiance flashed in Ginny's eyes. "If Wiley wants his ashes
blasted into the sky, that's what we'll do! Right, Missy?"

Missy fiddled with the gold chain I so admired, her gaze

flitting back and forth between her grandfather and her mother, as if trying to decide whom to side with.

"It's what your Daddy wanted," Ginny urged with a spunk I hadn't seen since Wiley's death. Far from depressing her, the letter seemed to have energized her by giving her a focus other than guilt-ridden grief.

Missy wavered a moment longer. Then, her mother's spirit proving infectious, she said, "Only Dad could've dreamed up something so way cool as this. I've had people ask me to make them mugs with glaze using their pets' ashes, but that's lame compared to Dad's Big Bang idea."

Ginny stood up. "Why're we wasting time? C'mon, girl, we've got calls to make, letters to write."

Randall's hand rested on the empty patch of carpeted stair where Ginny had sat. He watched them leave with a bemused expression. "You think you know, or at least have some idea how it is all going to turn out," he murmured. "But people keep surprising you and behaving in ways you could not possibly have foreseen. And sometimes that is not an altogether bad thing."

A faint smile played over his handsome face. Then like someone proffering an invitation to dance, he rose and took my hand. "Shall we see what we can do to help?"

FOURTEEN

"It is always a good idea to buy either from a trusted sutler who will stand by the piece or have someone knowledgeable with you when you choose your weapon."
Reliving the Civil War, A Reenactor's Handbook

"THERE'S PLENTY OF TIME before your flight. Why don't I park and come in with you?" Beau suggested as we approached Reagan National Airport.

"Thanks, but I don't want to put you to more trouble," I demurred.

"It's no trouble. I enjoy your company."

I smiled at him, thinking again what a good person he was. He had stopped by Ginny's yesterday evening to see what he could do to help and promptly been enlisted in the preparations for Wiley's Big Bang, as it was now called. This event wouldn't happen for at least a week. Since Ginny, aided by Missy, Beau, and Randall, who had a friend at the National Park Service, seemed to have matters in hand, I'd decided to return to Cambridge and get back to work.

We entered the terminal and, at Beau's suggestion, headed for the nearest bar. He ordered two glasses of Stroh's. When the bartender brought them, Beau raised his glass in a toast: "Here's to a safe flight. Bet your honey will be glad to have you back."

I shrugged. "As I said before, it's complicated and right now we're in an 'off' phase."

Beau nodded. "From my own experience, I know how hard it is to start up with someone new after a divorce. Unless you've got somebody waiting in the wings."

The bitter note in his voice gave me pause. He'd had a strong negative reaction to the discovery that Ginny had a lover and to my own role in that betrayal.

"If you mean Ginny, you should know she feels a lot of guilt about her affair."

"I'm sure she does. Unlike my ex who didn't think twice about taking a lover while we were married. She's still with him, as a matter-of-fact. On a live-in basis. The only reason they haven't married is that she'd lose the big chunk of child support she's been hitting me for all these years."

His round, good-natured face turned grim, reminding me that despite his placid exterior, Beau had his share of difficulties. "I'm sorry," I murmured. "Seeing Ginny with another man must've brought back painful memories."

"It was like déjà vu. Except that I caught my wife in bed with her boyfriend." He bowed his head, as if oppressed by the memory. When he looked up again, his expression had changed and he was once again the open, friendly man I knew and liked. "Getting back to your honey, things can't be all that bad between you."

"Why do you say that?"

Beau grinned. "Call it male intuition, but you don't give the impression of a woman who's stuck in a difficult relationship. On the contrary, you've got this glow."

If I possessed a glow, it was because of Randall, not Nate. My mind circled back to our farewell. He had been on the telephone, working out a detail connected with Wiley's Bang. "Excuse me a moment," he said to the person on the other end. Then he took both my hands in his. "You cannot leave until I have told you again how much it has meant to have you here during this difficult time. You have been such a comfort to Virginia. I cannot begin to thank you for…" His voice faltered as emotion overcame him. "Everything you have done. Oh, and before I forget, here is the copy of your Civil War chapter." He picked up a manila envelope from the table and handed it to me. "I made a few notes on the manuscript and I thought you might like to have them—for what they are worth." He gave me a self-deprecating smile. "If you have other chapters you would like my rather old-fashioned opinion on, feel free to send them."

Now, remembering the earnest look in his dark eyes, the deep, thrilling gravity of his voice, and the warm pressure of his hands on mine, I felt as if a switch had been triggered within, illuminating me not with a faint glow but with high-beamed brilliance.

"…replica musket, if you were on the outs."

Beau's words brought an instant dimming. I stared at him in bewilderment. "What?"

"You wouldn't have bought his kid a replica musket, if you two weren't still pretty solid."

At the mention of the gun, I squirmed inwardly. Amazing how one well-intentioned gift had turned into a nightmarish tangle of troubles from which I wasn't entirely free, even though the gun was in Jake Euell's possession. But Beau didn't know this. And there was no reason he should.

"Oh, *that*. I didn't want to disappoint the boy just because his dad and I quarreled. I have a relationship with him, too."

"Sure, but what did you do with the replica?" Beau frowned at my regulation-size carry-on luggage.

Following his gaze, I saw what he must, that the gun couldn't possibly fit in my bag. "I didn't think they'd let me take even a replica musket on the plane, so I mailed it to my boyfriend's son."

"Ah."

We finished our beers and made small talk until my flight was called. Beau walked with me to the security check-in. I deposited my suitcase and shoulder bag onto the conveyor belt, where they were drawn in by the X-ray machine's long plastic fangs.

Beau slipped an arm around me and drew me close. "You take care now," he murmured. "When you come back for the Big Bang, maybe we can have dinner."

MY CAMBRIDGE APARTMENT was as cluttered as ever. But at least this time I'd remembered to take out the garbage, so no unpleasant odors greeted me. I straightened a few piles of books and papers, then went to look for my cat, Love. After making a cameo appearance at the window when I first arrived, she'd immediately disappeared to show her displeasure at my absence. I lured her out from under my bed with kitty treats and promises not to abandon her again for such a long time. Then I turned to the phone messages, e-mail, and pile of snail mail that had accumulated.

Nate had left a message saying he was having such a great time on Martha's Vineyard that he'd decided to stay through the coming weekend. Thanks a lot, I thought with a prickle of annoyance. Maybe I should have stayed in Alexandria, where my presence was more appreciated than it obviously was by Nate right now.

Sam had e-mailed a reminder about the replica musket. Kids, I'd discovered, had remarkable memories and were relentless when it came to stuff they wanted. I replied that, having discovered a defect in the model I'd purchased, I needed to get a replacement.

By Friday afternoon I was ready to get back to work on the chapter on Reconstruction I was writing for *America: The Republic's Glory and Greatness,* otherwise known as *ARGG.* First, though, I decided to check in with Ginny. Missy answered the phone.

"How's it going?" I asked.

"Pretty well. The National Park Service won't let us use parkland for the Bang despite Randall's connections. But the Yingling family has given us the green light to use the field on their farm where this year's reenactment was held, provided we keep things small."

"That's good news. How's your mom holding up?"

"Okay."

"Was she able to reach your dad's doctor?"

"Not yet. When she tried him a few days ago, he still hadn't come back after the long weekend."

"Too bad. It would be good to know whether your dad had a heart condition or not."

"Yeah, that's been bothering me. There's something else, too."

"What?"

"Mom's boyfriend, Greg Jefferson, keeps calling. She won't speak with him, but it's upsetting her."

Apparently, grown-ups could be just as persistent as kids when it came to getting what they wanted. "Tell him to back off."

"Are you kidding?"

"I thought you didn't approve of your mother's affair."

"I didn't realize she was involved with such a celebrity. Greg Jefferson and his wife were one hot couple."

"Who was his wife?"

"Chantal Mornay."

"Who?"

"You don't know who Chantal Mornay was! I can't believe this."

"Okay, maybe I'm not as with it as I could be," I replied testily. "Will you please tell me who she was?"

"Chantal Mornay was just possibly the most gorgeous model to grace the pages of fashion mags in recent years."

No wonder I had never heard of her. The only women's clothing publication I consulted regularly was the L. L. Bean catalog. "You used the past tense. What happened to her?" Now that I thought about it, I remembered Ginny mentioning Greg's wife had died.

"You don't know?"

Missy's astonishment at my ignorance was becoming annoying. "If I knew, I wouldn't be asking."

"It was awful, just awful. She was mugged in front of their loft and died in Greg's arms."

"I'm sorry to hear that. But think of your mother. His calls are upsetting her and need to stop. The next time he telephones, hang up on him."

"I'll try," Missy promised.

What Missy had told me about Chantal Mornay piqued my curiosity. I turned on my computer and did a search on her. As might be expected for a supermodel, even a dead one, there were plenty of entries, including a Web site devoted to her memory. I clicked onto the Web site and was rewarded by a selection of her most famous covers for *Vogue, Cosmopolitan,* and *Elle.* I had glimpsed some of these while on the supermarket checkout line.

I just hadn't connected a name with that striking face and figure. Like Veruschka, the fashion model I'd idolized as a pre-teen painfully aware of towering over the boys in my class, Chantal Mornay was a giantess. Six foot, seven inches of long, gleaming, café-au-lait-colored limbs ended in a sculpted face with pale green eyes and a mane of wavy black hair. No wonder Ginny was worried about her weight; Chantal Mornay hadn't an ounce of fat on her. Lean on the early covers, she looked almost skeletal on the later ones.

I turned to the text. Born on the French-speaking side of St. Martin, Chantal Mornay had lived in poverty and obscurity until discovered by a vacationing fashion photographer who brought her back to the U.S. and helped launch her career as a model. She had hobnobbed with the rich and famous, including football superstar, Greg Jefferson. After a fairytale courtship, they were married. Several years later, the fairytale turned tragic when Chantal was mugged and badly beaten outside the couple's loft in New York City's fashionable SoHo section.

Here, Missy was mistaken. Chantal hadn't died then, but her recovery was long and difficult. Afterward there were hints of trouble within the marriage. Greg was rumored to be having an affair with a woman he'd met on the road. Chantal was often seen in the company of a well-known black anchorman.

Whether to squelch these rumors or repair their unraveling relationship, Greg and Chantal took a skiing vacation in Aspen. Chantal never made it onto the slopes. Riding up on the lift with Greg, she suffered a sudden heart attack and died in his arms. Doctors attributed Chantal's death to anorexia, a condition she had developed during her years as a model, which had lately grown worse. Greg told reporters that despite plastic surgery after the mugging, Chantal was convinced she'd lost her looks. He said she vowed she wouldn't be "fat, as well as ugly."

Poor Chantal. Evidently she had subscribed to the dangerous dictum that one can never be too rich or too thin. Someone had spouted that same dictum recently. Voluptuous Ginny who yearned for a more svelte shape? No. It had been her rail-thin husband refusing Jake Euell's offer of pretzels at Herr Tavern the night before he died.

From Wiley my brain ricocheted back to Greg. Probably it was only a coincidence that both Greg's wife and his rival had suffered violence at the hands of another, then died suddenly. In the case of the wife, there was a time gap between the mugging and the death, whereas Wiley's death had followed close on the heels of the shooting. But the similarities bothered me.

I checked the other entries under Chantal Mornay's name and found nothing to indicate that Greg had ever been under suspicion for the mugging or for his wife's sudden death in the chairlift. Still... Maybe in a few days I would give Detective No-Relation a call to find out if he'd come up with any information about the source of the large amount of cash Dred Davis had on him when mowed down by the eighteen-wheeler.

Meanwhile, I had my own work to do. I threw myself into the chapter on Reconstruction, working until midnight Friday and putting in a sixteen-hour day on Saturday. By Sunday I was ready for a break and a trip to the beach with a woman friend. We swam, lazed lizardlike in the sun, and shared a picnic lunch. Returning home late in the day, I felt more relaxed than I had in a long time. I was just about to step into the shower when the phone rang. Wrapping a towel around me, I hurried to answer it.

The voice on the line was low, sexy, and unmistakably male: "Where've you been all day, Miranda?"

"Who is this?" I demanded, my sense of well-being rapidly vanishing.

"Where've you been?" he repeated smoothly.

"At the beach. Now will you tell me who you are?"

"One-piece or two?"

"What?"

"Your bathing suit. Got it on now?"

I felt each grain of sand as a needle prick in my scorched skin. I slammed down the handset. The last thing I needed was an obscene phone call. When the phone rang again a moment or two later, I let the answering machine respond.

"It's Jake, Miranda," the voice on the other end said. "Sorry about that. Will you please pick up? I need to talk to you."

Reluctantly I reached for the handset. "You sure like playing games. What's it tonight? Are you the soldier, sailor, tinker, or spy?"

"I guess you'd call it the spy," he said. "Has anyone contacted you about the gun?"

"No," I replied without a moment's hesitation.

"Will you let me know if they do?"

"What's the point? You've got the gun, not me."

"Ah, but if they want it, you'll have it and offer to turn it over to them—for a price, of course."

"You'd use me as bait for a trap?" I demanded furiously.

"Calm down. I'd see you were well protected."

"Nothing doing."

"It was just an idea. You probably won't hear from them, anyway. Are you coming back to town for Wiley's Big Bang?"

"Yes."

"See you then."

"Jake?"

"What?"

What indeed? I had a sudden sense of him as a little kid in a grown-up's body, playing his games of cops and robbers the way he played at being a Civil War surgeon. But such games could be dangerous, I thought, remembering the teenager from the shop's smashed face and Wiley's dead body.

"Be careful."

He laughed. "You sound like my mother."

"I mean it. Sometimes I think you take unnecessary risks just for the hell of it—that it's your way of getting your kicks."

"What unnecessary risks have I taken recently?" He sounded amused, but also curious.

I thought a moment. "Pretending you were a cop on the road the other night."

In the silence that followed I could almost hear the wheels whirring as he considered this.

"I shouldn't have done that?"

"No. Why did you?"

"I wanted you on the bike," he said simply.

"Because you were worried about what would happen to me otherwise?"

"I wanted you on the bike," he repeated.

I wrapped the towel more tightly around me, as if I needed to shield myself from him and this odd declaration of desire. Which was ridiculous, because he wasn't there, couldn't see me, was nothing but a disembodied voice.

"It wasn't a good idea." I meant his pretending to be cop. But he might think I was talking about being on the bike.

"We'll see about that," he replied.

Then I was the one who was confused. Did he mean the cop part, or my getting onto the bike? *One unclear pronoun referent leads to another!* I heard a former English teacher of mine exclaim.

Before I could clarify what I'd meant in order to clarify what he meant, he said, "I have to go now. See you at the Bang."

I thought I would feel better after I'd showered. The lukewarm water soothed my sunburn, and I was glad to get the grit off my skin and out of my hair. But the conversation with Jake left a residue of unease. From inauspicious beginning to ambiguous end, our exchange had been rife with misunderstandings, each of which constituted its own peculiar source of embarrassment. But beyond the awkwardness of our actual words, I sensed something else, something missing, something that should have been said, but hadn't. By him, by me?

A French phrase leapt into the void: *mal dans son peau.* It explained how I felt—uncomfortable in my skin.

FIFTEEN

"Sometimes, when the unit marches past, soldiers can be 'resurrected' and can rejoin the regiment. Keep resurrections to a minimum, however."
Reliving the Civil War, A Reenactor's Handbook

NATE CALLED MONDAY NIGHT to say he was back from Martha's Vineyard. We talked awhile and even made plans to see each other. Missy's phone call the following evening put the kibosh on those plans. Right away I could tell something was wrong.

"It's Mom," she burst out. "She's in a bad way, and I—we— don't know what to do."

"What happened? I thought she was busy with the preparations for the Bang."

"We'd finished with that by Sunday afternoon," Missy explained. "Mom seemed at loose ends. I suggested we go out to dinner and a movie. She said she'd rather stay home, so I went with a friend instead. I came back to a dark house. I knew Mom was there because her car was parked in the driveway. But when I called to her, she didn't answer. I searched everywhere. Finally I found her curled in a corner of the walk-in closet she and Dad shared. She was holding one of his smelly, old socks and crying."

My heart wrenched at the image of Ginny crawling into her lair to mourn her dead mate like a wounded animal. From my own experience after my father died, I knew that you could go along, thinking you were okay, until some seemingly trivial reminder of loss triggered a fresh onslaught of pain. In Ginny's case, it was the discovery of a stinky sock in the closet; in mine the death of a character in a novel I'd been reading.

"I got her to come out and go to bed," Missy continued. "But the next day the package arrived and that really tipped her over the edge."

"Package?" I repeated.

"From the hospital in Pennsylvania. Mom was out when they called to see what we wanted done with the clothing Dad was wearing when he died. They said his pants were bloody and torn, but that his uniform jacket was still in okay condition. I thought Mom might want it as a keepsake, so I had them send it to the house. Big mistake! First Mom yelled at me for not having the jacket burned with Dad's body. Then she buried her face in it and started crying again. Granddaddy and I tried to comfort her, but she shook us off. Granddaddy said we'd best leave her be, that she'd come round eventually. The next thing we knew, she'd gone to the den and put on the video of the movie, *Gettysburg*.

"She's been there ever since. Just sits there on the couch, wearing Dad's jacket and watching the part where he gets shot in Pickett's Charge over and over again. We've begged her to come out, but except to use the bathroom, she won't budge. I don't know, Miranda. Granddaddy thinks that maybe if you…"

"I'll be there tomorrow."

RANDALL MET ME at the airport, his handsome face drawn and pale. "Thank you so much for coming. I would not have asked Missy to call you if we were not at our wits' end. Sometimes what is needed is a different touch. And Virginia is so fond of you."

"I'll try but…" I shook my head, not wanting to give the impression that I could succeed where he and Missy had failed.

"Her going back to Coldwell Banker is out of the question right now," Randall said on the drive from the airport. "But perhaps you could involve her in your work. Tell her you need help with the research for the chapter you're currently writing. See if you can't get her to accompany you to the National Archives or the Library of Congress. Anything to get her out of the house and focused on something else for the next few days."

I promised to do what I could. The rest of the ride passed in silence. As we were about to leave the car, Randall reached over and gave my shoulder a quick squeeze. "Good luck." Hope flickered in his brown eyes like a lightbulb that's almost run out of juice.

I had been warned what to expect. Still, I was shocked by the sight of Ginny in the darkened den. The shadowy figure slumped on the couch, dressed incongruously in an oversized gray army jacket over a faded cotton nightgown, bore little resemblance to the lively, fun-seeking woman who had been my college roommate. Her hair was uncombed and her complexion sallow. She might have been a well-worn and once-loved doll, cast aside when her owner ran off in search of newer, brighter playthings. A plate of food lay untouched on a nearby table. The Ginny doll stared at the TV screen with fixed, glassy eyes, immobile but for the hand gripping the remote control like a doomsday detonating device.

Her silence and stillness contrasted sharply with the noise and frenetic movement on the TV screen. In the flickering light, a gray-clad soldier exploded into the air, then miraculously reconstituted himself in nonstop replay. Wiley's performance was as riveting as ever: He pitched backward, arms and legs flailing while his face registered his agony.

I spoke Ginny's name softly, then more loudly. No response. *Oh, my poor, dear friend.* I sank down beside her, intending to say something to break her trance. Instead, I fell into a trance myself as Wiley jerked back and forth between life and death. *Spring forward, fall back. Spring forward, fall back.*

The action was so hypnotic I could have sat there for hours. After several minutes, a faint but unmistakably rank odor roused me from my stupor. Coming from Wiley's jacket, it was the same sweaty, urinelike stench he had given off as he stormed past Randall and me the morning of my arrival. The odor filled the stuffy room like a noxious gas. I had to open a window before it overpowered me.

Dragging myself from the couch, I crossed the room and opened a high, small window. The air that wafted in was warm and humid, but thankfully fresh. The window also provided a peephole into the world beyond the den. On the front lawn above me, a plump robin poked in the grass. Across the street, two little girls in bathing suits piled into a station wagon. Ordinary scenes of a summer's day, but viewed from the dungeon where I now was, they appeared nothing short of miraculous.

"Ginny, look!" I cried, "Where do you think those little girls are headed?"

She was too absorbed in the action on the screen to notice. I'd have to do something more drastic to get her attention. Before Wiley took the fatal hit for the nth time, I snatched the remote from her and hit the rewind button.

"What're you doing? Stop it!" she cried, grabbing at the instrument. I held it out of reach, finger pressed on rewind while Wiley back-flipped through Pickett's Charge and into oblivion as frame after frame rushed past.

"Give me that!" Ginny held out her hand furiously.

"No. You're not doing yourself any good with this."

"What *am* I supposed to do?"

It was a real question for which I didn't have a ready answer. When she realized I didn't, Ginny's gaze shifted from my face to the remote. She eyed it greedily. What else could I offer her? In her present state, I couldn't see involving her in any trumped-up research project related to my work. No. Her focus was on her dead husband, and that was as it should be. But how to help her find a more constructive outlet for her grief?

The images on the TV continued to career crazily backward. I shut off the set. Ginny stared bleakly at the blank screen. I had seen her upset before, but never this withdrawn. Maybe if I involved her in a different sort of research, I could bring her back from the dark place into which she'd retreated.

"Were you able to reach Wiley's doctor?"

"What?"

"Wiley's doctor—did you speak with him?"

"I left a message, but he hasn't called back."

"It couldn't hurt to try him again."

"What's the point? Wiley's dead."

"Yes, but don't you want to understand what happened? He

died of a heart attack, but as far as we know, he didn't have a heart condition."

She glanced at me, then back at the screen. "All right, I'll give his doctor a call. But not just now."

"What about Detective Seeger—have you heard anything from him?"

Ginny shook her head.

"Too bad. I was hoping he might've found out where the man who shot Wiley got all that money they found on him."

Ginny frowned. "That reminds me of something I've been meaning to do."

"What?"

"Return the overpayment for the work on the Battlemobile to Chad and Peg. They deserve the extra money. If it hadn't been for Chad, Wiley wouldn't have had a steady job. He and Peg put up with a lot from Wiley over the years. They even let him camp out in the garage after I asked him to leave."

"Then let's—"

A click signaled that the tape was rewound. Ginny started. I pounced on the protruding cassette and tore it from the slot. If I'd ripped her heart out, Ginny couldn't have looked more desperate.

"Miranda, please!" She held out a hand.

"No, but you can have this back." I gave her the remote. She tossed it aside and looked up at me pleadingly. "C'mon," I urged gently. "Let's take care of your errand."

Ginny fingered a button on the jacket, releasing another whiff of eau de Wiley. "You go. I can't face them yet. The money's in an envelope on my dresser."

I hesitated, loath to leave but unsure what more I could accomplish by staying. "Okay, but I'm taking this with me."

I held the cassette aloft like a trophy. For a moment Ginny looked as if she would make a grab at it. Instead, she sank back onto the couch. I left her as I had found her, staring fixedly at the screen as at the void into which Wiley had vanished.

Missy was in the dining room sorting through a large stack of mail. "How did it go with Mom?" she asked anxiously.

"I got her to stop watching the video, but that's about it."

"Sounds like progress to me," Missy said. "One step at a time."

I told Missy about the errand to the Yagers. She gave me directions to the garage and told me the keys to her mother's car were in the basket on the front hall table.

As I was leaving, she said, "Would you mind picking up a prescription for me at the neighborhood pharmacy on your way back?"

"Not at all."

"There's a refill for one of Granddaddy's medicines waiting there, too. I told him I'd get it when I picked up mine, but with Mom in such bad shape, I've been afraid to leave the house."

"Don't worry, I'll take care of it." Then on an impulse, I said, "Okay if I take the Battlemobile instead?"

Missy looked at me curiously. "Sure, if you want."

SIXTEEN

"The hardcore movement is often misunderstood and sometimes maligned."

Reliving the Civil War, A Reenactor's Handbook

DRIVING THE BATTLEMOBILE WAS a unique experience. People gaped, laughed, honked, and waved—so much that I had trouble concentrating, and made wrong turns a few times. Eventually I found my way to the Yagers' garage. It was located at the end of a dead-end street in an area of warehouses not far from the Rockville Pike. When I arrived around 4:30 p.m., Peg was seated at a computer in the office, speaking with a young woman in shorts and a tank top who had come to pick up her car.

"Here's what we did," Peg said with a glance at the computer screen. "We changed the oil and filter, checked all the fluids, and checked the brakes. The pads are okay, but the rear rotors are worn and the left outer tie-rod end has too much play, so you might want to consider…"

An ignoramus about cars, I was impressed. As the front woman of this operation, Peg obviously knew her stuff. While she continued with her spiel, I glanced around. Both the office and what I could see of the garage through the open door behind Peg were remarkably neat and clean. What a contrast to Gallic Motors in Cambridge, where I took my ancient Peugeot for servicing. But then my car, like my apartment, was hardly neat and clean itself.

The phone rang before Peg was finished with the young woman. She listened intently, then said, "We close at six, but if you want to drop your car off afterward, put the key in an envelope and drop it in the mail slot."

While Peg was on the phone, another customer, a harried-looking man in a business suit, came in. He slapped a check on the desk and headed for the pegboard where the keys to various vehicles hung. "I'm in a big hurry, so I'll just—"

Peg stood up, blocking his way. "You'll have to wait your turn. These two women are ahead of you," she said, including me.

"But I'm late for—" the man started to protest.

"You wait," Peg commanded.

She was one strong woman, I thought, and not someone you would want to cross. The man looked unhappy, but did as he was told.

When Peg had finished with the other woman, she turned to me. "How can I help you?"

"I didn't come on car business, and I'm not in a hurry," I explained. "Why don't you take care of this man first?"

Despite the man's rush, Peg insisted on going over all the work that had been done on his car before surrendering the keys. When the door had shut behind him, she turned back to me and asked, "What did you want to see me about?"

"I'm a friend of Ginny Cross's. She asked me to—"

"I remember you," Peg said. "You were there the day we brought back the Battlemobile. Marilyn, right?"

"Miranda. I'm here because Ginny wants you to take back the overpayment for the work on the Battlemobile." I rummaged in my purse for the envelope.

"Nothing doing," Peg said quickly, holding out a hand to stop me.

"Please. Ginny feels indebted to you and Chad because of all you did for Wiley."

The phone rang again. Peg listened, asked a few questions, and dispensed advice to a clearly distraught car owner in the calm, measured tones of a therapist. She wore earphones and doodled on a pad while she spoke with the caller. She drew fluffy kittens, puppies, and flowers, creating a parallel universe of soft fuzziness that contrasted with the smashed metal, snapped belts, and leaky hoses that figured in her conversation.

"Don't worry," she said finally. "Have it towed here and we'll fix it." Turning back to me, she said, "We did for Wiley because we were fond of him. He was something of a fuckup, but lovable and one of the few people—" She got up and shut the door behind her. "One of the few people Chad could bear to be around. They were both in Nam. Both wounded in different ways. Wiley brought Chad out of himself, made him laugh."

She cast an anxious glance toward the door. Wondering how Chad would get on now that Wiley was dead? At least he still had Peg to deal with the outside world for him.

"How's Ginny holding up?" Peg asked.

"She was doing okay when she had the arrangements for Wiley's Big Bang to work on, but now that it's all set, she's having a hard time. She blames herself for his death."

Peg looked at me with surprise. "Why? He had a heart attack, didn't he?"

"Yes, but Ginny thinks that if they had stayed together and she'd tried harder to help Wiley, he might still be alive."

"He was very upset about their breakup in the beginning," Peg said thoughtfully. "But then just before he went to Gettysburg, his mood changed. He told us he had a surefire plan to win her back and even took us out to a fancy restaurant to celebrate."

Missy, I recalled, had said something similar. "Did he tell you what his plan was?"

Peg shook her head. The phone rang a third time. Peg listened, made a diagnosis, and scheduled an appointment. While she spoke, Peg began to sketch another cat.

The call over, she said, "Getting back to Ginny and Wiley, if anyone was responsible for their breakup, it was her dad." The paper cat's mouth opened in a snarl.

"Randall? How?"

"He undercut Wiley at every turn," Peg said. Claws sprouted from the cat's paws; its back arched, fur on end. "Spending money was one of the ways he did that, by making sure they were beholden to him."

I felt she was adopting a very one-sided view of things but

saw no point in arguing. "Won't you reconsider taking this?" I extended the envelope with the money. "Ginny will be very disappointed if you don't."

"It's her money and she should keep it," Peg said firmly.

"But I thought the money came from Wiley."

"Yes, but it had to have come from her originally. Where else would Wiley have gotten that much cash? He didn't make a lot as a mechanic, and most of what he made went to support his hobby. Chad and I were surprised she would shell out so much for repairs on the Battlemobile, though."

"How come?"

"She kept him on a tight allowance after they split up. Her dad saw to that." Peg sharpened her scary cat's claws. "And the dinner he insisted picking up the tab for must've cost a bundle, too. So either he won the lottery without telling us or—" She broke off as another customer walked into the office.

Won the lottery. Detective Paxton had used the same phrase about Dred Davis. Both Davis and Wiley had managed to obtain surprisingly large amounts of cash. I couldn't help wondering if it came from the same source.

"Did Wiley have any special visitors at the garage over the last few weeks?" I asked when the customer was gone.

Peg thought for a moment. "Beau stopped by a couple of times. There was another guy, too. Jack somebody."

"Jake? Jake Euell?"

"Yes, odd sort of guy."

I could vouch for that.

"If there were others, they came after business hours," Peg said. "We close at six and don't open again until eight in the morning. Why do you ask?"

"Just curious." Behind us, a garage door rumbled open and an engine revved. "Ginny was really insistent about you taking back the money. How about it?" I put the envelope on Peg's desk.

She stared at it, then at her doodle pad. A tear dropped from one of the fluffy kitten's eyes. "All right," she said finally, "but tell Ginny not to be a stranger. It was bad enough losing him without her, too."

Chad's long, thin torso was bent like a bowstring over the hood of the Battlemobile when I went outside. He appeared to be focused on the array of gray plastic figures marching across the metallic surface in a scaled-down version of Pickett's Charge. He scraped at something on the hood. Then, with whatever it was balled in his fist, he stood up, giving me his profile rather than his full face.

Chad had positioned himself by the driver's side. I approached cautiously, as I might have a wild creature that would attack at the first wrong move. I had no idea what he wanted, what I should say to him. When I reached the car door, I said, "Drives just fine now." My words echoed into the silence, unnaturally loud and falsely upbeat. Chad's face remained turned away from me. With his free hand, he twisted the side mirror slightly, as if deflecting the flow of ions in the air between us.

I tried again, softly with genuine feeling: "I'm sorry about Wiley."

Chad's jaw worked. Something shifted in the smoky blue depths of his eyes. "Harpers Ferry," he got out in a voice hoarse from disuse.

"What?"

"Went to meet someone at a bar there."

"When?"

"Few days before he died. Asked to borrow a car 'cuz he didn't think the Battlemobile would make it."

Chad's clenched fist wavered in the air. I imagined him smashing it through the windshield. Instead, stuffing the fist into his pocket, he strode quickly to the garage and vanished inside. I peered at the surface of the hood. There was a gap in the gray line marching forward to meet the enemy. Examining the spot more closely, I found a cracked crust of glue where a Confederate soldier had stood.

SEVENTEEN

"Be sure to tip your hat when passing ladies, and watch your manners and language."
Reliving the Civil War, A Reenactor's Handbook

THE ENCOUNTER WITH CHAD rattled me so much that on the drive back I became seriously lost. Coming to an unfamiliar area of vacant lots and boarded-up buildings, I realized I'd better turn around and retrace my steps. I had just swung into a driveway when a dark green minivan with tinted windows pulled up in front of me, blocking my way. A man left the van and walked toward me. He wore dark glasses, a short-sleeved sport shirt, and chinos. For all I knew he was a law-abiding citizen who meant no harm. But appearances can be deceiving. I rolled up the windows and locked myself in, feeling suddenly vulnerable and afraid. The man came over and rapped on the window. I didn't open it, though I was now drenched with sweat and would have welcomed a breath of air.

The man thrust his face at the glass. "Lost?"

I shook my head.

"Driving like you are."

Had he been following me? I felt another thrill of fear. The man patted the heads of several gray-clad soldiers on the hood.

"Great car. Couldn't help noticing it. Why I followed you," he added. "That and…" He muttered something, shook his head, and moved away from the window. "Well, I'll be going."

I took a deep breath and let it out slowly. Thank God!

Halfway between the Battlemobile and his van, he stopped and called back to me, "If you really are lost and need to get back to Alexandria, follow me. I'll get you headed in the right direction."

I followed the van, hesitantly at first, then more confidently when I realized that he was taking me where I wanted to go, was a Good Samaritan after all. As we approached the city limits, he gave me a thumbs-up signal, made a quick U-turn, and drove off. Only then did it occur to me to wonder how he knew I was going back to Alexandria. Could he have tailed me from Ginny's house to the garage, waiting while I was inside speaking with Peg before picking up my trail again? Or he could have been driving along, recognized the car, and decided to follow it. That meant he knew Wiley and where he lived. The strange encounter made me made me even more curious about what Wiley had been up to in the days before he died.

A welcome blast of frigid air hit me when I stopped at the pharmacy to pick up Missy's and Randall's prescriptions. I glanced quickly at the labels of each to be sure I had the right medicines before slipping the vials into my tote.

I had barely pulled into Ginny's driveway when Randall arrived in his Lincoln. I got out and waited for him on the brick path leading to the house. "Is everything all right?" he asked with a puzzled glance at the Battlemobile.

"I was just out on a couple of errands. Before I forget, here's the refill of one of your prescriptions. Missy asked me to pick it up."

"Thank you." Randall pocketed the vial, then his gaze returning to the Battlemobile, he said, "There's a problem with the Toyota?"

"No, I decided to take the Battlemobile instead."

"Really? I would not have thought a car like that was your style."

He wouldn't have said that if he saw my ratty Peugeot. "You know the saying that you can't really know a person until you've walked in his shoes? The same might hold true for cars."

Randall was silent a moment, pondering this. "What did you learn about Wiley from driving his car?" he asked finally.

"He definitely wanted to call attention to himself. I got a lot of stares and even caused one near-accident."

"Oh, dear."

"But I also got a lot of smiles, honks, and waves. The sight of such a funky car seemed to give people a lift, lighten their spirits."

"Yes," Randall said, "Wiley possessed a remarkable ability to amuse and delight those he came into contact with." He gazed at the car with a pensive expression. Then, turning back to me, he said, "I would like to look in on Virginia now. When I telephoned earlier, Missy said there had been a change for the better."

We opened the door onto Dorcas Nutley and Missy standing in the hallway. Dorcas greeted Randall and me, then thrust her bulldog face back at Missy.

"I'm sorry I couldn't come sooner," she apologized. "But you know how hard it is with Carl. I'm going to do my best to get to the Big Bang, though. Even if it means dragging him along."

"If you can't make it, we'll certainly understand," Missy said, giving Dorcas a hug.

"I hope she doesn't bring Carl," Missy remarked after the door had closed behind Dorcas.

"That is not very nice," Randall scolded.

"Well, I don't like him. Mom says he turned bitter and angry after the accident. But he's so negative about everything, it's a real downer."

"Carl is her husband?" Randall asked.

"No, her older brother."

"You mentioned an accident?"

"An explosion at an industrial plant several years ago. He lost the use of his legs and has been confined to a wheelchair ever since. Dorcas takes care of him, so it's difficult for her to get out. Reenacting is one of her few outlets," Missy explained.

"He sounds like the same person we heard being interviewed when they were about to blow up the National Observation Tower in Gettysburg," I chimed in. "The one who said the National Park Service could take their explosives and—"

"He did strike me as an unpleasant sort," Randall conceded. To Missy he said, "Do you suppose we can persuade your mother to come to my house for dinner? Luise is making some of her Caribbean specialties."

GINNY WASN'T WILLING to have dinner at her father's house, though she did let us coax her out of the den for a meal of Caribbean treats. She said little and ate less, but we were all thankful that she seemed to be taking the first baby steps toward resuming a normal life. We were further pleased when, afterward, she told us she was tired and would go to her room to lie down. I didn't doubt she was exhausted from her three days of almost nonstop video viewing. But Missy convinced her to take a couple of Elavils just in case.

Randall went home soon after dinner, and I settled in the living room with my laptop. After a while, Missy joined me.

"I was just on the phone with a friend from California," she said, flopping into a chair and putting her bare feet onto the coffee table. "He's a filmmaker, and when I told him about Dad's Bang, he thought it would be cool to film it. What do you think?"

"I don't know, Missy. I'm not sure your mom's up for that. She's still pretty shaky."

"Yeah, but this would be done as a tribute to Dad. It's just the kind of thing he loved. And I think that once Mom understands that, she'll enter into the spirit of things. Look how much better she was when she was busy with—"

The doorbell's ringing interrupted Missy midsentence. She frowned at her watch.

"That's odd. It's almost nine o'clock. We don't usually get visitors this late."

Her footsteps sounded in the hallway, followed by the creak of the door being opened. I heard a sharp intake of breath, then Missy's worried voice, "You can't— She doesn't want—"

I hurried into the hall just as Greg Jefferson brushed past Missy. At the foot of the stairs I intercepted him. "You've got your nerve barging in here. Ginny doesn't want to see you."

Greg glared at me. He reached out as if to shove me aside. Instead, his hand closed around the decorative wooden globe at the end of the banister. "I only want to talk to her. She won't speak to me over the phone. I thought if I came here, she'd have to see me, let me explain."

"Explain what, Greg?" I asked quietly.

"This is between Ginny and me," he insisted.

"You can't see her right now. She took a sleeping pill. She's out cold."

At least I hoped she was, hoped the commotion hadn't awakened her, and that she wouldn't appear bleary-eyed at the top of the stairs. The same thought must have occurred to Greg, because he glanced in that direction. He leaned forward, breathing heavily. Again I sensed he was about to steamroller over me.

I braced myself, determined to face him down. "You need to leave."

His grip tightened on the wooden globe of the banister, then abruptly he let go, and turned around. On the way to the door, he noticed Missy regarding him warily.

"Sorry if I frightened you," he said softly. "I love your Mom, and when she shuts me out, it's hard."

He left without another word. I leaned against the banister. "Whew! That was a close call. I was afraid he was going to storm upstairs, waken your mom, and then who knows what would've happened."

Missy stared open-mouthed at the door. "So that's Greg Jefferson," she said finally. "Wow!"

A half hour later, I was back in the living room, trying to concentrate on my writing, when the phone rang. Missy picked up in the hall. "Oh…*hi*." Something in her voice suggested it might be Greg. He was no fool; he knew he'd made an impression on Missy. Still, I hadn't expected such a quick follow-up. I scurried into the kitchen and grabbed the extension in time to hear him say, "When your mom wakes up, I want you to give her a message from me. Tell her I'm really sorry about your dad, and that I didn't mean what I said that night in Gettysburg. I was angry and—"

"What did you say?" Missy demanded.

"I—I," Greg fumbled, but only for a moment. "This would be so much easier if I could explain in person. Could you meet me at…?" He gave the name of a bar in Alexandria.

Over my dead body, I thought. A chill shot through me. Wiley had used those same words with Ginny.

I went into the hall. "Where're you going?" I asked Missy.

"Out to see a friend," she fibbed with a nervous jiggle of car keys.

"Uh-uh. I'll meet Greg instead."

"But it's me he—"

"That's just it. I'm less likely to fall for his sweet talk."

EIGHTEEN

"One word of warning to Union troops: Southern men seem to congregate naturally on the side with the women. If you don't invite the women to dance first, you may find that the Southern boys have cut you out."
Reliving the Civil War, A Reenactor's Handbook

THE BAR WAS TRENDY, with modern art on the exposed brick walls, lots of leafy plants, and stylish young couples posed like mannequins around little zinc tables. Greg's kind of place, I thought. He was waiting at the rear in one of the few booths. He stood up as I approached.

"Where's Missy?"

"I decided to come instead. You can just as well tell me whatever you were going to say to her."

Greg didn't reply. Yet while he summoned a waitress to take my drink order, I imagined I heard the grind of mental gears, as he adjusted to a less sympathetic listener.

"There's something you wanted to explain?" I asked, cutting to the chase.

"Yes. Thank you." Greg smiled appreciatively at the waitress as she slid my glass of wine and its landing pad napkin onto the table. He shifted restlessly in his seat, knees knocking against the tabletop, as if he felt trapped in the booth. "That night after Ginny and I met up with Wiley at the tavern, we went back to my motel, and, I don't know what she may've told you, but…" He paused, tugged at the gold bracelet band of his Rolex watch.

"She mentioned you said something that really bothered her," I interjected, curious to hear his version of the conversation.

Greg tugged at his watchband and rearranged his long legs. "I was angry. She was pushing me away again. I couldn't take it, so I lashed out at her." He looked up at me, eyes soft and liquid.

"What did you say?" I inquired, though I remembered perfectly well what Ginny had told me.

"That her crazy husband didn't have much longer to live."

"He looked ill to you?"

"He looked like Chantal," Greg said grimly. "Smelled like her, too."

"I don't understand."

"Chantal was my wife. A fashion model and a real looker until she started starving herself to death. Should've seen it coming, but I didn't. Thought she was just on another one of her diet kicks. And that the sweet scent came from perfume." The gold bracelet band was now stretched to the breaking point.

"It didn't?"

"No, godammit!" Greg burst out. "It was the smell of her flesh feeding on itself." The gold pieces snapped back around his wrist like biting teeth.

Omigod. This must explain the peculiar odor of overripe fruit I'd noticed on Wiley.

"There's thin and there's anorexic," Jake Euell had said. People died from anorexia, I knew. Pop singer Karen Carpenter, Boston Ballet dancer Heidi Guenther, and supermodel Chantal Mornay.

"He reminded me of her," Greg said. "That's why I said he didn't have long to live. It was cruel, I know, but I was desperate. I'd finally gotten Ginny back, only to lose her a second time." He gazed mournfully at the bright yellow cosmos blossom in a bud vase on the table.

"You care about her that much?"

His eyes met mine. "Yes, though I never expected to." He paused, staring off into space. "Hard to believe the whole thing with Ginny started because of a bet."

"Huh?"

Greg plucked the cosmos from its vase and twirled it by the

stem. "The fall of sophomore year she showed up in poli-sci 101." He paused again, rapt with memory.

Ah, yes, good old poli-sci 101. A gut course popular with jocks. But Ginny hadn't taken it because she wanted an easy "A" or because she wanted to meet jocks. She had been genuinely interested in the subject.

"Thought she was kinda cute," Greg continued, "but not really my type. I was into tall, willowy blondes then and the occasional redhead. So I wouldn't have bothered asking her out if one of the guys from the team hadn't pointed to her and said, 'See that brunette over there? That's Ginny Longford. Half the guys on campus would like to get into her pants, but she won't give 'em the time of day.' Why, I asked, what's her problem? Is she stuck up or something? My teammate told me no, the buzz was she had a boyfriend back home in Virginia she was determined to be true to. Then he slapped a bill on top of my notebook with the words, 'Twenty says even you can't get her to go out with you.'"

"That's why you pursued her? For a lousy twenty bucks!" I flared.

"No," Greg replied with a shamefaced look. "It wasn't the money, but the challenge. I was a big man on campus, had women swarming around me like bees around honey—all except this little brunette who kept turning me down. But the funny thing is that once I finally did persuade her to go out with me, I fell for her hard. Surprised me more than anyone, because before that my motto had been 'love 'em and leave 'em.'"

"What was different about Ginny?" I asked out of genuine curiosity.

Greg stopped twirling the flower and stared at me with surprise. "Hell, you were her roommate, you knew her."

"Yeah, but…"

The twirling resumed. Greg shifted in his seat. For a man who could turn on the charm at a moment's notice, he seemed uncomfortable talking about his true feelings. "Okay," he began after a long moment. "She was pretty." He tapped a petal on the flower for emphasis. "And funny. And sexy. And…" He hesitated, finger suspended over a fourth petal.

"What?"

"It was her spirit that made her special," he said finally. "She was so alive, so vital, so gutsy for such a small person. She cared deeply about things like poverty and injustice that growing up in a middle-class black family I hadn't given much thought to. She really wanted to make the world a better place. 'So, Greg,' she'd say in that half-teasing, half-serious way of hers, 'what're you gonna do when you can't play ball anymore? You've been fortunate, had your share of advantages, but one of these days you need to start thinking about how you're gonna give back at least some of what you've had.' Wasn't just talk with her, either. No. She practiced what she preached. Wanted to take her to Hawaii winter break, but damn if she didn't go work with migrant farm workers instead." He shook his head with exasperated fondness. "Had a mind of her own all right. I admired her for that, even when the choices she made went against what I wanted. Even when they caused me a lot of pain."

He squeezed the cosmos's stem so tightly that it gave way. The blossom drooped lifelessly like the head of a person whose neck has been broken. "The night she told me she was leaving college and going back to Virginia to be with him was one of the worst nights of my life."

"You didn't act very broken up," I challenged. "Seems like every time I saw you on campus, you had a different girl, sometimes two, on your arm."

"I put on a good front, but deep down I was hurting. Like I'm hurting now."

He stared moodily at the drooped cosmos in his hand. Instead of putting it back into the vase, he placed it beside a demitasse cup containing a votive candle. It curled around the base of the candle like a flower left at a shrine.

"I know you're wondering why someone like me who seems to have it all would pine after an old flame from college. But you have to understand that she meant a lot to me then and still does.

When we got back together, it was like a rebirth, at least for me. I vowed I wasn't letting go of her again."

Never gonna let you go. Never gonna let you go. The words of an old love song came back to me, making me wonder to what lengths Greg might have gone in order to keep Ginny.

"You went back to Cleveland that night?"

"What?"

"The night before Wiley died, did you go back to Cleveland?"

"Well, no. At least not right away. I was angry and very upset. I stayed at the motel for a while to—to calm down." But his legs, moving this way and that under the tabletop, belied his claim of inactivity.

"You didn't try to see Ginny again?"

Greg reached for his brandy snifter and managed to knock it over. Brown liquor spilled onto the tabletop.

"I'll take care of that." Our waitress appeared out of nowhere with a towel.

"Sorry." Greg flashed her an apologetic glance.

"Accidents happen. Can I get you another drink?"

"No, thanks."

"You haven't answered my question about what you did afterward," I prodded when the waitress had gone.

"I'm not gonna, either. It was a night from hell and one I'd rather forget."

He rose, put bills from his wallet on the table, and headed for the door. The waitress watched him go with a bemused expression. Then she gave me a quick, sidelong glance, as if to say: *What did you do to set off such a nice, handsome man?*

What indeed? Except ask a question he didn't want to answer.

NINETEEN

"If you are truly sick or injured, shout 'Medic!' The use of the twentieth-century term lets the other reenactors know you are not acting."

Reliving the Civil War, A Reenactor's Handbook

"So Greg was here last night," Ginny said when I walked into the kitchen the next morning. She was still wearing Wiley's Confederate jacket, but her face had lost its couch potato pallor, and overall, she looked more alert than the day before. Missy sat opposite her mother at the kitchen table, fooling with the Cheerios in her milk-filled bowl like a child with an armada of toy boats.

"Yes, he barged in, demanding to see you."

"He was frantic," Missy interrupted, taking Greg's side as I might have known she would. "And he apologized. Last night and this morning."

"He came back today?" I asked incredulously.

"No," Ginny said. "He sent two dozen roses with a note saying he was sorry."

When in doubt, send roses, I thought wryly. And double the order. But maybe I was judging Greg too harshly. He had sounded genuine when he'd spoken of his feelings for Ginny.

"Missy says you met him at a bar afterward, so he could explain something he'd said to me. What was that?"

I told her. When I finished, Ginny said, "So Wiley reminded him of Chantal. That must have been painful for him." She paused, twirling her spoon in her coffee cup with a wistful expression. "He never spoke much about her except to say they hadn't been getting along, but were attempting a reconciliation when she died. Sounds like me and Wiley. Except for the reconciliation part. If only I'd tried harder to make that happen, maybe…" She stared gloomily into the muddy, swirling vortex of her coffee.

"You don't know that," I cut in, fearing she was about to sink into another morass of self-blame. "What we do know is that Wiley died of a heart attack. Which could have been brought on by any number of things—anorexia, the stress of battle and being shot, or a previously existing heart condition. You were going to try his doctor again, right?"

"I'll do that now," Ginny said.

The line was busy. Ginny waited a few minutes before hitting the redial button. She did this several times with no luck. I had another idea. "An autopsy was done, wasn't it? It might be helpful to know what they found."

Again we had a hard time getting through. Ginny was put on hold and had to listen to a lot of canned music before reaching a live person who gave her another number to try. Since there were three of us, we decided to do the phone work in shifts—when one of us got tired of holding the receiver, she would pass it to the next person. Missy, I noticed, had developed an odd habit of kneading the bare flesh of her arms and thighs.

Eventually we got through to the medical examiner's assistant, who had performed the autopsy on Wiley. She promised to send a copy of the report, but also agreed to give us the gist of it over the phone. Missy was on the line with her, fingers working the flesh of her thigh until it was red and blotchy while they spoke. Missy's side of the conversation consisted mostly of a string of unenlightening "uh-huh's." These were broken by a brief explanation of how Wiley's left leg had been shattered by pieces of an exploding grenade during a firefight in Vietnam. The "uh-huh's" ended with, "Could you spell that please?" Two unfamiliar words appeared on the pad Missy used to take notes: "Felodipine" and "Plendil."

Ginny and I pounced on the words. "What do they mean?" we demanded as soon as Missy was off the phone. She kept us in suspense while she related the conversation verbatim.

"The doctor talked about the bullet wound first. She said that Dad was shot in his left leg, where she found evidence of previous injury. That's when I explained about Vietnam. She told me he was underweight, but otherwise appeared to be in good physical condition. His heart and other organs were perfectly normal. But she wondered if he had a problem with high blood pressure."

Ginny looked puzzled. "Really? Why?"

"I'm getting to that," Missy said. "Toxicology tests were also done. They found a high concentration of this." She pointed at the word "Felodipine."

"What is it?" I asked.

"It's a calcium-blocking agent that's used to treat high blood pressure. By restricting the movement of calcium into the cells of the heart and blood, it relaxes the blood vessels and increases the supply of blood and oxygen to the heart while reducing its workload."

"And Plendil is…?"

"The brand name for Felodipine," Missy replied

Ginny shook her head in bewilderment. "Wiley never had a problem with high blood pressure, as far as I know. I don't understand why would he have been on that drug."

"Maybe he was taking it for some other reason?" Missy suggested.

"We really need to talk to Wiley's doctor," I said.

The line was still busy, but finally, around lunchtime, our call was taken by an answering service, which at least enabled us to leave a message. We hung around the phone, frustrated and dejected. Ginny, in particular, seemed so disconsolate that I half regretted prodding her to make these calls. Why this need to get to the bottom of things, to know the truth? I'd spent the first twenty years of my life in sunny California, land of the laid-back. Why couldn't I take a more carefree approach to life? Perhaps because I'd been away from my home state so long now that the dark roots of my New England ancestry were beginning to show. Not just show—dominate.

The ringing phone pulled me from these grim musings. In the scramble that ensued, Ginny came out the winner.

"Yes? It's for you." She handed the phone to Missy. "Collect from California."

While Missy pinched her arm, we listened to another string of "uh-huh's," ending with, "I haven't had a chance to ask her, but I'll get back to you when I do."

"What was that all about?" Ginny asked when Missy was finished.

"This probably isn't a good time," Missy began.

"What?" Ginny persisted. "You might as well tell me."

Missy told her about her filmmaker friend and his idea of making a movie of the Bang.

"I'm not sure I can handle having a whole film crew underfoot," Ginny said.

"There won't be a crew," Missy assured her. "Just Dylan and his camcorder."

"In that case, I suppose it'll be okay."

Missy beamed. "Thanks, Mom." Then, her expression changing, she said, "One thing I forgot to mention. Dylan's been kinda underemployed lately, so he's going to need airfare."

Ginny rolled her eyes and looked resigned. "All right, I'll pay his way. Now that's settled, can you tell me why you keep massaging your arms and thighs? Is it a nervous habit or some kind of isometric exercise?"

Missy looked baffled. "I'm not sure why I'm doing it. All of a sudden I felt this urge to mold something with my hands, and my skin was the most readily available medium."

Her words gave me an idea. "How long since you left California?"

Missy thought a moment. "Over a week."

"And during this time you haven't done anything with clay?"

"No."

"So it's possible you're starting to go through withdrawal."

Ginny shook her head and laughed her wonderful laugh that came from deep within. It seemed like ages since she'd laughed like that. "Clay withdrawal—now why didn't I think of that? You go out and get yourself some clay, girl. There's a craft store over on—"

"I'll wait until after Dad's doctor calls back."

"Lord knows when that'll be!" Ginny exclaimed. "But if you're set on waiting, we can always make up some Play Doh. I've still got the recipe I used when you and Mandy were little."

Ginny got out flour, cream of tartar, salt, and food coloring. We threw ourselves into the project, dividing the dough into batches of red, green, blue, and yellow. I was glad to be doing something with my hands instead of simply waiting for the phone to ring. Though childish, the activity was a form of art therapy, like Peg's doodling while she listened to customers' car problems. Following Peg's example, I shaped a cat out of yellow clay. Missy made a miniature tea set. Ginny worked on a figure, which she crushed in her fist when the phone rang.

This time, Ginny took the call. It was Wiley's doctor's secretary. When Ginny explained why she wanted to talk to the doctor, the secretary said she thought it would be best if Ginny came in and spoke with him in person. Unfortunately, the earliest available appointment wasn't until the beginning of next week. Still, the secretary promised to let Ginny know if there were any cancellations.

"So that's it for now," Ginny announced glumly. "More waiting."

Missy groaned. "I think this calls for more Play Doh."

Beau's appearance an hour or so later gave us another project to focus on. "I was in the neighborhood and thought I'd stop by to see if you needed help with anything," he said.

"Thanks, but we're set as far as the Bang is concerned," Ginny said.

"So, you've got the…uh…ashes?"

"In a cardboard box in the den," Missy informed him.

"That's fine, but…" Beau seemed to have trouble getting his words out.

"Omigod!" Ginny cried. "I forgot about that part. You can't just shoot the ashes into the sky; they've got to be loaded into cartridges."

Beau nodded. "I'd be happy to do it myself, but some of the others might want to be included, too."

"I'm sure they would," Ginny replied. "I think we're looking at a cartridge-rolling party like we used to have in the old days. The Bang's this Sunday, so we'd better do it tomorrow, Friday. I just hope we can get a hold of people on such short notice."

Beau volunteered to make some of the calls on his cell phone. We divided up Ginny's list and went to work. By dinnertime we were finished. Ginny invited Beau to stay for a meal of Caribbean leftovers.

"I'd like that, but I was kinda hoping…" He had another bout of tongue-tiedness. "I promised Miranda I'd take her out to dinner when she came for the Bang. You and Missy are welcome, too," he finished awkwardly.

Ginny glanced curiously from Beau to me and back again. I knew what she was thinking, that after all these years, Beau and I were finally getting together. Sometime I'd have to tell her, and Beau himself, if he harbored similar illusions, that it wasn't going to happen. Much as I liked him, there were no sparks between us like the ones that crackled between me and Nate, bursting into dazzling tongues of flame. Still, I was glad to go out with Beau, and even had a particular reason for doing so.

"What're you in the mood for?" Beau asked when we were seated in his Crown Victoria. "French, Italian, Chinese, Japanese, Indian, Ethiopian, or good old Southern home cooking?"

"Harpers Ferry," I replied without a moment's hesitation.

TWENTY

"After the 1859 raid on Harpers Ferry, many militia regiments were formed in the South in preparation for insurrection or the coming conflict."

Reliving the Civil War, A Reenactor's Handbook

"A PENNY FOR YOUR THOUGHTS," Beau said during a silent stretch on the trip to Harpers Ferry.

I shrugged. "Nothing much."

"Sure? From the grim look on your face, I figured you were brooding about poor, crazy, old John Brown. Or Wiley."

"I was thinking about Wiley some," I admitted. Thinking about him and wondering who he had met at Harpers Ferry. If this person were connected with the gunrunning ring, then Harpers Ferry, the site of John Brown's Raid on a federal arsenal, was an appropriate rendezvous point. Wiley's involvement with the ring could explain where he'd gotten the cash to take Chad and Peg out to dinner at an expensive restaurant and overpay them for repairs on the Battlemobile. He could've been shot because someone decided he was no longer trustworthy. Or maybe he'd gotten greedy and started demanding too large a share of the profits.

If so, the ringleader had chosen the wrong hit man when he'd picked Dred Davis. Instead of blowing Wiley away, Davis had shot him in the left leg, the same leg that had been injured in Vietnam. Had Davis, knowing about Wiley's earlier injury, deliberately selected that spot? Or was it merely a coincidence, like lightning striking twice in the same spot? And why the leg instead of the chest or head, if Davis was supposed to take Wiley out?

I also wondered about the high concentration of Felodipine in Wiley's system. That part would have to wait until Ginny spoke with Wiley's doctor. In the meantime, I decided to ask Beau if he knew anything about the drug.

"Are you familiar with a medicine called Felodipine that's sold under the brand name of Plendil?"

"It's not one of my company's products," Beau said quickly. "Why do you ask?"

"The autopsy done on Wiley revealed the presence of a large amount of this medicine. Apparently it's used to treat high blood pressure, but Ginny's not aware that Wiley suffered from hypertension. We wondered if he might have been taking Felodipine for some other reason."

"I can't think of any reason offhand," Beau said. "But I can look into it for you."

"Thanks. And thanks, too, for driving me all this way on what might turn out to be a fool's errand."

I had been deliberately vague about my reasons for wanting to go to Harpers Ferry. I had told Beau only that I'd learned from Chad that Wiley had met someone there, and that I thought the meeting might be somehow related to his being shot.

"I couldn't very well let you go alone. That bar in Harpers Ferry is a real dive, and no place for a lady without an escort," Beau said gallantly. "Besides, I'm hoping we'll find a good place for dinner once we've finished our business."

EVEN IN THE LONG twilight of a summer evening, Harpers Ferry was depressing. John Brown's Raid seemed to have cast a permanent pall over the town. Or maybe the place had always been that way. There was a starkness about the landscape that contrasted sharply with the gently rolling farmland we'd driven through. The main street roller-coastered down a steep hill onto a peninsula surrounded by bluffs like brooding giants. The town owed its original importance to its location at the confluence of the Potomac and Shenandoah Rivers, but progress had bypassed it a long time ago, leaving a run-down tourist trap.

At Beau's urging, we drove down the hill to look at the historic sites, such as they were. These included the oblong, brick engine house, where Brown and his men had holed up until captured by Robert E. Lee, then a U.S. Army officer, and his marines, and the John Brown Wax Museum, featuring his story, "Youth to Gallows." The engine house and museum were already closed for the day. Even if they had been open, I wouldn't have cared to go in.

The bar was located up the hill from the historic section on a road leading out of town. It was a squat, bunker-like structure with a broken Budweiser sign. What we could make out of the interior through a thick haze of cigarette smoke was equally unattractive. No plants could have survived long in the blighted atmosphere, which reeked of stale beer, urine, and nicotine. And the only artwork decorating the smudged and stained walls consisted of faded Harley Davidson posters and a few battered playgirls of the month that looked as if they'd been used for target practice.

The place was a far cry from the trendy bar where I'd met Greg last night. I doubted that he, as a black man, would be welcome here. At a bar like this, you had to be a white male of the genus *Americanus redneckus* to feel at home. Everyone else entered at his own risk. Beau was hardly a redneck, yet he could play the part if he had to. I was glad he was with me, glad, too, that we'd arrived at a slow time. There was only the bartender, two men playing pool in the rear, and a third man slumped at the counter. A thuggish sort with a shaved head atop a bull neck, the bartender gave us a quick once-over when we walked in. The pool players were too intent on their game, and the man at the bar too far gone, to pay us any mind.

Beau ordered beers, then got down to business. "Buddy of mine was in here a couple of weeks ago." He showed the bartender a snapshot of Wiley. "'Member him?"

"Who wants to know?" the bartender asked warily.

"I'm a concerned friend, not a cop," Beau replied. "My buddy told me he was gonna meet someone here. Been missing ever since. I'm trying to find him."

"Whaddya want him for?" the bartender demanded.

"His kid was in a car accident a few days ago. He's in the hospital crying for his daddy."

"Yeah?" The bartender appeared unmoved by this tale of woe.

"Yeah," Beau said. "So if you could just tell me if you remember seeing him, I'd be much obliged. Also, if you remember anything about the guy he met, that'd be—" he broke off as the door swung open.

Four bikers, clad in black leather, burst in, the trouble I'd sensed in the air made manifest. They swarmed around us like crows around road kill. Two took stools beside Beau, the other two next to me. Beau made a move to get up, but the biker closest to him growled, "Whatsa matter, man, doncha like our company?"

"Jest thought y'all would like to set together," Beau replied in his best good ol' boy voice.

"We're fine, ain't we, boys?" the biker said.

His fellows agreed. Beau and I weren't fine, though. We were stuck between the proverbial rock and hard place. If we tried to leave, there was bound to be unpleasantness. But staying wasn't an appealing option, either. Not once the jostling started.

It began with a brush here, a nudge there—kids shifting restlessly in line. The touching escalated. A brush became an unmistakable rub as the biker seated beside me sideswiped my bare arm with his. My flesh recoiled at the contact. Hot and damp with sweat, his arm left a slug trail of slime. I wanted to wipe it away, but was afraid he'd turn nasty. I moved closer to Beau. My biker neighbor jabbed me with his elbow just as Beau's neighbor gave him a shove. Our shoulders knocked. Beau and I exchanged nervous glances.

Behind us, I heard the crack of a wooden cue against an eight ball. The pool players were too caught in their game to notice what was going on. The bartender had already signaled his non-involvement by turning his back and pretending to examine the labels of various bottles on the shelf. Surprisingly, the drunk who'd been slumped at the end of the bar now sat up straighter. He even turned his grizzled, derelict's face in our direction. Yet if his brain were as bleary as his eyes, he would be little help.

"I'm hungry," I said to Beau, hoping the bikers would buy this excuse for our departure. "Let's go get something to eat."

"Good idea," Beau agreed.

I started to slip from my seat, but the biker on my left grabbed me by the chin, whiplashing my head around in his direction.

"Don't like me, do you, girlie-girl?" he demanded.

I heard another crack from the pool table; then it was quiet again. I met the biker's eyes steadily. "I'm hungry, that's all."

His mouth opened in an evil grin. He fumbled with the zipper of his pants. "Then eat this!"

Seizing me by the hair, he yanked my head downward. My scalp stung with pain. With a supreme effort, I jerked free and rammed my head into his chest. He teetered backward and tumbled to the floor. Beau crooked an arm around me. We scooted toward the door.

A biker blocked our way. "Not so fast, fat boy," he growled at Beau. "Your old lady owes Billy here an apology."

The biker who had grabbed me slowly picked himself up from the floor. We tried to dart past the man in front of us, but we weren't fast enough. A knife snapped open in his hand. He waved it in the air like a surgeon gone berserk.

"What d'you think, Billy?" he called. "Want me to cut her?" He brought the blade in close to my face.

I held my breath. The steel tip swam before my eyes. I couldn't look at it. Instead, I focused on the biker's upraised arm. A series of letters was tattooed on his inner forearm. I stared hard at them, as if they were a code on which my survival depended. "SSRA," I made out before his arm swung away and the letters vanished.

"Or maybe I oughta slice some of the flab off this bozo?" He pointed the knife at Beau's belly.

"Okay, boys, that's enough fun and games for tonight." The drunk at the end of the bar stood up and pulled a gun on the bikers. "Drop the knife and put your hands up. All of you," he ordered.

The biker with the knife exchanged glances with the others. Billy nodded, and he obeyed. The other two raised their hands. Billy's hand slid downward.

"You, too, Billy," the erstwhile drunk commanded. Another knife clattered to the floor. "Check the others for weapons," the drunk ordered Beau. Two more knives landed on the ground. The drunk kicked them to one side. "Now git!"

The bikers left with a show of false bravado, Billy knocking over a chair on his way out. Moments later, we heard the roar of revving engines. Beau put his arms around me. I sagged against him.

"Thanks for the help," Beau said to the drunk. "You law enforcement?"

The man jerked his head upward, whether nodding or merely stretching his neck. "Let's go into the back. Wanna have a chat with you two."

Relief switched to unease as he steered us to the men's room and opened the door. "What's going on?" Beau demanded.

"Do as you're told," the other man rasped.

Out of the frying pan into the fire, I thought, as he pistol-herded us into the men's room, a cesspool of a place. Obscenities were scrawled on the walls, stinking pools of urine lay on the floor, and a cigar-shaped piece of excrement floated in one clogged urinal.

"Oughta be ashamed of yourself, bringing a lady to a hellhole like this," the man scolded.

Beau and I stared at him with amazement. Had he brought us here to deliver a lecture on good manners?

"It was my idea to come," I said. "We're looking for a friend of ours."

"Show me the picture you showed the bartender," the man demanded.

Beau and I exchanged glances. Obviously, he hadn't been as far gone as we'd thought. Who was he? He hadn't really answered Beau's question about being a cop. *Dear God.* What had I gotten us into? For all I knew, this man, now examining the snapshot of Wiley, was a member of the gunrunning ring and the very person Wiley had come to meet.

"He was here, all right," the man affirmed.

"What about the guy he met?" Beau asked eagerly. "Remember anything about him?"

"I might," the man replied cannily. "But it's gonna cost you."

Beau gave him a twenty. The man examined the bill carefully before pocketing it. "Your buddy met a biker who drops in from time to time."

"One of the guys who was just here?" Beau asked.

"Different one. Name of Davis. Real lowlife," he added contemptuously.

And what does that make you, I wondered, scum of the earth? Still, I was intrigued by the information. Wiley's meeting Davis suggested that the ring was behind the shooting.

"Do you have any idea what the meeting was about?" I asked.

The man glanced at Beau, who handed him another bill.

"Davis and your buddy sat down at a table together and talked in low voices. I couldn't hear what they were saying till the end. Your buddy handed Davis an envelope and asked if he's got it straight. Davis nodded and said something I couldn't hear. Obviously, he didn't have it straight. Your buddy got mad and called Davis a fucking idiot. Said he told him the left, not the right, and that he'd better not mess up."

Beau looked bewildered. I was equally confused. It sounded like Wiley and Davis had been plotting something. But what did Wiley mean by "the left, not the right"? And what was in the envelope he gave Davis? If it was money, then…? Omigod. I had never considered this possibility. But the more I thought about it, the more it made sense.

"Now get the hell out of here before those bikers come back," our informant warned.

We took his advice. Beau drove like such a madman I was amazed we weren't stopped for speeding. If we had been, it would have been a fitting finale to a terrible evening.

When we were well past the city limits, Beau pulled off onto a side road and parked. He switched on the overhead light and turned to me, his face ashen. "Holy Moley, Miranda, I had no idea it was gonna be that bad. Guy was right, I had no business bringing you to a hellhole like that."

"It was my idea, remember. And in spite of everything, I'm

not sorry we went, because now I understand why Davis shot Wiley—Wiley paid him to do it."

"What?" Beau looked flabbergasted.

"The envelope Wiley handed him contained Davis's payment. When Wiley told him the left, not the right, he meant his left leg instead of his right one. He'd already taken a hit in his left leg in Vietnam, and he didn't want two bum legs."

"But why have himself shot in the first place? Unless…" A horrified expression came over Beau's face. "Wile used to say that the one big thing missing from reenacting was the experience of dying in battle. Still, I never dreamed he'd actually try to get himself killed."

"That may have been an element of that," I said. "But mostly I think he did it to win over Ginny. Both Missy and Peg Yager mentioned Wiley spoke about a surefire plan to get back together with Ginny. The shooting was the centerpiece of this plan. When Wiley was wounded in Vietnam, Ginny broke off with Greg Jefferson, the same man she was with at Herr Tavern, and dropped out of college to be with Wiley. He must've figured what had worked before would work again."

"But that's so twisted."

"Yes."

I'd found out what I wanted, but the knowledge didn't make me feel any better. Rather it filled me with a sense of bleakness verging on despair. Beau was right: Wiley's plan was twisted. But mainly it was sad.

"And I thought he was shot because—" I broke off.

"What?" Beau asked quietly.

I hesitated. He'd had a knife, then a gun, pulled on him so I could satisfy my curiosity. Surely he deserved some sort of explanation.

"I thought Wiley was shot because he was involved in something illegal."

"Drugs?"

"No, guns."

"Guns?" Beau looked shocked. "Whatever made you think that?"

"Remember that replica musket I bought for my boy-friend's son?"

He nodded.

"When I took the package back to the B and B that night, I found out it contained an assault rifle instead of a replica."

"You're kidding!"

"I wish I were."

"Why didn't you tell me this before? When I asked about the replica at the airport, you said you'd mailed it to your friend's son."

"I didn't want to involve you. Besides, by that time the rifle was already in the hands of the police."

"You turned it over to them?"

"Jake did." I hadn't meant to mention him, but the name slipped out.

"Jake? I don't get it."

"I was looking for a policeman to turn the gun over to at the reenactment site when these two guys jumped me. Jake saw them and helped me escape. He said he'd give the gun to the police."

Beau was silent a long moment, digesting this. Finally he said, "And you thought Wile was involved with people dealing in illegal guns?"

"Right."

"How come?"

"It just seemed like something he might've gotten into. I mean, he was pals with Davis and—"

"What about Davis?" Beau asked sharply.

"I'm not positive, but I think he was one of the guys who jumped me."

"Probably was—I wouldn't put anything past that scum," Beau said grimly.

I shivered, as the scenes in the bar replayed themselves in my mind. I'd kept myself under control then. But now all I wanted was to be held and comforted. Beau opened his arms and I collapsed into them.

"It's over," he soothed. "Everything's going to be all right now."

TWENTY-ONE

"When you take a hit and pretend to be wounded, you can make all the noise you want and call for your mother, friends, or sweetheart. Avoid overacting or clowning, however. This is a reenactment of a real event where real men died, and they should not be satirized or mocked."

Reliving the Civil War, A Reenactor's Handbook

GINNY'S FACE CONTORTED with pain and shock. "Wiley paid Davis to shoot him?"

"I know it sounds crazy, but everything I've learned points in that direction."

I had dreaded telling her. I had been relieved when I returned to the house last night and Missy told me Ginny had gone to bed. Now, at 8:30 a.m., Ginny and I sat alone in the kitchen. Missy had left to pick up her friend, Dylan, who was coming in on the redeye.

"It *is* crazy," Ginny echoed, "but something I can imagine him doing. How awful that he felt he had to resort to such a drastic measure." She shook her head.

"I'm sorry, Ginny." I clasped her hand across the kitchen table. "But at least this shows he wasn't suicidal. He wanted to be wounded, not killed. Otherwise, he would've had Davis shoot him in the head or chest."

"Yes, but…" She stared mournfully into space. The phone rang and Ginny picked up the extension. "Good, I'm on my way," she said. "That was Wiley's doctor's secretary," she explained. "They had a last-minute cancellation. The doctor can see me at nine."

Everything conspired to make us late. Construction along our route to the VA hospital slowed traffic to a snail's pace. In the hospital garage, a white Mercedes cut ahead of us to take the first available parking space. We had to climb all the way to the rooftop to park. By the time we dashed into the glass carousel door at the hospital entrance, it was already 9:15 a.m.

The carousel moved with such glacial slowness that I was tempted to disregard the instructions not to touch the glass panels and shove the one in front. We'd barely stepped inside when the carousel stopped to let a wheelchair with a departing patient enter from the hospital lobby. A slight, dark-haired woman, dressed in street clothes but wearing a hospital ID tag, had already stepped into the slot ahead of the wheelchair. Like us she was temporarily trapped. When she looked up to determine the cause of the stoppage, I thought I recognized Linette. She glanced quickly away. Perhaps it wasn't Linette after all. I knew she was a nurse, but according to Beau, she worked at a hospital on Long Island. The door moved forward, freeing us all. The woman skittered off down the sidewalk, a live specimen escaping from its glass container.

Dr. Walter Jantz's waiting room resembled an airport terminal at peak travel time when bad weather has caused countless delays and canceled flights. Rumpled and disgruntled, the patients looked as if they'd been camped there for hours. I was surprised the doctor's secretary had bothered to call us when they had such a backlog. I half expected the harried-looking woman at the reception desk to tell us to take a number. Instead, she told us to have a seat and gestured vaguely into space, as if trying to conjure up two vacant chairs.

Nearly an hour later, a silver-haired, bespectacled man in a white coat poked his head into the waiting room. "I apologize for the wait," Dr. Jantz said as he ushered us into his office. "My regular secretary has been out on maternity leave, and her replacement has a bad habit of overbooking. Runs the office like an HMO." He shook his head disgustedly. "So," he continued after we'd sat down, "what can I do for you, Mrs. Cross?"

"You've heard about Wiley's death?" Ginny queried.

"Yes, and I'm truly sorry," Dr. Jantz said. "He was my patient for, let's see now…" He tapped his forehead as if to awaken dormant memory. "At least twenty years, possibly more. Nice young fellow. Very funny, too. I'd come into the waiting room and find him entertaining the nurses and patients. Had them in stitches a lot. Wish I could remember some of the jokes he told." He beat a staccato rhythm on his forehead. "There was one about stitches, I think." The tapping accelerated. "Now I remember. What do a surgeon and a comedian have in common?"

Ginny and I exchanged glances. Someone should tell the good doctor not to give away the punch line.

"It really was funny when he told it," Dr. Jantz said sheepishly. "But I suppose you didn't come to hear me repeat your husband's jokes."

"I'd like to get your opinion of his general health," Ginny said. "He died of a heart attack, but as far as I know he never had any trouble with his heart. He was also apparently taking a medication for high blood pressure, which I knew nothing about. And he'd gotten very thin recently."

"Thin, yes." Dr. Jantz seized upon the adjective. "I remember telling him at his last visit he ought to eat more and switch to a healthier diet. He told me he'd been living on hardtack, salt pork, and green corn because that's what Confederate soldiers ate. Interesting hobby, reenacting, though I sometimes thought he went overboard."

"Getting back to his heart," Ginny said, "do you think his sudden weight loss could have brought on the attack?"

"It's possible, because frankly I don't recall any problems with his heart."

"What about high blood pressure?" I asked.

"I don't remember that he had a problem there, either."

"You didn't prescribe anything for it—like Felodipine?" Ginny asked.

"Not that I recall. But I can check his file to be sure." Dr. Jantz pressed a button on the intercom. "Miss Silvera, could you please bring me Wiley Cross's file? Yes, that's Cross with a '*C.*' *C-R-O-S-S*," he spelled out.

"Was he on any medication that might have affected his heart?" I inquired.

"He took painkillers right after his injury. But that was a long time ago."

"Nothing more recently? Are you sure he wasn't on Felodipine?" I probed.

"Positive. But it will be in my notes." He pressed the intercom button again. "Have you got the Cross file, Miss Silvera? What do you mean you can't find it?" Dr. Jantz excused himself and left the room. A few minutes later, he came back empty-handed. "I'm afraid your husband's file has been misplaced."

Ginny and I looked at each other with dismay. "We have to find his file," Ginny said. "I have questions about Wiley's death that your notes may help me answer. Please have your secretary conduct a thorough search and call me when she finds the file."

Dr. Jantz promised he would see to it.

"That was disappointing," I remarked in the elevator.

Ginny nodded glumly. "I know it's just a record. But I can't help feeling it's another piece of Wiley that's gone."

"Strange that the file should vanish just when we want to see it. Maybe I'm being overly suspicious, but I can't help wondering if there's something in it Dr. Jantz doesn't want us to see." I had an even stranger thought. "I noticed a woman who looked a bit like Linette in the carousel when we came in. Do you suppose…?"

"Let's go back to Dr. Jantz's office," Ginny said, jabbing the button for that floor.

Miss Silvera did not look pleased to see us. "I haven't had time to—" she began.

"Of course not," I said. "But can you tell us if a slight, dark-haired woman dressed in street clothes with a hospital ID came to the office this morning?"

"There was someone like that," Miss Silvera replied slowly. "She told me she was the nurse of another doctor in the building. The other doctor needed a file on a patient of Dr. Jantz's whom he was treating for a different problem. I've been so busy this morning that I let her get it herself."

"Thank you," Ginny said. "You don't have to worry about searching for Wiley Cross's file anymore, because we're pretty sure we know where it is."

"What on earth would Linette want with Wiley's medical records?" I asked when we were back in the elevator.

"She's such a weirdo, who knows?" Ginny replied.

"Maybe she has questions about why he died, too," I speculated. "I mean, she is a nurse and she *was* with him the night before he died."

"True, but…" Ginny shook her head.

Back at Ginny's, we telephoned several of the big hotels in the area, but no Linette Peters showed up in their registers. We also made calls to everyone Ginny could think of in the reenacting community with whom Linette might be staying or who might have heard from her. No one had except Beau, who said she'd called a few days ago to find out if there would be a service for Wiley. Without an address or phone number, Ginny had been unable to contact Linette about the Bang. None of the other reenactors knew where to reach her, either. Even Beau didn't know where on the Island she lived, or which hospital she worked at. He did, however, suspect she intended to come to the Bang.

Reluctantly I turned to the one person I hoped could get information about Linette on short notice. For privacy's sake, I made the call from the den, where Dylan was now staying. He was in the kitchen with Missy, lingering over a late breakfast. But his presence was apparent in the trail of dirty underwear, socks, and three damp towels along the floor. Three damp towels? That meant one for his head, his upper body, and his lower body. And why on the floor? Evidently his mama hadn't taught him proper manners when a guest in someone else's home. Perching on the edge of the pullout couch, I dialed the number Jake Euell had given me.

"I was wondering when I was gonna hear from you," he drawled.

"I've been busy."

"So I hear. Enjoy the trip to Harpers Ferry?"

Despite the cool of the den, a prickly heat engulfed me. "How did you find out? That wasn't you who—" I broke off, appalled at the notion that he was last night's drunken derelict-turned-informant. Jake Euell, "the man of a thousand faces."

"Nope. Buddy of mine. Should've called me before you went out there. Could've saved you a lot of trouble."

"You mean that drunk who took money from Beau was an—"

"Buddy of mine," Jake interrupted before I could say the word "agent." "You calling from the house or a pay phone?" he asked quickly.

"The house, but I'm down in the den by myself."

"Okay, but watch it. Never know who could be listening in."

I thought Jake was getting carried away with the cloak and dagger bit, but I followed his advice. "Your buddy ought to return Beau's money."

"Don't worry. I'll see that he gets it back," Jake assured me.

"Then you can help me with another problem. What do you know about Linette Peters?"

"Works as a nurse on Long Island, acts kinda strange sometimes."

Look who's talking, I thought. Aloud I said, "I already know that. I need the kind of detailed information you got about me."

"Ah, but I was interested in you," he said smoothly. "I made it my business to find out."

Like his earlier declaration, *I wanted you on the bike,* this one caught me off balance. I picked at the edge of a pillow. "I want you to make it your business to find out about Linette."

"I suppose I could do that," he said carefully, "but what's in it for me?"

My fist clenched around the pillow. "Nothing. I'm asking as a favor with no strings attached."

"All right, all right," he responded irritably. "I'll see what I can come up with and bring the info with me tonight. You'll be there, won't you?"

"I'm not planning on stuffing cartridges, but yes, I'll be here."

TWENTY-TWO

"During the late winter or early spring, many regiments have a cartridge-rolling party…. This can be a lot of fun, and even a small number of people working together can roll an enormous number of cartridges."

Reliving the Civil War, A Reenactor's Handbook

WHEN I CAME BACK UPSTAIRS, Ginny was playing the polite hostess with Dylan. He seemed pleasant enough despite slovenly habits, spiked hair, and multiple piercings. But all he wanted to talk about was film, and after an hour or so, he had exhausted even Ginny's patience.

"Why don't you take Dylan out and show him some of the sights?" she suggested to Missy.

After the two of them had gone, Ginny said, "I don't think Linette's going to turn up until the Bang. So I'll have to wait till then to get Wiley's file back. But in the meantime, I'd like to find out more about that drug, Felodipine. There's a medical Web site I consulted when Daddy had his heart attack. It might be a good place to begin."

I followed her into her home office where her computer was set up. She logged onto *medlineplus.org,* and clicked "Drug Information." As the medical examiner had explained to Missy, Felodipine belonged to a class of drugs known as calcium channel blocking agents, which included a number of other medicines with names like Flunarizine and Nicardipine. Different drugs were used to treat different conditions, ranging from migraine headaches to hypertension.

Zeroing in on Felodipine, we scanned the information about

risks to consider before taking the medicine, proper use and dosage, and precautions while using. We learned that Felodipine should not be taken with grapefruit juice, and that the tablets should be swallowed whole without breaking, crushing, or chewing. We also learned that the medicine shouldn't be taken along with other, over-the-counter medicines for such things as appetite control, colds, and hay fever, as these tended to increase one's blood pressure.

The mention of appetite control pills gave me an idea. "Maybe Wiley was taking appetite control pills to help him lose weight, along with Felodipine, and that created a serious problem."

"It's possible," Ginny said, "but I still don't understand why he was on Felodipine in the first place."

We moved on to side effects. Difficulty in breathing, pounding heartbeat, headache, swelling of the ankles and feet, drowsiness, dizziness, nausea, constipation, diarrhea—the list went on and on. Ginny glanced up from the screen and made a face. "Reading stuff like this makes you wonder why anyone would want to take any medicine at all."

I agreed. I was also starting to feel somewhat ill. "I'm ready for a break. Want to go for a walk?"

Ginny shook her head. "I'm going to print this out and then there's another Web site I want to check."

The walk wasn't a good idea. I'd barely gone a block before I was dripping with sweat. I considered turning around then and there, but knew I'd feel like a wimp if I did. People had survived for centuries without air-conditioning, and some adventurous souls even went jogging in weather like this. I forced myself to go a little farther. When I did turn around, the air was so thick with humidity I almost could have swum back to Ginny's. Beau was waiting on the walkway to the house. In one hand he held a cooler, in the other a shopping bag filled with newsprint. "Jeez, Miranda, I hope you weren't out jogging."

"Just a walk. That was bad enough."

"Here's something that should help." He handed me a beer can from the cooler. I took a long drink, then pressed the frosty can

against my burning face, luxuriating in the coolness as Beau
fanned me with a piece of newsprint.

I smiled. "You're like a one-man oasis."

"What are friends for?"

His tone was casual, but not the look he gave me, a lingering
look with just enough wistfulness to make me suspect he wished
we were more than friends. He had gone beyond the bounds of
mere friendship last night by seeing me through the ordeal at the
bar, then letting me unburden myself to him.

"Why the newsprint?" I asked in an effort to return to
familiar ground.

"Oh. This." He seemed momentarily flustered by the shift.
"It's paper for the cartridges. Just have to cut it down to the right
size and shape."

"I can help with that part."

"You're on." Like me, Beau seemed relieved to be back on
our old footing.

RANDALL WOULDN'T BE joining us for the party. He had promised
to attend a retirement dinner for a colleague from the bench. I
suspected he was glad to have a prior engagement. I had a hard
time imagining elegant, dignified Randall stuffing cartridges
with his son-in-law's ashes. Missy, on the other hand, had no
qualms about pitching in. When I came downstairs, showered
and changed, she was seated at the kitchen table, cutting little
trapezoids out of newsprint and chatting with Beau, Paul, and a
few others as easily as if she were one of the guys. Dylan
hovered on the fringes of the group, a silent eye behind his
video camera.

Ginny stood at the kitchen counter, arranging cold cuts on a
platter, and every now and then casting a fond glance at the gath-
ering at the table. "It's just like old times," she confided when I
went over to help. "We used to have cartridge-rolling parties at
the house. Everyone would bring a dish or drinks to share, and
we'd make a night of it."

Missy and the men had the paper cutting well in hand, so at

Ginny's direction, I busied myself filling bowls with potato chips, popcorn, and pretzels.

"You see that e-mail about doctors and guns that's been making the rounds?" Paul asked. Missy and the others shook their heads.

"Too bad because it was a good one," Paul chuckled. "I can't remember the exact figures, but the gist of it is that there's a far greater likelihood of your being accidentally killed by a doctor than you are by an accident with your gun. So what we ought to be doing is banning doctors, not guns."

"Hear, hear!" someone else cried.

Missy made a face. "Come off it, guys."

"Gun control means hitting where you aim!" Paul proclaimed, ignoring her. He pointed his scissors at Dylan, who'd moved in with his camera for a close-up.

"I think we've cut enough of these," Beau said quickly. "Time to roll 'em and fill 'em. Got the ashes ready?" he asked Ginny. She gestured toward a cardboard container on the windowsill among various potted plants.

The phone rang. Ginny picked up and listened. "That was Jake," she said after she'd hung up. "He's running late and said to go ahead without him."

Ginny put the urn on the table. Beau, Missy, and the others rolled the cut papers into tubes on short wooden dowels. The tubes were then placed in a wooden stand with circular holes to hold them upright, and the excess paper tied off to create a cone-shaped tip. The cartridges were now ready to be filled.

Beau opened the cardboard urn. The room grew suddenly quiet. Ginny edged toward the door. She had been fine until now, but I sensed this part would be hard for her. This was not ordinary black powder but her husband's ashes. Another piece of Wiley soon to be lost.

Beau understood this. He caught Ginny's eye and nodded sympathetically. She left the room and he turned to Missy. "You want to start, sweetheart? He was your daddy."

Missy's lip quivered. She glanced from Beau to the urn and back again. "You go. You were his oldest friend."

Beau dipped a measuring spoon into the container and carefully filled a cartridge with a small quantity of ashes. He passed the urn and the wooden cartridge stand to the next person and the process was repeated.

When it was Missy's turn, she hesitated. Then she stuck her finger in the ashes and made a gray mark on her forehead like a good Catholic observing Ash Wednesday. "I—I don't know why I did that," she stammered.

"He was your daddy," Beau repeated. "You loved him."

"Daddy," Missy echoed in a little girl's voice.

She looked as if she were about to cry. Dylan moved toward her, but remained an impersonal eye behind his camera. Beau reached out a comforting hand. Missy took his hand and gripped it tightly like someone dangling from a precipice, holding on for dear life. Then abruptly she let go and bolted. From the hall came muffled sobs.

The men at the table were silent, heads bowed as if in prayer. "Think we oughta finish this later?" Paul asked.

"We'll get it done now." Beau nodded at the man sitting next to Missy's empty place.

The work continued. Conversation resumed, fitfully at first, then, like a stream that's found a new channel after being temporarily blocked, it began to flow more readily. The men were comfortable with one another and, after an initial awkwardness, with the task itself.

And why not? Better this homey scene of men filling cartridges with their dead buddy's ashes around a kitchen table than the creepy atmosphere at the funeral home after my father's death. "Something in cloisonné, perhaps?" the unctuous "bereavement specialist" had suggested. My mother, brother, and I had flipped dispiritedly through a binder with pictures of urns decorated with flowery designs, swans, or hands clasped in prayer, each a monument to bad taste. In the end, we had chosen the plainest receptacle we could find.

A rumbling noise in the street caught my attention. Jake? I peered out the window. It was only a boy on a motorized scooter.

"I'll start putting the spread out in the other room," I announced to no one in particular.

When the last of Wiley's sooty remains had been transferred into cartridges, the men moved to the dining room. They were joined by Missy and Ginny, looking blotchy-faced, but brave.

"I wonder what happened to Jake," I remarked to Beau, as he took a seat beside me with a plate filled with food.

"He's probably on his way," Beau said.

"Right."

I glanced around. Across the room, Dylan managed to eat and film at the same time, camera in one hand, while the other reached robotically into a bowl of chips. Why bother filming us eat? Or rather, some of us eat. Missy picked at her food. Ginny's plate was untouched, as was mine.

"Were you put off by the business with the ashes?" Beau queried.

"It seemed odd at first, but then I felt okay about it," I said.

"Same here," Beau agreed. "And it's what Wile wanted." He tilted his head back and took a long drink of beer, Adam's apple bobbing as he swallowed.

I couldn't relax as I usually did in his company. Instead, I felt unaccountably restless. "I'm going to try Jake at home," I said. I went into the kitchen and dialed his number. After six rings, the answering machine kicked in. I left a message.

"You reach him?" Beau asked when I returned to the living room.

"I got his machine."

"He must be on his way then," Beau assured me.

"Yes, but what's taking him so long?"

I forced myself to eat, drink, and make conversation. But Jake's absence was like a broken fingernail; my mind kept snagging on its jagged edge. He'd said he was coming, so why wasn't he here? I wanted him to come so I could satisfy my curiosity about Linette. But that wasn't the only reason.

"You were married to the sheriff too long," Nate had once said. "That's why you like hanging with outlaws like me." Nate was no outlaw, but as an Indian activist, he'd had his brushes with the law. Jake wasn't an outlaw, either; rather he was a government agent who, I suspected, didn't always play by the rules. Although I hated to admit it, Jake, like Nate, had an edginess I found attractive. I made another phone call and left another message.

BY 10:00 P.M. EVERYONE had gone and Jake was still a no-show. I couldn't stand it any longer.

"Where does Jake live?" I asked Beau, who had stayed to help with the cleanup.

"In the District, Adams-Morgan."

The doorbell rang. It was Randall returning from his dinner. In a dark suit with a red carnation in his lapel, he looked especially dashing. He smelled of cologne and expensive cigars.

"I am so sorry I was unable to come sooner," he apologized. "But the speeches went on and on, and I felt it would be rude to leave in the middle. How did everything go?"

"Fine," I said, "except one person never showed. I'm going out to look for him."

"Now? At this time of night?" Randall sounded horrified.

"I don't think it's a good idea, either," Beau chimed in.

"Can't this wait until tomorrow?" Randall asked.

"No. I'm worried something's happened to him."

"In that case, one of us will accompany you," Randall said.

"I'll be fine."

"Absolutely not," Randall protested. "I will not hear of your leaving unescorted."

"He's right," Beau agreed.

Oh, these southern gentlemen and their mistaken chivalry! Only the knowledge they were dead serious kept me from laughing out loud. For them it was a point of honor that I not be allowed to venture into the night alone.

"You just came back from town, Mr. Longford," Beau said, "whereas I've been sitting on my fanny all evening. I'm happy to take Miranda. Besides, I know where this person lives."

"Well, all right, if you insist," Randall conceded reluctantly. "But do be careful."

In the car, Beau turned to me with a ghost of the look he'd given me earlier in the evening. "Miranda…"

"What?"

"Never mind."

TWENTY-THREE

"No hobby is worth losing an eye or getting powder burns."
Reliving the Civil War, A Reenactor's Handbook

AT TEN-THIRTY ON A steamy summer night, the intersection of 18th Street and Columbia Road NW, in the heart of Adams-Morgan, was one big block party with a multinational flavor. Vendors sold everything from food to vintage clothing, and people thronged the sidewalks. They ate, drank, and danced to reggae and rock music blasting from boom boxes. The festive atmosphere was infectious. Under other circumstances, I would've happily mingled with the crowd, bought a snack at one of the stands, and sidewalk-shopped.

Parking was at a premium, though. After cruising the streets for several minutes, Beau pulled into a spot in front of a fire hydrant. Jake lived on the third floor of a building with an Ethiopian restaurant on the street level. There was a separate entrance to one side of the restaurant. The door was locked and when we rang Jake's buzzer, no one answered. We tried the other buzzers just in case. Again no response.

"What d'you want to do?" Beau asked.

"I guess we should go back to the car, but..."

While we hesitated, a man with dreadlocks and dark, luminous eyes appeared before us. "Who you want?" he demanded.

Beau told him. The man pressed Jake's buzzer three times in rapid succession. Nothing happened. He did the same to another buzzer, and we were buzzed in. Holding the door open with one hand, the man made a sweeping gesture with the other. Thinking he wanted money, Beau reached for his wallet. The man shooed

us in, shutting the door behind us. Beau and I exchanged mystified glances. As we started up the stairs, we heard the creak of a
door above us. "Omar?" a voice called.

Beau didn't answer. By the time we reached the landing, the
door had closed. We could still hear faint noise from the street;
otherwise it was quiet. The silence made me uneasy. Who was
Omar and why had he let us into the building? I hoped we hadn't
been set up for a mugging. I followed Beau cautiously up to the
third floor, relieved to find the hallway empty.

Jake's door was decorated with decals bearing slogans
ranging from "Shit Happens" to "My Daughter Is an Honor
Student at Morgan School." Daughter? He'd never mentioned a
daughter, let alone being married. Perhaps the decal had belonged
to a previous tenant.

Beau called Jake's name and rapped his knuckles on the emblem
of a clenched fist. The noise echoed through the still hall. Beau
shook his head. "I'm sorry, Miranda, but he's obviously not here."

"Wait a minute." Maybe I only imagined this, but the door
appeared to give slightly at Beau's knock. I pushed it open onto
a scene from hell. The room looked as if a tornado had swept
through. Furniture had been knocked over and books and papers
were strewn everywhere.

Jake lay on floor in the midst of the mess, a bloody mess
himself. Knife slashes covered his arms and chest. They looked
like the work of a very sloppy Civil War surgeon. Only this time
the cutting was all too real. I staggered into the room, Beau right
behind me. He put his arms around me and held me close. His
chest was like a cushion, muffling the screams that rose in my
throat, his body a buffer absorbing the waves of shock and horror
that swept over me.

TWENTY-FOUR

"The people of the last century saw perspiration as a natural function, the prevention of which was considered dangerous. A cold dip, for example, would 'check the perspiration' and was not considered healthy."

Reliving the Civil War, A Reenactor's Handbook

A QUICK BITE OF COLD, then balm as the water enveloped me. I swam under the surface, arms arcing forward, legs jackknifing back. Gawky on land, I felt graceful in the water and took pleasure in the buoyant medium, which I considered my natural one. Diving deeper, I skimmed the bleached bottom of the pool, surfacing only for air.

Growing up in Southern California, I had spent hours in the family pool. For me swimming had been a form of therapy. I'd used it to work through the unruly emotions of adolescence, just as now I used it to help me deal with yesterday's nightmare. In the crystalline waters of the pool at the Gettysburg Hotel, I sought release from the horror of Jake's knifing, which had landed him in the Intensive Care Unit. Release, and for some reason I didn't fully understand, absolution.

In the water around me, I was dimly aware of the others. Ginny plowed doggedly back and forth inside a roped-off lane, a tugboat version of *The Little Engine That Could,* doing the laps she hoped would trim down her Rubenesque figure. For her the pool meant work, but for Missy and Mandy, back from New York for the Bang, it was play and another venue for their tango of separation and union. They dove into the pool from opposite ends, cavorted briefly in the middle, then switched ends and repeated the process. I paid just enough attention to the twins to avoid bumping into them. Otherwise, I concentrated on my stroke until the rhythm took over, my mind cleared, and I reached a calm, quiet place. I didn't stay there long.

A partially deflated plastic beach ball splatted into the water ahead. Missy pounced on the ball, plucked it from the water, and lobbed it to Mandy. The ball made a sucking sound when Mandy caught it, reminding me of the sound Jake had made when the EMTs gently lifted him onto the stretcher, though his was more like a cross between a gasp and a groan.

Mandy threw the ball back to her twin, who missed it. "Butterfingers," Dylan called from the edge of the pool, where he stood with his video camera trained on the twins.

He films everything, feels nothing, I thought irritably. Missy splashed him and he hopped backward.

"Watch it!" he cried.

"Watch it, yourself." Missy laughed. "And see if you can find us a better ball. This one barely floats." She tossed the ball from the pool. It bumped along the ground like a flat tire before coming to rest against the base of the umbrella table, next to which Randall sat.

The ball could be repaired, and so could Jake—I hoped. I left the pool and went to sit with Randall. He was settled in a lounge chair under the umbrella with a tall, iced drink. He smiled at my approach, then gazed fondly at his determined daughter and his frolicking granddaughters, a proud *paterfamilias*.

"If I had known how much you ladies enjoy the pool, I would have booked us here the last time instead of that B and B," he remarked. When I didn't respond, he asked, "What is it, Miranda? Are you worried about your friend?"

"Yes. I wish Beau and I'd gotten there sooner, so he'd have a better chance of recovery."

I also thought, but didn't want to tell Randall, that if only I hadn't asked Jake to get me information about Linette, he wouldn't have been delayed and might have kept out of harm's way.

"Please," he chided. "You are starting to sound like Virginia—

blaming yourself for something over which you had no control. It was not her fault Wiley took part in the reenactment when he was unwell, any more than it is your fault you didn't get to your friend sooner. We all make choices in life, and often it is those choices that determine what happens to us. If your friend had chosen to live in a safer neighborhood, he might have avoided the break-in and knifing."

Semiconscious and barely able to talk, Jake had only been able to tell the police that he'd been attacked by a couple of guys wearing ski masks. So, for now, the police were treating the attack as a robbery turned violent. But I couldn't help wondering if people from the gunrunning ring had found out about Jake's undercover activities and gone after him.

"I am sure the doctors are doing the best they can for him," Randall continued, "so try not to dwell on it."

I sat with him until the sun had warmed me to the point where I either had to go back into the water or seek deeper shade. I decided to return to my room to shower and change. As I was leaving the pool area, Missy yelled after me, "Oh, Miranda, I forgot to tell you. Peg called last night when you were out."

"Did she leave a message?"

"Just that she wanted to talk to you. Maybe you can still reach her in Rockville. If not, she and Chad will be at the Bang tomorrow."

I opened the gate of the wooden fence enclosing the pool area and stepped into the alley between the pool and the rear of the hotel. I had neglected to put my sandals back on, and now the hot macadam scorched the soles of my feet. Wincing with pain, I balanced first on one foot, then the other, while I slipped the shoes on. When I looked up, I noticed a wheelchair coming toward me from the direction of the parking garage. An old-fashioned sunbonnet covered the pusher's bent head. What I could see of her face was red from the heat and effort. The man in the chair was inert except for his hands moving restlessly in his lap, as if shuffling and reshuffling a deck of cards. Dorcas Nutley and her brother Carl.

When Dorcas introduced us, Carl Nutley acknowledged me

with a bob of the white plastic sun visor he wore above pink-tinted glasses. "You must be here for Wiley's Bang," Dorcas said.

"Yes. Ginny and her father and the twins are over by the pool if you want to say hello."

Dorcas glanced toward the pool enclosure. "Maybe we will."

"I'm roasting in this heat," her brother complained. "I need to get inside where it's air-conditioned."

Dorcas stared at my still-damp bathing suit and the towel wrapped sarong-style around my hips with envy. *It's all very well for you and the others to enjoy yourselves in the pool,* her gaze seemed to say, *but it's a luxury I can hardly afford. And my brother certainly can't use the pool.* With a last, longing glance toward the enclosure, she turned the wheelchair toward the hotel. I walked along, unsure what to say and half wishing I hadn't run into them. Unpleasantness emanated from Dorcas and her brother like a bad odor.

"Terrible about Jake," Dorcas remarked after a moment or two.

"How did you hear about it?" I was surprised she'd found out so quickly. News must travel fast on the reenactor grapevine.

Dorcas's bulldog face met mine impassively. "Beau told me."

"What're the doctors saying about the odds for recovery?" Carl asked abruptly, his gambler's hands temporarily stilled.

"They're cautiously optimistic." This wasn't exactly true. But Carl's tone and the way he peered at me behind the sun visor and the odd, tinted glasses made me suspect he hoped to hear otherwise. He seemed like a person who, far from surmounting his disability or at least coming to terms with it, remained angry and embittered and all too ready to take pleasure in the misfortune of others.

"Cautiously optimistic!" Carl snorted. "That's doc-speak, for sure. They were cautiously optimistic in my case, too, weren't they, Dory? And look at me! Confined to a wheelchair and in spite of all the drugs they've given me, I haven't had a day without pain. Take it from me—the guy's better off dead."

"Carl," Dorcas murmured reprovingly.

"I'm sorry." I muttered an excuse about leaving my sunglasses at the pool and turned back. A graceless leave-taking, but I wanted to get away from them. Although I had never particularly warmed to Dorcas, I'd accepted her because she was a friend of Ginny's. Now, stripped of that protective coloration, I saw her differently. She and her brother struck me as crabbed and mean, people who wore their resentment on their sleeves.

TWENTY-FIVE

"Officers should encourage their troops to take casualties when the fighting becomes intense. There is no shame in taking hits; it is part of the hobby."
    Reliving the Civil War, A Reenactor's Handbook

BACK IN MY ROOM, I tried Peg at the garage and at home, but got an answering machine both places. Too bad. I wondered what she wanted to talk to me about. The last time I had spoken with her, we'd speculated about where Wiley had gotten the cash to pay for the repairs on the Battlemobile and take her and Chad out to dinner. Maybe now she had solved that particular mystery. I'd have to wait until tomorrow to find out.

Beau joined us for dinner at the hotel restaurant. He and Randall made attempts at polite conversation, but otherwise the silence dragged. The twins and Dylan finished first. After a quick exchange of glances, they stood up on cue, napkins dropping like parachutes over their picked-at plates.

"We're off to show Dylan Gettysburg," Missy announced.

"Enjoy yourselves," Randall called after them. "Would you like to go someplace else for coffee and dessert?" he asked the rest of us.

"No dessert for me," Ginny said. "I'm going for another swim to work off the calories I've just eaten."

Randall raised an eyebrow, but didn't try talk her out of it. He and I adjourned to the pool area for coffee and dessert while Beau left to take care of some last-minute Bang details.

"He looks tired," Randall remarked after Beau had gone.

I thought so, too. And no wonder: in the space of a few weeks

Beau's best friend had died and another buddy had been seriously hurt. Through it all, he had remained a source of comfort and support. The only chink in his seemingly invincible armor had appeared last night.

After we discovered Jake, Beau insisted I wait outside in the hall while he dialed 911. I heard him make the call. Then silence, followed by retching noises, the flush of a toilet, and running water. Mouthwash barely masked the smell of vomit on his breath when he told me an ambulance was on its way.

Much later, after we had left the E.R. and driven back to Ginny's, I caught another whiff of that acrid odor as we sat in the car. "I'm sorry," Beau said then. In the dim light of the car, all the good humor had drained from his face, leaving it fixed and grim.

"Virginia is a strong swimmer, isn't she?" Randall remarked as we sipped brandy and watched Ginny make furrows in the water. "I don't have to worry about her drowning now. But I will never forget the terror of her first swimming lesson. She was five, six maybe, when she announced that she was not going to wear her orange life jacket anymore. She wanted to swim like the older children."

I'd had an orange life jacket, too, but my parents had decided when I was ready to learn to swim. I smiled at the image of little Ginny, even then setting her own agenda.

"So I signed her up for lessons at the club," Randall continued. "And made sure I was on hand for the first lesson. They taught swimming differently than they do now. There was no coddling of the children, no coaxing them gradually into the shallow end with toys. They simply lined those little things up by the pool and had them jump into the deep end, one by one. When it was Virginia's turn and the lifeguard told her to jump, she hesitated for a heartbeat. Then in she went. I held my breath, counting the seconds. When she didn't surface, I ran to the edge, ready to dive in and save her. Miraculously, her head bobbed from the water, all bubbles and giggles. 'I did it, Daddy, I did it!' she cried."

At my first swimming lesson, my mother had sat under an

umbrella, gossiping with the other mothers while I waited fearfully in line. I still remembered my panic when the water closed over me. I thrashed desperately before I surfaced, gasping for air, eyes and nostrils stinging from the chlorinated water. "You didn't even watch!" I accused my mother. "Oh, I knew you'd do fine," she said with a dismissive wave.

My mother's casual attitude contrasted with Randall's acute concern. Did that make her a worse parent? Not necessarily. Perhaps the right approach lay somewhere in-between. Still, I couldn't help wishing my mother had dashed to the pool's edge like Randall.

"Growing up in Southern California, you probably learned to swim before you learned to walk," Randall commented.

"In fact, I didn't learn until I was eight. But then I practically lived in the family pool."

"You must have missed having a pool in the backyard the summer you spent with us," he went on. "But at least you girls had the pool at the club. Speaking of that summer, I realized that you were right—Virginia did not accompany us to Gettysburg. I simply assumed she was with us, because she came to all the other battlefields. Also, I was so worried about her then that, looking back, I could not imagine leaving her on her own for an entire day."

"Why not?"

"I was terrified that she would elope with Wiley the moment my back was turned. I am surprised you don't remember. Surely, I shared my concern with you."

"You seemed distracted that day at Gettysburg, but I thought you were preoccupied by a court case."

Randall shook his head. "How odd that I never told you, as their elopement was my worst fear that summer. I was so relieved when I had gotten Virginia off to college again and Wiley off to Vietnam. I felt as if an enormous weight had been lifted from my shoulders."

"*You* got Wiley off to Vietnam? I thought he enlisted."

"He did, but when he went for his physical, there was a

problem, flat feet or something. They were not going to send him into combat. He was upset about it. So I made some phone calls, had lunch with a good friend at the Pentagon, and lo and behold, Wiley was on his way to Vietnam in a front-line unit!" Randall clapped his hands in self-congratulation.

Ah, yes, the old boy network. Wiley had wanted to fight for his country, and Randall had used his connections to make this possible. Nothing wrong with that. Then why did I suddenly feel uneasy?

Randall's dark eyes clouded with concern. "Is something the matter?"

"I'm feeling kind of restless. I think I'll go for a walk." Alone, maybe I could figure out just what was bothering me.

"Why not take the car? You will be much more comfortable with the air-conditioning." The keys clinked like coins as he dropped them into my hand.

I drove aimlessly, my mind preoccupied. Randall had had his own reasons for shipping Wiley off to Vietnam. Without his intervention, Wiley might have sat out the war behind a desk. He would have been safe and able to elope with Ginny at any time. But not once he was overseas. In Vietnam, Wiley was not only in another part of the world from Ginny, but in a hot spot, as well. He might be wounded, captured, or killed.

An ugly suspicion insinuated itself into my consciousness: perhaps Randall had secretly hoped that Wiley would never come home, or if he did, in a body bag. *You bastard, you wanted him dead.*

This possibility was so awful I didn't dwell on it long. But other disturbing thoughts soon rushed in. I couldn't help but see the events of that long-ago summer in a different light. I was aware of a shift taking place within me, the clash of tectonic plates marking the start of a major upheaval. When it was over, I might never view certain things the same way. Parts of my mental landscape would be irrevocably altered.

On a family trip to Yellowstone National Park years ago, we had driven through an area where an earthquake had struck. The course of a river had been diverted. Where once there had been woods, now there was a lake, Earthquake Lake, product of the cataclysm. Something similar was happening to me now.

I had been a fool to imagine Randall had any interest in me beyond furthering his purpose of preventing Ginny's elopement with Wiley. The invitation to spend the summer with her and her father had come from Ginny. Yet I didn't doubt Randall had played a part in it. He probably figured there was safety in numbers, that relations between Ginny and Wiley were less likely to come to a head if I was there. I had provided companionship for her during the day, and at night served as a chaperone, along with Beau. I had thought Randall a kind and loving father. I still did. But now I realized he had also been a puppet master, quietly pulling strings behind the scenes to ensure that Punch and Judy didn't run off together.

Yet his plan had backfired. Wiley had been wounded, not killed, in Vietnam. His injury had produced the very outcome Randall dreaded. I recalled what he had said about thinking you know how things are going to turn out and being surprised by what actually happens. How often he must have brooded about the unpredictability of life in the years since.

But if life was often unpredictable, so was death. Wiley's death was a case in point. Neither Randall nor Wiley himself could have foreseen that he would collapse during Pickett's Charge. Randall hadn't even expected Wiley to show up at Gettysburg. He didn't know that by having himself shot at the reenactment Wiley hoped to win Ginny back, just as he had years ago.

Wiley's plan was risky, though. He had taken a big chance when he'd chosen Davis as his hit man, because what if Davis, whether by accident or on purpose, mortally wounded him? Also, given his poor physical condition, Wiley might have put himself in jeopardy simply by taking part in the reenactment.

Randall believed that Wiley had brought his death on himself. Without his medical records, we couldn't determine whether this was so.

The thought of the missing records brought me back to Linette. When she came to the Bang tomorrow, Ginny and I could confront her about the records and recover them. But I might be able to locate her sooner. If Linette were already in Gettysburg, I thought I knew where to find her.

TWENTY-SIX

"There was a small but active number of women who worked as professional (paid) mourners at funerals."
        Reliving the Civil War, A Reenactor's Handbook

IN THE DUSKY LIGHT, the Yingling Farm looked very different from the last time I'd seen it. No tent encampment sprawled on the rise to one side of the road. No parked cars were massed beside the barn opposite. Only the trampled grass remained as mute evidence of the reenactment. A dark blue Neon was parked off the road on the battle side. It blended so well into the shadowy landscape that I almost drove past without noticing it. The car could belong to someone connected with the farm, or a passing driver who'd stopped to enjoy the view. But if my instincts were right, it was Linette's.

I parked a little ahead of the Neon and got out. The car was empty and so, as far as I could tell, was the field before me. No crowlike figure picked its way through the grass. The only sign of life was a real bird. A hawk hovered in the air over the field, on the lookout for rodent prey. Perhaps I was wrong about Linette coming here. I was about to return to my car when the hawk veered sharply to the right and flew toward the clump of trees at the far end of the field. Wiley had camped behind that clump of trees, I remembered. He had spent the last night of his life there with Linette. That's where I suspected she'd go now.

I hurried across the field and into the clump of trees. Branches snapped back at me, scratching my arms and legs. Then the curtain of wood opened to reveal Linette. Dressed in her Civil War widow's weeds, she sat on a blanket in the clearing. An old-fashioned, unlit kerosene lantern stood on a camp stool in front of her. I wondered if she intended to spend the night.

"What're you doing here?" she demanded when she saw me.

"Looking for you and Wiley's medical records."

"Go away."

"Not until you hand over his records."

"I don't have them with me."

"Where are they?"

"In a safe place."

"Then you need to get them."

"They're mine. He wanted us to have them."

"Us?" I felt a brush against my arm as a mosquito made its landing. I slapped the insect dead before it could bite, hoping it was a lone scout and that the rest of the troops were far behind.

"The child and I."

My jaw dropped. Could she and Wiley have had a love child no one knew about?

"Where is this child?"

Linette patted her belly. "Our baby has a right to know about his father," she said.

Was this the reason she had swiped the records? If she were really pregnant with Wiley's child, I could understand why she would want medical information about the father. This didn't excuse the theft, but it did give me a line of reasoning I might be able to use to my advantage.

"Sure, he does," I said. "But your baby hasn't been born yet. It'll be years before he's able to understand what's in his father's records. In the meantime, Wiley's other children, his grown children, have a right to those records, too."

Linette drew herself up like a haughty librarian. "They'll have to apply to me for permission."

A needle prick on my leg told me reinforcements had arrived. Bare-legged, I was the perfect target. I hoped I could finish here before the mosquitoes launched a major offensive. I was disappointed that Linette didn't have the records with her. But maybe I could get her to tell me what was in them.

"Suppose your child were old enough to understand the records, what would he learn about his father?"

Linette's expression softened. "He had a good heart."

"In a medical sense?"

"He had a good heart," Linette said, "but bad medicine killed him."

An inner alarm went off. Did she mean the Felodipine? As far as I knew, that was good medicine, provided you had high blood pressure. "What medicine?"

"There's one right there," Linette cried, pointing at my right cheek.

I slapped hard, my cheek smarting from the blow.

"Missed!" Linette crowed.

The note of glee in her voice made me suspect she had deliberately misled me. I felt a strong urge to hit her, but suppressed it. We were now surrounded by a cloud of mosquitoes, whining for blood. They were attacking Linette, as well, but she didn't seem to mind.

"What medicine?" I repeated.

"The medicine in the water."

"Water?" I felt idiotic questioning her every other word, but how else could I follow her?

"You'd better leave before you get eaten alive," Linette advised.

"Speak for yourself. Have you got bug spray?" I demanded frantically.

"Wiley wouldn't approve. Too farbish."

"Jeez, Linette, how did you expect to survive the mosquitoes?" I was appalled that, even after Wiley's death, she was determined to be true to his hardcore standards.

"They're a scourge sent to punish me, sinner that I am," Linette muttered grimly. .

Again I felt at a loss. "Why are you a sinner? What have you done?"

"It was an accident. Same as the other time."

"What other time?"

"You've got to stop blaming yourself, Karen," Linette said in the deep voice of a man.

Now I was truly bewildered. Linette seemed to have assumed a different persona, and in this guise she was addressing someone called Karen.

"It's me, Miranda," I said, hoping to bring her back.

"Not my fault," Linette said in her own voice.

What on earth? It was impossible to carry on a coherent conversation with her, especially while the mosquitoes continued their feeding frenzy. My arms, legs, and face were covered with itchy, stingy bites. But I wasn't giving up yet. I tried a different tack.

"Of course, it wasn't your fault," I soothed. "Now why don't you tell me what happened?"

I'd chosen the right approach. Linette made room for me on the blanket. I settled beside her. She even let me light the lantern. I hoped the odor of kerosene would repel the mosquitoes. It worked, at least awhile.

"You said that bad medicine killed Wiley," I prompted.

"Yes. It wasn't my fault. I—I—" When she spoke again, her words had a strange, incantatory effect. "I wanted to take care of him. When he was lost, I would help him find his way. When he was weary, I would bid him rest. When he was sick at heart, I would comfort him."

The phrases had a familiar ring. Where had I heard them before? After a moment's reflection, I realized they came from the Bible, were part of a prayer. In the lantern light Linette's face had the rapt look of a true believer.

"When he was hungry, I would give him bread," Linette continued. "When he was thirsty, I would give him drink. I wanted to be an angel of mercy, not an angel of death." Her voice quavered and she began to cry.

I waited for her to calm down; then I asked, "How were you an angel of death?

"The water I gave him had bad medicine in it."

Images fast-forwarded through my mind: Wiley collapsing on the battlefield, Linette rushing over and giving him water from his canteen, then in a panic summoning Jake and the other medic when she discovered the gunshot wound. I saw them bearing him away on the stretcher, saw him rise up and flail wildly in what I'd thought was a reprise of his movie death. That final image froze in my brain. The sequence leading up to it made sense, but one thing puzzled me.

"How did you find out the water in Wiley's canteen contained bad medicine?"

"Samvaran told me."

"Who?"

"A very wise man. He can look at water and see what's in it."

She must mean a chemist at a lab. But why take the canteen water to him in the first place unless she suspected it was poisoned?

"You took the canteen because...?"

Linette thought I was asking a different question. "I wanted something of his. Why should she have everything and I have nothing? It wasn't fair."

"No, it wasn't," I agreed, humoring her. "I don't blame you for taking the canteen, but what made you go to Samvaran with it?"

"We had a visitor that night, a visitor who was up to no good."

My heart raced. Who could she mean? As far as I knew only Dorcas Nutley and Ginny had been at Wiley's campsite that night. Surely neither of them meant Wiley harm. Ginny had been upset when she'd found Wiley with Linette, but not so much that she would try to kill him.

"Who was it?" I demanded, struggling for composure.

"The devil," Linette hissed.

Angels and now the devil—she had to be crazy. Still, I decided to play along with her. "What did he look like?"

"I didn't see a face, only a pair of shoes."

"How did you know it was the devil?"

"The shoes were devil's shoes."

Devil's shoes? She was definitely delusional.

"It was the Evil One. I wanted to help Wiley, not hurt him. When he was weary, I would bid him rest. When he was sick at heart—"

"Yes, yes, I know. Those shoes were all you saw?"

Linette nodded. "I was having a nightmare. Wiley was leaving me and going back to her. I begged him not to. I opened my eyes and saw the shoes. I thought they were Wiley's. Then he groaned in his sleep. I realized Wiley was lying beside me, that it was all a bad dream. I was so happy I hugged him. When I looked again, the shoes were gone."

"The shoes could have been part of your dream, too," I suggested.

"No," Linette insisted. "The Evil One was here. I know because he's come before."

This was getting weirder by the minute. "When?" I asked.

Linette glared at me. "Why are you tormenting me? Can't you see how painful it is? Go away—now!"

She made a growling noise that became a high-pitched wail. Then she lunged, fingernails raking the air inches from my face. I stepped quickly out of the way. Linette lost her balance and collapsed in a heap on the ground. I moved farther away, keeping an eye on her and bracing for another onslaught. She pushed herself into a sitting position. But instead of standing, she swiveled around until her back was to me. Then, wrapping her arms around her, she began to rock and hum, softly at first, then more loudly. She hummed the tune "Dixie" so slowly and sadly that it sounded like a dirge rather than the spirited song it was meant to be.

I considered trying to approach her again, but decided against it. Her sudden fury had frightened me, and now she seemed to have withdrawn into a place where I doubted I could reach her. I left her making her eerie music, a lone figure in a field of deepening shadows.

I crashed through the trees and dashed up the slope to the road. What a relief when I reached the Lincoln and could escape inside. I settled back on the cool leather seat and heard the doors click shut with a satisfied sigh. Linette gave me the willies. I was glad to be here in this fortress-like car, safe from her, the mosquitoes, and other predators. I turned on the headlights, cheered by the friendly glow they shed on the road. Their light would see me safely home.

I put the key in the ignition. A shape shifted behind me. I wasn't alone.

TWENTY-SEVEN

"Reenactors in Confederate uniform outside the Confederate camp area and not on the field should salute the U.S. flag as it passes by. Although you are representing a Confederate soldier, you are also a U.S. citizen and should render honors to passing colors."
Reliving the Civil War, A Reenactor's Handbook

I GRABBED THE DOOR HANDLE. The next instant, an arm dropped around my neck like a huge snake. Terror choked the scream in my throat. "Not so fast," a voice rasped. "You and me need to have a little talk."

When he leaned forward into my line of vision, I saw the grizzled, derelict's face of Jake's "buddy" from the bar at Harpers Ferry. "Who are you?" I gasped.

"Agent Mulinari, ATF." He flashed an ID at me. "Who'd you meet out there?"

I gestured at my neck to show him I couldn't very well talk while he had me in a headlock. He let go but kept a hand on my shoulder. "Who'd you meet?"

"Linette Peters, a reenactor."

"Why?"

"She stole the medical records of Wiley Cross, the guy I was asking about at the bar. I wanted them back."

"Did you get them?"

"She didn't have them with her."

"Sure this wasn't about illegal guns?"

He had scared the bejesus out of me, and now he was calling me a criminal. Indignation replaced fear. "Of course not!"

"But you were in possession of an illegal gun."

"It came into my hands by accident. Jake knows that."

"Yeah, but he's in the ICU. How'd you wind up with that gun?"

I repeated the gist of what I had told Jake. Mulinari listened intently, every now and then questioning me on a particular point, such as why I didn't realize sooner that the replica musket was really an assault rifle. When I had finished, he was quiet briefly before firing another question at me: "How'd you know to go to that bar in Harpers Ferry?"

"The mechanic Wiley worked for told me he'd gone there to meet someone shortly before he was shot."

"This mechanic was the guy with you?"

"No. That was Beau Johnston, an old friend of Wiley's."

"Why'd he come along?"

"Misplaced chivalry."

"Say again?"

"Southern gallantry. When I told him where I wanted to go, he insisted on taking me. Said the bar was no place for a lady without an escort."

Another silence, this time longer than the first. Mulinari's hand rested lightly on my shoulder now. I could almost relax. Almost but not quite. His next question jolted me as much as if he'd put me in another headlock: "Your phone call to Jake yesterday—what was it about?"

"How did you—?"

"Why'd you call him?" he repeated.

"I needed some information and I figured Jake could get it for me fast."

"This?" He waved a plain business-size envelope in my face.

"If what's inside has to do with Linette Peters, yes."

"You turned to Jake because you knew he was ATF?"

I nodded.

"How'd you find out?"

"He told me."

"Christ!" Mulinari whacked his head with his palm. "I might've known he'd do something stupid like that. It's just like him, always upping the ante, increasing the risk. You tell anyone else?"

"No."

"Sure you didn't accidentally let it slip?"

"No, but—" My intestines knotted.

"What?"

"I did tell someone that Jake turned the rifle over to the police."

"Who was that?"

"Beau Johnston."

"When?"

"Thursday night after we left the bar."

"And the next night they get Jake," Mulinari said. "Now, either it's pure coincidence, or your friend Beau put two and two together and tipped them off."

"He wouldn't!" I protested hotly. "He was with me when I found Jake, and he was as upset as I was."

Mulinari's fingers drummed on my shoulder. "Maybe so. But there's something fishy about the way he always seems to be there at the right time."

"What do you mean?"

"First he goes to the bar with you. How'd he know it was no place for a lady unless he'd been there before?"

"He could have gone to the bar with Wiley," I suggested.

"Or met Davis or another member of the ring there," Mulinari countered.

"Beau and Davis hated each other. I can't imagine them being partners in anything."

"Then he goes with you to Jake's last night," Mulinari continued. "Was he just doing his southern gentleman thing? Or did he know in advance what you were going to find?"

"This is crazy."

"I don't think so. Look at the business with the assault rifle. You told me just now he carried the package with the rifle to the car. He must've realized you'd been given a real gun instead of a toy. But he said nothing, because he didn't want to alarm you? Or because he hoped to make an exchange without your knowing?"

"I don't—" I broke off.

Beau had asked about the replica musket at the airport. At the time, I hadn't thought anything of it, but now I realized this could have been a way of sounding me out about the rifle. Jake had warned that someone from the ring might contact me. I had never dreamed that person would be Beau. I had just undergone a seismic shift in my view of Randall. Now another upheaval was occurring. Couldn't anyone in this collection of southern gentlemen remain true to my image of him? The displacement of men I liked and admired made me dizzy.

Yet Mulinari's version had a certain credibility. It explained Beau's odd apology last night after we left Jake at the hospital, his rueful expression when we met in front of Ginny's earlier, and other things, as well.

"Terrible about Jake," Dorcas Nutley had said this afternoon. I'd been surprised she'd found out so quickly. Now I wasn't so surprised. She'd said Beau had told her about the attack on Jake. What if, instead, he'd shared his suspicions that Jake might be an undercover agent with Dorcas and her brother? They could've known about the attack because they'd been the ones to plan it.

Angry, embittered, and filled with hate for the government, Carl Nutley was just the kind of person I would expect to get involved with a gunrunning ring. For all I knew, he was the ringleader. I remembered seeing Beau talking with someone seated in a chair that first night in Gettysburg. Carl? This could explain why Beau and his companion had suddenly disappeared, and why later Beau had denied being in town. He didn't want me to know about his connection with Carl and the ring. But my brain balked at the notion of someone as straight-arrow as Beau being part of a gun-smuggling ring.

"You may be right. But why him, of all people?"

Mulinari shrugged. "Either he buys the right-wing, neo-Nazi crap, or he's in it for the money."

I couldn't see Beau subscribing to an ideology based on hate. It had to be the latter. He'd complained about the hefty chunk of child support his ex-wife had been hitting him for, also the high cost of college educations for his children. Still...

"One way to find out," Mulinari said.

"How?"

"You're going to ask him."

He actually had the gall to expect me to entrap an old friend. "No way!"

"Calm down," Mulinari soothed. "All you have to do is meet with the guy and ask him a few questions. Maybe he's innocent, maybe he accidentally told the wrong person that Jake turned the gun over to the police. Once we know who that person is, we can take it from there."

"If he's not innocent?"

"There will be…uh…consequences," Mulinari replied carefully. "I know you're having trouble with this. But think about what those bastards from the ring did to Jake. Do you want them to get off scot-free? Do you want them to go on supplying guns to hate groups like the SSRA?"

The initials had a familiar ring. I remembered the tattoo on the biker's arm at the bar in Harpers Ferry. "What does SSRA stand for?" I asked.

"The South Shall Rise Again. It's one of several militia-style organizations we think the ring supplies weapons to."

"I see."

"The Quartermaster is probably a front for the gun-smuggling operation," Mulinari continued. "The fact that they gave you an assault rifle by mistake certainly suggests that. And a shop like The Quartermaster would be good cover. When they make shipments to clients, they can conceal the real weapons under a bunch of toys. Anyway, we've been keeping a close watch on their operation ever since. But after they messed up with that rifle, they've been lying low. They may slip up again. But in the meantime, more innocent people may get hurt if you don't cooperate."

"I get the message."

"You'll speak with your friend?"

"Yes, dammit!"

Mulinari grinned, the gold in his teeth gleaming like pirate's loot.

I SAT ACROSS FROM Beau at a table in the rear of Herr Tavern. It was the same spot where Wiley had discovered Ginny with Greg, an irony that wasn't lost on me. Now as then, we had the back room to ourselves. I wore a wire; in fact, I was double-wired, and felt so jittery that I, rather than Beau, might have been on trial. I knew what I was supposed to do, but not how. When it came to entrapment, I was a rank amateur.

"You'll be fine," Mulinari had assured me. "Hell, you women are a lot better at this than many of the men. Just turn on the charm, and he'll get loose as goose."

"So," I said to Beau with a forced smile, "is everything set for tomorrow?"

"As ready as it's ever gonna be," Beau replied. "But I'm keeping my fingers crossed that nobody's gun misfires or some other glitch occurs."

He smiled. I smiled back. An awkward silence followed, broken only by sipping and swallowing sounds as we drank our beer. In that silence I heard Beau's unspoken question: *Did she ask me to meet her at this bar just to find out about the preparations for the Bang, or does she have something else in mind?* I pictured Mulinari sitting in his van, listening to the same silence and thinking, *Get on with it already.* He was undoubtedly waiting impatiently. Beau, meanwhile, was looking at me expectantly.

"What?" he asked.

"It's Jake," I said, my expression turning serious. "I'm still very shaken by what happened to him."

"It was bad," Beau agreed. "We just have to hope he pulls through."

"Yes… The why of the attack's been bothering me, too."

"It's pretty obvious what happened," Beau said. "Robbers broke in, Jake put up a fight, and they knifed him. Happens a lot in that neighborhood."

"Maybe, but I'm not sure this was the work of robbers."

"Who then?"

"Those guys selling illegal guns—they could've found out Jake was on to them and gone after him."

Beau shook his head. "Nah. It was robbers, believe me."

"I wish I could, because then I wouldn't feel responsible."

"You—responsible? How?"

"My big mouth—I shouldn't have blabbed about finding the assault rifle and Jake turning it over to the police."

Beau shifted uneasily in his seat. "You tell anyone besides me?"

"Ginny, Randall, my boyfriend back in Cambridge, some other friends, too." I figured that if I cast a wide enough net, Beau wouldn't feel cornered.

"You don't seriously think one of them…?"

"No, but the information might've been passed along until eventually it reached the wrong person." I paused to take a drink of beer. "You didn't mention it to anyone, did you?"

"Nope."

"What about Dorcas and her brother?"

"What about them?"

"When I ran into them today, they brought up the attack on Jake. I was surprised they'd found out so quickly. Dorcas said you told them about it."

"Well, now that you mention it, I guess I did. Dorcas telephoned with a question about the Bang and that's when I told her."

"Ah… She said something else, though, that made me wonder about her."

"What was that?" Beau asked sharply.

"As she and her brother were walking away, I overheard her say to him, 'Bastard got what he deserved.'"

Beau's face turned red and beads of sweat sprouted on his brow. He wiped them away.

For a moment I thought he'd take the bait, but I was wrong.

"Dorcas said *that?* I don't believe it. You must have misheard her."

"Maybe so," I backpedaled. "Because what could she have against Jake that would make her say such a thing?"

"I have no idea." Beau made another swipe at his brow and

gulped down the last of his beer. "Kinda warm in here, don't you think? How about another cool one? Or better yet a ride in my air-conditioned car?"

A car ride was the last thing I wanted, but maybe it would be easier to get Beau to open up when we weren't in a public place. I just hoped Mulinari would be able to follow us all right.

We drove into the open countryside, past miles of shadowy farmland. Once I thought I heard a car behind us, but when I glanced over my shoulder, I saw no pursuing headlights. Either Mulinari was keeping his distance, or he'd lost us. Finally Beau pulled off onto a dirt road and parked under some trees. He took a deep breath and let it out slowly. "So much better out here in the country than in that stuffy bar."

"Mmmm."

"Like old times, too," he said, draping his arm around the back of my seat. "You and me in the front, Wiley and Ginny in the back. I am fond of you, you know, Miranda. Always have been."

"I'm fond of you, too."

"Then I hope you won't take what I'm about to say the wrong way."

"I'll try not to," I said, curious about where this was headed.

"Because you do have a tendency to get carried away about certain things."

"Such as?"

"The notion that Jake was attacked by guys dealing in illegal guns—it's pure baloney."

So we were back to that again. Obviously, Beau was worried that I'd stumbled upon the truth. "Why do you say that?" I asked innocently.

"Just because you happened on one assault rifle doesn't mean there's a whole bunch of bad guys out there dealing in illegal guns."

"No?"

"Of course not. We're talking one guy, one gun. And for all you or I know, the owner of that gun has a permit for it."

"Yes, but why bring an assault rifle to a reenactment?"

Beau shrugged. "Some guys are just so attached to their guns that they don't like to go anywhere without them. I know it's probably hard for a lady like you to understand, but that's just the way it is."

"I suppose you're right," I said slowly. "And I do have a tendency to get carried away. Other people—my boyfriend included—have told me that. Thanks for setting me straight about Jake."

"Anything for a friend," Beau said, giving my arm an affectionate squeeze.

"It's a big relief to know I wasn't responsible."

"You just put that whole nasty business out of your mind, y'hear?" He drew me close and gently tilted my head so that it rested on his shoulder. "Sweet," Beau murmured, stroking my hair.

It was so nice and peaceful in the car with Beau that I wished we could have stayed that way. But somewhere out in the silent landscape Mulinari was listening and waiting, and in the very lull I saw my chance.

"Did you have any idea they'd hurt Jake so badly?" I asked softly.

"Nuh-uh. They told me they were just going to rough him up a—" Beau sat bolt upright, dislodging my head from his shoulder. He knew he'd said the wrong thing, and it was painful watching him scramble to cover up his mistake.

"What did you ask me just now? I'm confused."

I repeated my question and his answer.

"I don't know why I said that. I mean, how could I have known what those robbers—"

I couldn't stand the charade any longer. "They weren't robbers, they were gunrunners," I exploded. "And you tipped them off. How could you get involved with people like that?"

"Look, Miranda, I don't like those guys any more than you do, but I needed the money, for Chrissake! I've got a blood-sucking ex-wife, two kids in college, and I don't make much as a sales rep. When they approached me about making some deliveries, I figured, well, I'm on the road a lot already so—"

"But guns to hate groups?" I cut in, my voice rising with my indignation.

"I know it's wrong, but those guys are gonna get their weapons one way or another."

"And you and your gang might as well supply them? I still can't believe you'd let yourself—"

"God, I wish that kid hadn't screwed up and given you that rifle," Beau cried. "Because now I've got to—what was that?" He glanced around with a panicked expression.

"I didn't hear anything," I said, though, in fact, I had—the snap of a twig, which meant that Mulinari could be nearby.

"Quiet!" Beau hissed, clamping a hand over my mouth.

It hadn't occurred to me to be afraid before, but now suddenly I was. Beau's hand was a tight band across my mouth, his fingernails dug into my cheek, and I could smell his fear. Footsteps crunched on the ground. With his free hand, Beau reached across me to the glove compartment. To get a weapon? Not if I could help it.

I slapped at his hand. He grabbed me by the wrist and tried to yank my hand down and out of the way. We arm-wrestled frantically until caught in glare of two flashlights beaming in through the windows on either side.

"Let her go and come out with your hands up," Mulinari ordered.

TWENTY-EIGHT

"Footwear is one item which has been allowed to slide in the past but will be closely monitored at Gettysburg."
Gettysburg Reenactment Regulations, 1988

BACK IN MY HOTEL ROOM, I removed the tiny microphone hidden inside my bra. I also removed from my pocket the mini tape recorder Mulinari had given me. Then I stole a glance in the mirror in case I'd morphed into someone else. But no snarling face glared back at me. I slipped both the microphone and the tape recorder into a zippered compartment of my tote, which also held the envelope with the information about Linette. Might as well have a look at it now.

Reading the printout helped me understand Linette's bizarre behavior tonight and earlier. For example, when she had addressed a person named Karen, she'd been talking to herself. Karen Phillips had been her name when, driving home from her senior prom in Towson, Maryland, she'd slammed into a tree. Her date, who was also her fiancé, and the other couple riding in the car were killed. So was the five-month-old fetus Karen was carrying. Only Karen survived. This was the tragic accident that even now, nineteen years later, she found too painful to talk about.

Shortly after the accident she suffered a breakdown. For the next several years she was in and out of mental institutions. Between hospitalizations she took courses at the local community college, eventually earning a degree in nursing. As Linette Peters, she moved to Long Island and got a job at a hospital there.

Given her history, I could understand her desire to portray a Confederate widow. I could only guess at why she had been drawn to Wiley. Maybe she saw him as another lost soul—a lost soul that she would save as she had not been able to save her fiancé and the baby she'd been carrying.

A knock on the door ended my foray into pop psychology. Ginny had exchanged her bathing suit for a nightgown and robe. "Mind if I come in?"

"Not at all."

"Daddy said you went for a drive," Ginny remarked as she sat down in an armchair.

"I felt restless and there were some things I wanted to think over."

"I've been thinking, too, while I was doing all those laps."

So swimming had been a form of therapy for her, as well. "What were you thinking about?"

"How I'm going to spend the rest of my life after the Bang."

"That sounds like a pretty tall order."

"Yes, but it's something I need to deal with. I've been Daddy's girl, Wiley's wife and mom, the twins' mom, and Greg's lover twice. Now I'd like to figure out what else Ginny from Ol' Virginy is about. I thought I'd go back to school, and see if I'm good at anything besides selling real estate to Daddy's rich friends."

"I bet you'll discover there are plenty of things you can do well."

"I hope so because, frankly, the whole business of making it on my own is kind of scary. But if I do get involved with another man, whether it's Greg or someone else, I want it to be for the right reasons. I don't want to enter into a relationship as an act of desperation, as I did with Greg. I want to feel strong and sure of myself again. But right now, I don't know, I feel like I've got a long way to go before that happens."

I reached over and patted her arm. "One step at a time."

Ginny smiled. "Thanks for listening, Miranda. What about you? You said you had some things to think over. They must have been important, because you were gone a long time."

I debated how much to relate about the evening's events. I decided not to say anything about the seismic shifts I had undergone with regard to Beau and her father. But I thought she should know about my strange encounter with Linette.

"I did do some thinking, but what's more important is that I found Linette. She's camped at the Yingling Farm in the same spot where she and Wiley spent the night."

Ginny's eyes narrowed. "Did you get Wiley's medical records back?"

"She didn't have them with her. But I did persuade her to tell me a little of what's in them. Dr. Jantz remembered correctly. Wiley's heart was fine but, according to Linette, bad medicine killed him."

Ginny leaned forward in her chair. "What! If he died of a drug overdose, it would've shown up in the autopsy."

"They did find a high concentration of Felodipine in his system."

"That's the bad medicine that killed him?"

"Linette didn't specify which medicine, just that it was bad and where it—" I broke off as the full implications of what Linette had said dawned on me.

Ginny crossed her legs and began to jiggle the top one. "What?"

I took a deep breath. "According to Linette, the bad medicine was in the water she gave him on the battlefield."

Ginny's jiggling leg stopped in midair, pointing outward like an accusing finger. "That means she killed him."

"She believes someone else put the medicine in the water."

The jiggling continued at an accelerated rate. "If Linette didn't put the medicine in the water herself, how does she know it was there?"

"She took the water in the canteen to a chemist and had it analyzed."

Ginny sprang to her feet. "This is incredible! First she swipes his canteen, then his medical records."

"She took the canteen because she wanted something of his," I said.

No need to tell Ginny now about Linette's reason for swiping the medical records. Besides, I didn't know if she were really pregnant with Wiley's child, or if she had confused "his" baby with the one she'd lost.

Ginny began pacing back and forth like a caged lioness. "Okay, but why take the water to a chemist?"

"Apparently she and Wiley had a visitor the night before he died."

"They certainly did—me!" Ginny cried. "So that's Linette's game. She wants to make it look like I killed Wiley. I knew she was twisted, but I never dreamed she would stoop this low." Her green eyes flashed angrily.

"Calm down. Linette didn't accuse you. I don't think she even knew you were there, because she didn't mention seeing you. The person she saw came toward morning, and you were there earlier in the evening, right?"

"Right, but who's to say I didn't come back later?"

I stared at her, dumbstruck, bracing myself for another earth-wrenching revelation. "*Did* you?"

"Of course not! But I was out a lot of the night driving around, so it's not like I have an alibi."

"Will you stop it? She's not accusing you. All she saw was a pair of shoes."

"What kind of shoes?"

I sighed. "I know this is going to sound crazy, but she called them 'devil's shoes.'"

"Devil's shoes!" Ginny snorted. "I've always thought Linette was loony, but this really takes the cake."

"She's not the most stable person in the world but—"

"What do you know about her mental state?" Ginny asked sharply.

"I did some checking and found out she had a serious break-down a while back."

Ginny's expression softened. "That's sad, though I can't say it surprises me."

"No. But she could still be telling the truth."

"You actually believe her nonsense about devil's shoes?"

"I'm not sure what to believe anymore."

I meant it. If Beau was involved in a gunrunning ring and Randall could get Wiley into a front-line unit in Vietnam, hoping he'd be killed, then what might another ostensibly good person do?

"Parts of Linette's story can be verified. If she took the water to a chemist for analysis, he'll have written a report. His report will settle the question of whether the water was drugged."

"True, but…" Ginny shut her eyes and chafed her forehead. Opening her eyes again, she said, "It's very disturbing to think that someone could have done such a thing."

"I know, but Linette's story still needs to be checked out. And we can't very well do that tonight. Try not to dwell on it and get some rest. You've got a big day ahead of you."

"I'll try."

I WISHED I COULD HAVE followed my own advice. But after Ginny had gone, I couldn't stop thinking about the scene with Linette and what had happened before and after it. In the space of a few hours, my world had been upended. I had been forced to make drastic revisions in the way I saw Randall and Beau. Also, my own role was questionable at best. I'd betrayed Jake unwittingly, Beau intentionally, and in this instance two wrongs didn't make a right.

Then there was Linette. Was I mistaken in granting her a measure of credibility? Sure, she had a history of mental illness, but people, I believed, could be crazy in stripes: layers of rationality coexisting with layers of complete irrationality. The trick was to separate these different strands.

Suppose Linette were right about bad medicine being in the water; then, who could have put it there? Who was this devil she claimed to have seen? This person had to be someone with both access to drugs and a reason to kill Wiley. As a doctor and Wiley's romantic rival, Greg scored in both categories. And his whereabouts that night remained unaccounted for.

But others had access to drugs, if not a motive for murder. Beau was a sales rep for a pharmaceutical company; he could have easily obtained a lethal drug. But why kill his oldest friend? Unless Wiley had found out about Beau's involvement in the gunrunning ring and had threatened to expose him. I didn't want to believe Beau was capable of murder, but I had misjudged him before.

As an EMT, Jake also had access to drugs, but I couldn't think of any reason he would want to knock off Wiley. Linette, on the other hand, had both access as a nurse and a motive of thwarted love. Maybe she viewed Wiley's murder as a mercy killing. But then why tell me about the bad medicine? Unless in her confused mental state, she had persuaded herself that someone else was responsible. According to her, the Evil One had come before. She must have meant at the time of her automobile accident. Probably she blamed the devil for making her drive into the tree.

Wiley was another possibility. He could have used the drug to commit suicide after he'd caught Ginny with Greg and despaired of winning her back. But why not simply change his instructions to Davis from shoot to wound to shoot to kill? And why go to the trouble of crushing the pills or caplets and dissolving them in water when he could easily pop them in his mouth?

Finally, if the bad medicine were indeed Felodipine, why that particular drug? Did Wiley already have a prescription for it, contrary to what Dr. Jantz had told us? Or if someone else had put the drug in the water, why had he selected Felodipine out of other potentially dangerous drugs?

Questions, questions. They wriggled like maggots in my brain, resisting my efforts to pin any one thing down. I got up and began to pace like Ginny, hoping to clear my mind with motion. Instead, yet another question blew into my consciousness like a bit of dust on a windy day.

Assuming that Linette had neither hallucinated nor fabricated the nighttime visitor, what did she mean by devil's shoes? Aside from cloven hooves, what was considered appropriate footgear for the devil? I pictured black, hobnailed boots. Beau and other reenactors attached horseshoes to their boots to keep them from slipping. So did Wiley. But that night he'd been wearing flip-flops. Perhaps the association with the devil came from the material the shoes were made of. Snake skin, alligator? I didn't recall seeing anyone wearing shoes of either material.

Maybe I ought to drive out to the Yingling Farm and try to cajole clarification from Linette. But the memory of how she had turned on me made me wary of approaching her alone and at night again.

Yet I felt an urgent need to talk to someone. Who? I had already spoken with Ginny, and I couldn't imagine having a conversation about bad medicine and devil's shoes with Randall; he would think I was as wacky as Linette. Missy, on the other hand, lived in California, where she'd probably heard of stranger things than devil's shoes. I knocked on her door. No answer. She was probably still out on the town with Mandy and Dylan.

Who did that leave? Detective Seeger? No. I needed solid evidence before I went to him. But I sure could use a sounding board. I picked up the phone and dialed.

"I was starting to think you'd disappeared from the planet," Nate drawled, reproach wrapped in a casual tone. "Left several messages on your machine, but you never returned my calls."

In the background I heard the mellow notes of Bill Evans. I imagined Nate lounging in his living room with the lights down low—alone, I hoped.

"I went back to Alexandria unexpectedly and now I'm in Gettysburg. I called because I need your help with something."

Nate sighed wearily. "Okay, but make it short. It's been a long day and I'm beat."

I told him about the encounter with Linette. When I finished, I said, "So, am I crazy trying to figure out what a clearly unbalanced person means by devil's shoes?"

"I don't know. I'm too tired to think straight. Maybe tomorrow…"

"Fine," I said with ill-concealed disappointment. "We'll talk another time."

I was about to hang up when Nate said, "About those shoes— my ex used to get this catalog for people with hard-to-find sizes. Each style had a special name in addition to the brand name. Like Serenity by Stride-Rite and so on. This woman could be referring to a particular style."

"Deviltry by Reebok?"

Nate chuckled. "Something like that. If I think of anything else, I'll let you know. Now I need to hit the sack. You try to get some sleep, too."

"Will do. Thanks for listening."

I felt better after our conversation. At least Nate hadn't dismissed the notion of devil's shoes outright. And there might be something to his suggestion that Linette was referring to a particular style of shoe. I'd look into it tomorrow. Too wired to sleep, I made myself lie still, inhaling and exhaling deeply to rid myself of all the turmoil of the day. Eventually my mind became a stream upon which thoughts landed like leaves. One by one, I watched them float away. The random clutter included a few half-remembered lines from a poem, something about how the naming of cats was a serious matter, not just a game. The naming of cats. The naming of shoes. Names for the devil. The Evil One, Lucifer, the dickens, the...

SOMETIME IN THE NIGHT, I was awakened by voices and scuffling sounds in the hall. "Shush, you'll wake everyone up." Missy and Mandy giggled, bringing to a halt Dylan's drunken rendition of "La Marseillaise." More giggles, followed by Dylan's muttered, "Shit! I'm going to be sick." Then the noise of retching outside my door. Thanks for waking me up and vomiting on my doorstep, I thought crossly. But mostly I was glad they were back safely. Alcohol, automobiles, and people their age were too lethal a combination not to feel relieved. Karen Phillips's prom-night companions hadn't been so lucky.

TWENTY-NINE

"All members of the regiment are responsible for keeping the area free of modern trash and non-period ('farbish') items."
    Reliving the Civil War, A Reenactor's Handbook

THE SCENE AT BREAKFAST in the hotel dining room the next morning was like déjà vu. Straddling a backwards-facing chair, Detective No-Relation-to-the-Folk-Singer had assumed his friendly-neighbor-leaning-over-the-fence pose. But his solemn expression told me this was no casual exchange about the weather. Like a rider posting in the saddle, Detective No-Relation half rose from his chair as I approached. He nodded and seemed about to speak. Ginny beat him to the draw.

"They found Linette's body at the Yingling Farm."

The news hit with the force of an eighteen-wheeler. *"Body?"* I slumped into a chair.

"A trooper noticed the car parked beside the road and stopped to investigate," the detective explained. "He found an empty bottle of sleeping pills and an empty fifth of vodka. Apparently she took her life."

I was stunned. Linette had behaved strangely last night, but I had never imagined she was contemplating suicide.

Turning back to Ginny, the detective asked, "Did you know Ms. Peters well?"

"Not particularly, but I always thought she was rather odd," Ginny replied.

"How so?" the detective probed.

"She played a Confederate widow, was obsessed with death and dying."

"I only met the poor woman once," Randall volunteered, "but she struck me as a fragile blossom, the kind that would blow away in the slightest breeze, or wither and die in the heat. I heard she had fainted the day before I saw her, and I was very concerned that it might happen again if she did not take better care of herself." To Ginny he said, "I believe you mentioned something about her having a breakdown a while back."

So Ginny had told him about our conversation. Last night after she'd left me, or this morning before Detective Seeger had arrived?

"That's right," Ginny said hastily.

"She had mental problems?" the detective asked.

Ginny nodded.

He made a note of this. Dismounting from his chair, he said, "That's it for now. I thought you should know about Ms. Peters because, judging from her costume, we figured she was a reenactor and here for your husband's...uh...service, Mrs. Cross. We've cordoned off the area where she was found. It won't affect your event, though, because the site is located on the other side of a clump of trees."

Randall stood up and held out his hand. "Thank you, Detective."

After the detective had gone, no one spoke for several moments. Then Randall said, "Well, this is indeed a sad development. But life must go on, and we have a busy day ahead of us. If you will excuse me, I had better go see about rousing Dylan and the girls. I gather they burned the midnight oil last night, and I want them to be ready when our guests arrive," he finished with a glance at Ginny.

"I'll help you," she said, getting up.

I watched them leave. Randall's arm was crooked around the small of Ginny's back, shepherding her like a lost lamb. A lost lamb that, judging from our conversation last night, was starting to find its own way. Or so I hoped. I poured myself a cup of coffee from the carafe on the table and helped myself to a blueberry muffin from the buffet table. I drank the coffee, but left the muffin untouched while I pondered Linette's suicide. Now that I knew her history, I realized she must have blamed herself for

Wiley's death, just as she undoubtedly blamed herself for the death of her fiancé and the baby she was carrying. That burden of guilt had probably tipped her over the edge. And yet, something was bothering me.

I glanced at my watch: 9:00 a.m. At noon, Randall and Ginny were hosting a luncheon at the hotel for family and friends. The Bang itself wouldn't take place until 5:00 p.m. I had time for another trip to the Yingling Farm.

WHEN I ARRIVED AT the farm, workers from a rental company were setting up chairs for the afternoon's event. Having borrowed the keys from a hung over Missy, I parked the Battlemobile behind the company truck and strode across the field toward the clump of trees. The sun was hot overhead. Soon I was bathed in sweat. Thank heaven I wasn't wearing a wool uniform like the reenactors who would be taking part in the Bang. I hoped the thunderstorms predicted for later in the day wouldn't interfere with Wiley's send-off.

The spot where Linette's body had been found was cordoned off by yellow crime scene tape. But no officers were around; apparently the local police had better things to do than guard the site of an apparent suicide. I walked over to the edge of the tape and peered inside. All that remained was a depression in the grass where Linette had lain.

I stared gloomily at the patch of flattened grass. Here one day, gone the next—first Wiley and now Linette. In her case, I was probably the last person to have seen her alive. The realization gave me an odd feeling. Mentally, I reviewed what she had said and how she'd looked last night, trying to figure out if there was anything that didn't jibe with the notion of suicide. Sometimes she had sounded crazy; other times she'd seemed perfectly lucid. Linette in her Civil War widow's weeds sitting on a blanket with an old-fashioned kerosene lantern on a camp stool. A lantern she had let me light to keep the mosquitoes from devouring us alive.

That was it! When I asked about bug spray, she said Wiley wouldn't approve—that it was too farbish. If she were so determined to be true to his hardcore standards, would she really bring a fifth of vodka and a bottle of sleeping pills to this place? I hadn't noticed any telltale paper bag, though she could have returned to her car for the vodka later.

The vodka was wrong for another reason. The day Linette had nearly fainted on the field, she had refused Beau's offer of a drink, saying she was temperance. This could have been part of her Civil War widow persona, but in her contemporary persona, she didn't drink, either. She'd ordered a soda at Herr Tavern. Linette and her friends had been drinking the night she'd driven into the tree. I wasn't surprised she had foresworn alcohol ever after. The more I thought about it, the more I was convinced that if Linette had wanted to commit suicide, she wouldn't have chosen vodka and pills.

If she hadn't taken her life, then what *had* happened? Could someone have killed her? Someone who'd arrived after me and who, having listened to Linette's story about drugged water and devil's shoes, decided she knew too much and needed to be eliminated. This theory was a stretch but not entirely implausible—especially if I could find some trace of my hypothetical killer, something the police had overlooked.

I walked slowly around the crime scene tape, scanning the area it enclosed. Nothing. I moved a few feet away and made another circle. I repeated the process again and again, each time fanning a little farther from the center. The sun beat down on me, making me sorry I hadn't brought a hat and a bottle of water. I wished someone would show up with a cooler and hand me a frosty can to press against my burning face, as Beau had the other day. I felt a pang. He was a good man who, against his better judgment, had gotten involved in a bad business.

Eventually I came to the edge of the clump of trees. Thank God! I needed a break from the sun. I plopped down in the shade. After a few moments, I became aware of an unpleasant odor. Glancing around, I spotted stray pieces of used toilet paper. Evidently reenactors had used this shady grove to relieve themselves. Yuck! I got up and was about to leave when a flash of white in the grass not far from my feet caught my eye.

More toilet paper? No. It was a round plastic lid with green lettering "Push Down and Turn." This could be the lid of the container of sleeping pills used to kill Linette. As the police already had the container, the lid wasn't much of a find. But wait a minute. The lid looked soiled. That meant it could have been here longer than last night. Maybe I'd hit pay dirt of another sort, the lid from the medicine that had been slipped into Wiley's water. But where was the vial itself? If the lid was here, the other, more valuable piece of evidence might be nearby.

I walked another set of concentric circles radiating out from the place where I had found the lid. No dice. And no wonder. By itself the lid was hardly incriminating. It could be discarded without a second thought. But the medicine container was another matter. Most likely, it had already been deposited in a trashcan, picked up, and compacted along with other garbage. Still, the fact that I'd found the lid gave me hope of finding the container itself. But not right now. A glance at my watch showed me it was past 11:00 a.m. Time to return to the hotel to shower and change for the pre-Bang luncheon.

The red light on the phone was blinking when I got back to my room. Peg had left a message asking me to meet her at the Gettysburg KOA Kampground on the outskirts of town. If I went there now, I'd be late for the luncheon. But Peg might have important information.

PEG SAT READING a book at a picnic table next to an older-model trailer parked in a spot surrounded by trees. In one of the few patches of sunlight, a young woman clad in a bikini lay on her stomach on a lounge chair. Her well-oiled body showed the beginnings of a serious sunburn. Chad was nowhere in sight.

"Welcome to our home away from home," Peg greeted me. "It isn't much, but it beats staying in a motel. Like some lemonade?"

"What's up?" I asked, as she poured me a glass from the pitcher on the table.

"The frying chicken over there is my niece, Affinity," Peg said, indicating the young woman. I smiled at both Peg's description and the young woman's name, which gave her away as the child of former flower children. "Do you want to tell her, or shall I?" Peg asked.

"Go ahead," Affinity replied without raising her head.

"Remember when you asked me if Wiley had any unusual visitors?" Peg said. "Well, it turns out he did, someone who came after-hours. Affinity knows about him because she stopped at the garage to drop off her car while he was there."

"Who was it?"

"She didn't actually see him but—"

"I heard him," Affinity broke in, propping her chin on her hands and turning in my direction. "He and Wiley were inside the garage arguing."

"What about?" I asked with growing curiosity.

"Money," Affinity said. "The other man offered Wiley fifty grand, but Wiley said it wasn't enough, that he wanted double that amount. That's all I heard because my boyfriend was bugging me to leave. He'd driven over to the garage with me and was anxious to get home."

"This person must be the source of the money Wiley used to take Chad and me out to dinner and pay for the repairs on the Battlemobile," Peg said.

And pay Dred Davis to shoot him, I thought. Who could it be? Obviously, someone with money to burn. Greg? It fit with my image of him as a man who used money and charm to get what he wanted, in this case, Ginny.

Then again, it could be someone connected with the gunrunning ring, though not Beau, I hoped. Maybe Wiley had found out about the ring, and this person was trying to buy his silence.

"It's all very mysterious," Peg continued, "but I suppose it's water over the dam now that Wiley's dead."

"You didn't notice anything else that could help identify him—his car perhaps?" I asked Affinity.

She shook her head. "I heard the arguing when I went to the mail slot to drop off my keys. When I didn't come back right away, my boyfriend started honking his horn. I dropped off the keys and ran."

Another dead end, I thought glumly. A lid without a container, and now a disembodied voice. Still, I wasn't ready to give up yet. "This voice you heard—can you describe it?"

Affinity shrugged. "It was a man's voice."

"You can do better than that," Peg said sharply. Affinity made a face at her.

I smiled encouragingly. "Did the voice sound young and sexy like your boyfriend or…?"

"More like my dad. An older guy."

"From the South?"

"Yeah."

"Did he talk like your dad does when he gets angry?"

"My dad yells when he's mad. Swears, too. This guy was soft-spoken, kept his cool."

I took a long drink of lemonade, then pressed the cold glass against my forehead. "You've been very helpful," I said, getting up. "You're a great observer." Affinity beamed. "But don't you think it's time to cook the other side?"

Affinity frowned at her shoulder, now an angry red, and rolled over onto her back. Peg followed me to the Battlemobile. "Who do you figure Wiley's visitor was?"

"I'd rather not say until I'm absolutely sure."

THE LUNCHEON WAS underway when I returned to the hotel, but in the interests of hygiene, I decided to shower before taking my place at the table. As I hurried along the corridor to my room, I noticed that breakfast trays had been left out to be picked up. Breakfast trays and a pair of shoes waiting to be shined. Brown loafers with tassels, they didn't look anything like footwear for the devil. But they reminded me of Nate's suggestion that Linette might have been referring to a particular style of shoe.

In my room I hauled out a local telephone directory. My fingers would have to do the walking. It was Sunday so I looked for stores in malls that were likely to be open. I struck out with the first couple of salespeople. I could tell they thought I was crazy to be asking such a thing. But then I found someone who was not only willing to give my question serious consideration, but provide an answer. Of course! Why hadn't I thought of it myself?

My elation at the discovery soon gave way to an awful sinking feeling. This wasn't what I had expected. But just because I'd observed one person wearing a particular brand of shoes didn't mean someone else hadn't worn them. Also, the shoes were only one piece of the puzzle. Without the other pieces, the picture would remain incomplete like the puzzle that, as a child, I'd spent an entire rainy day working on only to discover that important pieces were missing.

Yet what if, in this case, the finished picture was too terrible to behold? Maybe I should store what I'd already learned in some far compartment of my brain, where eventually I'd forget about it. Linette, the sole witness to the apparition in devil's shoes, was dead. The police and almost everyone believed Wiley had died of natural causes. They would go on believing this unless presented with compelling evidence to the contrary. *Don't do it, Miranda.* Even as I thought this, I knew I couldn't simply walk away. I had to put together the puzzle, whatever the cost.

With pen and notepad in hand, I let my mind range freely over everything that had happened since my arrival at the Washington airport for the first visit. My ex-husband had once called me a mental pack rat because of my tendency to retain large quantities of what he considered trivia—snippets of conversation, random observations, details of dress, meals, the weather. This capacity served me in good stead, enabling me to recall bits of information that had seemed unimportant at the time, but now became significant. I jotted these things down and made connections until a pattern began to emerge. I also thought about what I had learned about Felodipine from the Web site, and called a couple of pharmacies to ask a "what if" question.

Eventually I reached the point where I thought I knew the who, how, and why of Wiley's murder. But one thing was missing: the proverbial smoking gun, or rather the empty pill container.

In my mind, I put on devil's shoes and tried to retrace the steps those shoes had taken that morning. I imagined stealing through the dew-wet grass to the spot where Wiley lay with Linette, imagined opening the canteen and pouring in the deadly powder from the vial. The lid was tossed into the trees, but the vial re-pocketed for disposal later on. Then the wearer of the shoes had stood awhile beside their sleeping forms—having second thoughts? I wanted to give this person that moment of doubt and reconsideration because he was not a cold-blooded killer. It wasn't too late to undo what he had just done. He could still dump the canteen water onto the ground. But then Linette opened her eyes and saw the shoes. He hurried away.

As he was leaving, I saw him stop to toss the vial into a trash can. I went over the sequence again. And again and again. In various scenarios, he discarded the vial at different places, but the result was the same: the vial was long gone.

Throwing the vial into the trash was the obvious thing to do. Each time I reviewed his movements that morning I came up against this hard fact, hit this same wall over and over again.

This same wall. That was it! Unwittingly I had stumbled upon the answer. I knew then that he hadn't done the obvious thing, but something else, something so quixotic that if I hadn't actually seen him do it, it never would have occurred to me.

THIRTY

"Over the wall then, with bayonet, and on to the crest of the hill!"
R. E. Lee, A Biography

A TOUR GROUP OCCUPIED the area between the copse of trees and the stone wall, behind which Federal troops had aimed their deadly fire at Pickett's advancing men. I waited in the shade of the trees until they were gone. Where to begin? Placing him at the exact spot where he had stood that morning was impossible. I'd have to start with a section of the wall and examine it before moving on to another section. As best as I could remember, he'd been somewhere in the area opposite the copse of trees.

Pretending I was a surveyor, I walked a straight line from the far end of the trees to the wall. I knelt and began to examine the stones, running my hands along the breaks between them and poking my fingers into the gaps. Weeds sprouted from spaces between the stones. Over time, the stones had shifted, making a jumble out of what had once been a careful arrangement. I scraped my skin against the rough edges of the rocks. Whenever I stuck my finger into a hole, I worried about disturbing snakes, lizards, a hornet's nest, or a hill of angry ants.

The search went slowly. I could have used a pair of work gloves. A water bottle, too.

The morning sun had disappeared behind thunderheads, but the heat was as oppressive as before. Sweat dripped down my forehead into my eyes. I wiped it away with grubby hands. At least I wasn't trying to build this wall from scratch.

"It's against the law to remove Civil War relics from federally owned land," a voice intoned from above. A park ranger stared accusingly down at me.

"I'm not," I protested.

"Then what are you doing? You've been combing this wall for nearly a quarter of an hour. I've been watching."

I debated what to tell him. The truth, that I was searching for a medicine container I hoped would solve a murder, would sound preposterous. Better to lie. "I'm looking for an earring I lost the other day."

He frowned at my earlobes, pierced but unadorned.

"This isn't just any earring," I continued shamelessly. "It's a real pearl and belonged to my mother. It's one of the few things of hers I have left."

The ranger humphed and shifted his weight. "All right," he said finally, "but see that you don't take anything you shouldn't. The penalties for removing relics from Civil War battlefields are up to five years in prison and two hundred fifty thousand dollars in fines. I'll be keeping an eye on you." He moved off toward the trees. I didn't doubt he would keep an eye on me, might even ask me to empty my pockets before I left. But right now the important thing was to find the container.

I went on groping among the rocks. After a while, noise from the field ahead made me look up. Barely visible in the haze, a small group of gray-clad figures headed for the stone wall. Diehard reenactors performing Pickett's Charge yet another time. They were still too far away to interfere with my search. But as I watched them struggle across the field, it suddenly dawned on me why Wiley's killer had chosen this spot to stash the vial. He had deposited it here, the way others left flowers, tiny flags, and other objects at the various monuments throughout the military park. He must have felt a deep ambivalence about killing Wiley. And so he had left the vial to mark the place where Wiley might have fallen if, in real life, Wiley had taken part in Pickett's Charge. For him, it had been an act of atonement.

An ominous rumble roused me from these thoughts. Glancing upward, I saw a thunderhead bearing down on me like the hull of an immense tanker. I attacked the wall in a frenzy, clawing at rock, soil, and weed. Dirt blew into my face, temporarily blinding me. I blinked and rubbed my eyes. The reenactors in the field were getting closer. I could hear their shouts and cries.

A huge raindrop splatted on my head, then another and another. The deluge was beginning. Lightning blazed across the sky, followed by an ear-splitting clap of thunder. Time to run for cover. The next instant, a gray monster came flying over the wall at me with a god-awful yell.

The impact sent me sprawling. I lay in the grass, shaken and sore, while the rain beat down on me. "Are you all right, ma'am?" a voice asked gently. I peered up through sheets of water into the concerned, young face of a Confederate reenactor.

"No, dammit! You plowed right into me!"

"I'm awfully sorry, ma'am. When I saw the wall, all I could think about was how I had to jump over before the Yanks—"

"What Yanks?" I demanded. No Union soldiers occupied this area. They hadn't been here for more than one hundred and thirty years. I felt a spiteful urge to point this out to him, to shatter the illusion, as my own illusions had been shattered. *Give it up,* I wanted to tell him. *You guys lost the war a long time ago, and no amount of reenacting is going to change that.*

"I thought…" He glanced around. But whatever ghosts he'd seen had vanished. His expression turned wistful. I'd ruined the experience for him. He looked so disappointed, I felt sorry. Perhaps I could still make amends. "Look, over there!" I cried, gesturing toward the equestrian statue of the Union commander, General George Gordon Meade, on the other side of the copse of trees.

The reenactor's eyes lit up with excitement. "Yeah, give 'em hell!" Then, turning back to me, as to a fallen comrade, he asked, "Will you be okay?"

"Yes, go get 'em!"

He dashed off in the direction of the statue. I dragged myself back to the wall, taking care to avoid the other reenactors as they hurled themselves over. Rain lashed at me and at the wall. Water ran down the rocks like dirty tears. The spaces between the stones resembled gaping wounds. As I stuck my fingers into the muck, I felt like a Civil War surgeon trying to extract a bullet from a mess of blood and guts.

Trying and failing. Maybe Wiley's killer had second thoughts about leaving the vial here and had returned for it. Maybe a park ranger or a tourist had noticed the vial and discarded it. If it was still here at the wall, it was in a place I had overlooked and would never find in this downpour.

Wet, cold, my vision obscured by rain, and my upper body aching from the collision with the reenactor, I was ready to quit. Before I did, I scanned the section of wall before me one last time, using my hand as a visor. Lightning illuminated the landscape like a bursting rocket. In its lurid glare, I glimpsed a small orange crescent wedged between two stones.

THIRTY-ONE

"What was Lee to do in the face of such temper and antagonism?"
R. E. Lee, A Biography

THE LUNCHEON WAS OVER when I arrived back at the Gettysburg Hotel. To avoid notice, I ducked behind a pillar on the verandah while Randall and Ginny said good-bye to the last departing guests. A tall, gaunt man in a flashy sport shirt was pumping Randall's hand. He looked like an older version of Wiley—his father, an uncle? Randall was smiling, but I could see the strain in his face. A horn honked and a voice yelled, "C'mon, Pa!" With a final jerk on Randall's arm, "Pa" lurched down the steps into an ancient Cadillac convertible jam-packed with a boisterous crowd of adults, children, and dogs.

Randall and Ginny stood on the verandah, smiling and waving as the Caddy pulled away.

When the car was gone, Randall turned to Ginny. "I hope you won't mind my saying this, but I am relieved that this part of the day's activities is over. Now I know Bud Cross means well, but I do wish he would not tell that story about being attacked by a rabid raccoon every time I see him."

"He is a bit much," Ginny agreed. "But you were a perfect gentleman, as always."

"Civility is never amiss—even with *those* people."

"Come, Daddy, let's get some rest before the Bang," Ginny urged. They went back into the hotel.

FORTY-FIVE MINUTES LATER, I stood in front of the door to his room, showered, changed, and armed with the tiny microphone and mini tape recorder Mulinari had given me the night before. I was all set. Still, I hesitated. Last night I had done the unthinkable to Beau. But only because Mulinari had badgered me into it. This time the impetus had to come from within. This time the stakes were much higher, at least for me.

Newspaper rustled nearby. I glanced down the hall at the plainclothesman Mulinari had provided for backup after I told him what I was planning. He jerked his head impatiently at Randall's door. I tapped a finger at my temple to signal that he should remove his dark glasses if he didn't want to call attention to himself. He got the message and pocketed the glasses. Steeling myself for the assault, I knocked on the door.

I had roused him from a nap. Shoeless, his shirt unbuttoned at the collar, silver hair slightly mussed, dark eyes unfocused, he looked vulnerable, so much so that I almost lost my nerve and fled. It took all my will just to stand and face him.

"Miranda, my goodness!"

The sound of my name in his soft Tidewater accent gave me even more of a pang.

"Is it really you or am I dreaming? We have not seen a hide or a hair of you since this morning. Wherever have you been? Missy said you borrowed the keys to the Battlemobile, but when you didn't return for the luncheon, we were afraid some terrible misfortune had befallen you."

"I'm sorry. I should have telephoned when I realized I'd be delayed."

"Well, now, I do not mean this as a reproach, but I wish you had. Poor Virginia was beginning to feel that all her friends had abandoned her."

"Other people missed the luncheon?"

Randall nodded. "There was that nice lady from the United States Sanitary Commission, Miz Nutley, I believe her name is."

Evidently Mulinari hadn't wasted any time rounding up Dorcas and her brother. Good. Whatever qualms I still harbored about my role in exposing Beau, I had no regrets about them.

"Beau Johnston, too," Randall continued. "Apparently something important came up at the last minute. He won't be at Wiley's Bang, either. It is a pity because he was such a good friend of Wiley's. But at least he had the good manners to call and let us know."

"Yes. May I come in? I need to talk to you."

"Why, of course. But you must excuse me a moment. I was taking a nap when you knocked, so I will just step into the other room and freshen up a bit. Do make yourself comfortable." He motioned me to one of two armchairs positioned on either side of a low round table. I took a seat. After he returned from the bathroom, shirt buttoned and hair combed, Randall sat down opposite. "What would you like to talk to me about?"

Speak now or forever hold your peace. The old-fashioned wedding ceremony exhortation rang in my ears. "Linette Peters didn't commit suicide," I blurted. "She was murdered."

Randall raised his eyebrows. "Really now? What a shocking idea! What led you to this conclusion?"

"Something bothered me about her suicide, but I didn't realize what it was until I went to the Yingling Farm this morning."

"Ah. So that is where you were."

"Part of the time. While I was there, it came to me that if she'd wanted to kill herself, she wouldn't have done it that way."

"I am afraid you have lost me."

"She went there in the guise of a Civil War widow. The mosquitoes were ferocious, but she didn't bring bug spray because it would have been inauthentic. Vodka and sleeping pills are just as farbish. If she'd planned to take her life in a manner that was true to the period, she would have overdosed on laudanum—or the contemporary equivalent—slit her wrists, or shot herself. The vodka wasn't right for another reason: Linette didn't drink."

"Well, well. That is a most interesting theory," Randall remarked. As if the mention of alcohol had triggered an inner craving, he got up and went over to the minibar. "Can I offer you a drink?"

"No, thanks."

He poured bourbon into a glass and swirled it before imbibing. "As I was saying, it is an interesting theory. But considering that the poor woman had suffered a breakdown and was rather unstable, it seems more likely that she took her life."

"Ginny told you about Linette's breakdown?"

"She mentioned something to that effect."

"Last night?"

Randall didn't reply. His gaze had strayed to the *Wall Street Journal* lying on the table between us. A story must have caught his eye because he reached into his pocket for his reading glasses. His inattention annoyed me. I pushed the paper away. Randall looked at me with surprise, his half-open glasses dangling in midair like a broken wing.

"Did Ginny tell you about Linette's breakdown last night?" I repeated.

Randall re-pocketed his glasses. "She may have. Or perhaps it was this morning."

"Then she undoubtedly told you about other parts of our conversation—about the devil's shoes Linette said she saw, and the bad medicine found in Wiley's canteen."

Randall shrugged. "I honestly do not remember the details. Virginia indicated that Miz Peters said things she thought were utter nonsense, but that you seemed inclined to believe. Is that correct?"

"Yes. I believe Linette did see someone wearing devil's shoes, did discover bad medicine in Wiley's canteen. I also believe that's why she was killed."

Randall smiled faintly. "So now we are back to this notion of murder. You do amaze me, Miranda. I had no idea that behind the earnest history textbook author there lurks an aspiring fiction writer, given to remarkable flights of fantasy."

"I wish it were only fiction."

Randall rose and moved restlessly around the room, coming to a halt before the unmade bed. "I apologize for the disarray, but as you can see, the maid has not made up the room yet."

His shoes were on the floor by the bed. He gave them a little push so they were partially concealed. Then he pulled up the covers and plumped a pillow, arranging the bed, as he had tried to arrange the lives around him.

"How do you know it's not fiction? I mean, this business about devil's shoes and bad medicine reminds me of something out of a fairy tale." He reached for another pillow to plump.

"Part of it is from a fairy tale, or rather a famous German legend."

"So you agree. And what, pray tell, is this legend?"

"Faust and Mephistopheles. When Linette spoke of devil's shoes, she meant Mephistos—like the ones you just shoved under the bed."

Randall laughed. "Really, Miranda! The next thing I know, you will tell me I have sprouted horns and that this pen I hold in my hand," he picked up a ballpoint from the nightstand, "is in reality a pitchfork."

"You don't look like the devil, but you're not the person I thought."

My words registered in a slight flinch of his handsome features, but he let the comment pass. "Do you know what I think? I think you ought to lie down and have a little rest. You have been under a great strain lately, as we all have. But in your case, this strain has affected your mind. It has made you imagine the most incredible things. Now, be a good girl and do as I say." He patted the bed.

I felt a chill deeper than any that came from the air-conditioning. Was this how he had spoken to Linette last night, concern masking his murderous intent? I imagined him gently coaxing her to drink the lemonade he'd brought, lemonade spiked with vodka, because it was a hot night and she needed liquid refreshment. By the same token, he could have convinced her to take the sleeping pills because she was tired and needed to rest.

If I lay down on the bed now, would he try to persuade me to take the same pills? Or would he smother me with one of his perfectly plumped pillows? He was watching me and waiting.

"I'm fine where I am."

Randall shook his head. "You are, indeed, a strong-willed young lady, and rather like Virginia in that respect." He pulled the spread up over the bed, as he might have shrouded a corpse. Then he came and sat opposite me again. Giving his drink another swirl, he said, "Now that you have solved the mystery of the devil's shoes, what do you suppose that poor woman meant by 'bad medicine'?"

"Felodipine—that's what killed Wiley."

Randall put down his glass with a clatter. "Pardon me for saying so, but this is utter rubbish! Wiley died of a heart attack."

"A heart attack brought on by an overdose of Felodipine."

"Since when did you become such an authority on drugs?"

"Only recently, after the toxicology test done on Wiley revealed a high concentration of Felodipine. It's a drug used to treat high blood pressure. According to Wiley's doctor, Wiley didn't have high blood pressure."

"That poor boy had a host of ailments. He was always running to his doctor for a new prescription. He may have been taking that drug for some other reason," Randall suggested.

"No. Someone put Felodipine in Wiley's canteen water. Someone who had a prescription for it himself."

"I, myself, take several different medications for my heart condition, but Felodipine is not one of them. Here, you can see for yourself."

He went into the bathroom and returned with a leather toiletry case. Removing several orange plastic vials, he lined them up on the table between us like a salesman displaying his wares. After peering at the labels, I selected a vial of the medicine I had picked up at the pharmacy in Alexandria and handed it to him.

Randall stared at the label, then at me. "This is for Isordil, not—"

"Plendil?"

"What is that?"

"The brand name for Felodipine. You had a prescription for Plendil."

"I most certainly did not!"

"Recognize this?" I took the vial I'd found at the wall from my pocket and showed it to him. "The label's a little the worse for wear but still legible. It shows your name, your doctor's name, the name of the medicine, and a dosage of eighty milligrams a day—the same as for Isordil."

"So?"

"The maximum recommended dosage for Plendil is only ten milligrams a day. The pharmacist misread your doctor's handwriting. He gave you Plendil instead of Isordil, but at the dosage for Isordil. It would have killed you, if you hadn't caught the mistake in time."

"Give me that!"

He lunged at the vial. I jumped up and held it out of reach. Randall glared at me, his expression turning so ugly that he might have been Dr. Jekyll morphing into Mr. Hyde. Hell hath no fury like a control freak thwarted, I thought.

He recovered almost immediately, but the damage was done. He had revealed his true colors, shown me that beneath the courtly façade there lurked someone small and mean. He sat down again and motioned me to do likewise.

"So," he said, leaning back in his chair and crossing his legs, "you picked up one of my old medicine containers. Wherever did you find it?"

"In the stone wall at the Bloody Angle where you left it."

"*You* saw me?"

"Yes." Obviously, he didn't realize that when I was with him, little he did escaped my notice.

"Well, well, you are quite the observer, Miranda."

He regarded me curiously as if seeing me for the first time. I caught a glint of something I had craved all along, his admiration. After years of riding the merry-go-round, of reaching and missing, I had finally caught the proverbial brass ring. And discovered it was nothing more than that, a circle of worthless metal.

"This ability of yours will surely be an asset on our trip," Randall said.

"What trip?"

"The one the three of us are going to take—provided you agree. I did not want to mention it until after Wiley's service, but I might, as well. Now that you and Virginia have renewed your friendship, I thought we might take a longer vacation together. Someplace farther away. To Europe or Japan. I have friends in various embassies abroad who would bend over backwards to see that you ladies met the right people and thoroughly enjoyed yourselves. But please do not let financial considerations deter you. I would be more than happy to pay your way."

As he spoke, I was aware of the tug of invisible strings, but felt them the way one feels a limb that has been severed, as a faint tingling instead of a genuine connection. He had lost his hold over me—my prince who'd turned out to be a toad.

"You can't buy me off any more than you could Wiley," I declared indignantly.

Randall stiffened. "I do not have the foggiest idea what you are alluding to."

"You offered Wiley money to go away to South Carolina for the flag protest or some other place. You didn't care as long as he was out of the picture."

Randall shook his head. "I am still at a complete loss."

"Peg Yager's niece overheard Wiley and another man arguing about money when she came to the garage to drop off her car. From her description of this person's voice, I guessed it was you."

"Oh, *that*. Reenacting is an expensive hobby, and Wiley was short of funds. He approached me for a loan. Unfortunately, he had one figure in mind and I another. Hence our dispute."

"You were very generous. But Wiley did just the opposite of what you wanted. He came to Gettysburg and used your money on a crazy scheme to win Ginny back by having another reenactor shoot him in the leg."

Randall stood up and began to pace. "It was very naughty of Wiley to disobey me. Foolish, too. He should have realized that I would find out he didn't go where he was supposed to."

"You hired someone to follow him, didn't you? Another guest didn't borrow the Freeman biography the first night we were here—it was your private detective. He returned the book with a message that Wiley was in Gettysburg."

Randall stopped pacing to stare at me. "How did you figure that out?"

"Your private detective followed me the day I drove the Battlemobile to the garage. When I got lost, he showed me the way back to Alexandria."

"So Evans did a good deed, but not on my dime, I hope. This whole business has ended up costing far more than I bargained for."

"Is that why you killed Wiley—because he wouldn't stay away from Gettysburg?"

Randall came and stood behind my chair, his hands resting on its cushioned back, inches away from my neck and shoulders. Once I would have felt a thrill of pleasure at his nearness. Now I felt a thrill of a different sort. Fear raked the hairs at the back of my neck. Only my sense that he was on the verge of an admission kept me seated.

"He would not listen to me," Randall said quietly. "Neither would Virginia. In spite of all the pain and sorrow he caused her over the years, she still had a hard time letting go. Our second night in Gettysburg, she came to me in tears because she had discovered him in the arms of another woman."

So Ginny had confided in him—though not about Greg, it seemed. This didn't surprise me. She had looked to her father for comfort and support ever since her mother's death when she was twelve. Longer probably, I thought, remembering that it had been Randall rather than her mother who'd taken Ginny to her first swimming lesson. But in this particular instance, she had turned to her father with deadly consequences.

"The other woman was the last straw," Randall went on. "I realized then that drastic action was necessary to ensure Virginia's future happiness. And time was of the essence. Virginia does not know this, but according to my doctor, my heart could give out at any moment. I had to act while I still could, because once I was gone, there would be no stopping Wiley. He would go on hurting her for the rest of his life. I could not have that."

"*You* couldn't have that," I repeated, appalled by his arrogance. "What gave you the right to—"

"I did what was best for both of them," Randall interrupted. "Virginia needed to be free of him once and for all. And Wiley—"

"Needed to die?"

"It was what he wanted. Remember what he said in that letter to Virginia? How if he had died reenacting Pickett's Charge, he would have died happy. He talked about that a great deal. 'What's the point of being a hardcore reenactor,' he would say, 'when I'm missing the ultimate experience of dying in battle?'" Randall paused briefly before continuing. "*I* gave him that."

Glancing over my shoulder, I saw that his face wore the same triumphant-general look it had when the National Observation Tower was destroyed. Beau, I recalled, had also mentioned Wiley's calling death in battle the ultimate reenactor experience. But Beau hadn't used Wiley's words as a rationalization for murder. Again Randall's presumption astounded me.

"What about Linette?" I asked.

"Why, that pathetic little thing was just waiting to be put out of her misery."

As he said this, I was aware of a slight movement. His hands left their resting place on the back of the chair and hovered in the air behind me. I sprang up and spun around to face him.

"I can't believe this! You murdered two people, yet you have absolutely no sense of wrongdoing. All those years on the bench didn't teach you humility. They only strengthened your belief in your own godlike ability to pass judgment on everyone else. You're a monster!"

Randall's outstretched hands clenched. "I am not accustomed to being spoken to in such a manner. I believe you owe me an apology."

"I don't owe you anything. But you—how will you ever apologize to Ginny for what you've done?"

"You would actually tell her?"

It was his turn to be appalled. His shoulders slumped, and he lowered his hands to his sides like a rider dropping the reins. I almost felt sorry for him, but my sympathy was short-lived.

Drawing himself haughtily up again, Randall declared,

"Virginia will never believe you. No one will. You're nothing but a neurotic middle-aged woman with an overly active imagination."

"I think she and the police will when they hear the recording I made of our conversation."

I showed him the mini tape recorder I'd concealed in my pocket.

Randall glared at me. For a moment I half expected him to make a grab for the tape recorder as he had for the vial. Instead, he strode furiously to the bed. With his back to me, he gripped the edge of the night table with both hands, spluttering, "Outrageous... No right... Illegal... Never hold up in court."

"We'll see about that." I started for the door.

In one fluid movement, Randall reached into the table drawer, pivoted, and aimed his great-great-grandfather's pistol at me. "I think not," he said. "Now give me the tape recorder and the vial."

I froze.

"I would hate to shoot you, Miranda, but you must understand that I cannot very well let you walk out of here with incriminating evidence. So, be a good girl and hand the items over."

I stared frantically at the door. Where was my backup? "The police are already on to you," I said. "There's a plainclothesman waiting in the hall to arrest you."

"Oh, really?" Randall mocked, though not without a cautious glance at the door. "Then why hasn't he come in and introduced himself?"

Why indeed?

"No, my dear," he continued. "You may be clever, but you are not *that* clever. The tape recorder and the vial, please." He held out his free hand and moved closer.

"You shoot me, they'll catch you red-handed for sure," I said.

"I beg to differ. I will say your death was an accident—that I had no idea the gun was loaded when you asked to see it. Rather like an incident involving a Frenchman at Gettysburg a few years ago. He didn't know his pistol was loaded either when he fired at a fellow reenactor. He just missed hitting the man's jugular, I believe."

Instinctively, my fingers flew to my neck.

"But unlike him, I won't miss," Randall said. "Now give me

the tape recorder and the vial. I do not like to be kept waiting."
He cocked the pistol.

I stole a last glance at the door. It remained steadfastly
shut. "Catch!" I cried, lobbing the vial and tape recorder into
the air. While Randall was distracted by the flying objects, I
swung a leg outward, silently thanking an aerobics teacher I'd
once had who'd drilled the class in Radio City Music Hall
Rockette-style kicks. Randall yelped with pain as my shoe hit
his hand. The pistol clattered to the floor. We both dove for it
even as the door swung open and the plainclothesman burst
into the room, gun extended.

"I'll take that." He pointed at the pistol.

Randall rose slowly and handed it to the plainclothesman.
"This pistol belonged to my great-great-grandfather, a brigadier-general in the Army of Northern Virginia," he said stiffly.
"I was just showing it to Miz Lewis here when we were so rudely
interrupted."

"Right," the plainclothesman said. "Better come with me,
Mr. Longford."

Randall glanced quickly around, desperation in his dark eyes.
"Very well then," he said finally. "But first I hope you will allow
me a few minutes alone with my daughter. She lost her husband
recently. I am all she has left."

Was this a ploy that would enable him to escape? If so, he
wouldn't get far. The plainclothesman looked at me questioningly. I nodded in reply.

"Okay," the plainclothesman said. "But I'll be waiting right
outside."

Randall picked up the phone to call Ginny. I collected the
tape recorder and the vial and started for the door with the
plainclothesman.

"Goodbye, Miz Lewis," Randall called after me.

His chill formality cut me to the quick. I left the room without
a word. The plainclothesman followed, and the door shut behind
us with the whoosh and thud a heavy object makes when it falls
from on high.

"What happened?" I asked the plainclothesman in the hall. "Why didn't you barge in sooner?"

"Lost you for a bit there," he replied sheepishly. "Equipment malfunction."

THIRTY-TWO

"...many reenactors have a mystical bent toward the hobby. Ghost stories and supernatural events are discussed around the campfire."

Reliving the Civil War, A Reenactor's Handbook

BACK IN MY ROOM, the tough stance I'd adopted crumbled. My heart was banging against my chest so hard I thought it would burst through my rib cage. I collapsed into a chair and took a series of deep breaths to calm myself. Confronting Randall had been even worse than I'd anticipated. And it wasn't over yet. I still had to face Ginny, who would probably be furious at me for going after her father.

Ten minutes later, I heard the knock I'd been expecting. Bracing myself, I walked slowly toward the door. From the other side, Missy called, "Miranda, are you in there?"

I opened the door. "What is it?"

"Granddaddy's not feeling well, so Mom's going to stay behind with him for a bit. I wondered if you'd like to ride over to the farm with Mandy, Dylan, and me."

Apparently, Randall was using the excuse of ill health to postpone the inevitable. He couldn't stall forever, though. Sooner or later, the plainclothesman would take him away. When that happened, I'd rather not be around.

"Okay," I told Missy.

THE YINGLING FARM was shrouded in mist when we arrived in the Battlemobile. "Way cool," Dylan commented. "You didn't tell me there'd be special effects."

"This isn't a special effect," Missy informed him. "It's real mist created by this afternoon's thunderstorm."

Missy exchanged glances with her twin in the front seat. Evidently Dylan's insistence on seeing everything in cinematic terms was wearing thin.

Dylan opened the car door and got out. "Shit!"

"Now what?" Mandy asked.

"I just landed in a huge puddle. Better watch out. There's water everywhere."

The twins stepped out gingerly. They had donned Civil War-era dresses in honor of their father's commitment to reenacting, and now they lifted their long skirts as they picked their way along the sodden ground. I followed at a distance.

Dylan's remark about special effects was apt. In the mist, the farm resembled a smoking battlefield. When my toe encountered something hard, I caught my breath, imagining it was the limb of a fallen soldier. It turned out to be a fallen branch. But the arms that clamped around me from behind were real enough.

"Gotcha!" a voice crowed. I screamed. The arms let go. I spun around to face a tall, gaunt figure. "Sorry if I scared you," he said. "Thought you were Missy. Tall like her. Got red hair, too."

"I'm Miranda Lewis, a friend of Ginny's."

"Bud Cross, Wiley's dad. Pleased to meet you." He pumped my arm as he might have an old-fashioned water pump. He had pulled on Randall's arm this way, too. The scene of their parting on the hotel porch came back to me. Fortunately, Bud Cross was ignorant of Randall's contempt for him.

"Gin-gin and her daddy here yet?" he inquired.

"They should be along in a little while," I fibbed. "He wasn't feeling well after the luncheon."

"Too bad," Bud Cross said. "Outta sorts myself. Too much fancy food. Specially that fish in the Jell-O. Missy and Mandy around?"

"Up ahead." I gestured to where barely visible rows of gray metal chairs rose like a last line of defense thrown up by a desperate army.

Bud Cross squinted in that direction. "Better go have a word with 'em. Rest of the family's waiting in the car, wondering if the Bang's gonna happen. Weather kinda puts a damper on things, doncha think?" He ambled off to find the twins.

"Miranda?" a voice called. Peg and Affinity walked toward me, Chad trailing after them like an errant shadow. "What's happening? Where is everybody?" Peg demanded.

I repeated what I'd told Bud Cross about Ginny and Randall.

"I'll bet he's not well," Peg muttered. "The whole notion of the Bang probably sticks in his craw. Just hope Ginny doesn't get hung up on his account."

This time I didn't rush to his defense. Peg was probably right about the Bang sticking in Randall's craw. We continued on to the rows of chairs. "I don't know what to tell you," Missy was saying to Bud Cross as we approached. "Mom's not here yet, and I don't see Beau and the other reenactors."

"Beau's not coming," I volunteered.

Missy looked at me with surprise. "Why not?"

"Something important came up at the last minute."

"Gee, that's too bad," Missy said.

She'd feel a lot worse when she found out her grandfather wasn't coming. And Ginny might be too shaken by Randall's arrest to come, either.

Peg swiped a chair seat. "Soaking wet. Lucky I thought to bring towels." Handing a towel to her niece, she went to work drying the chairs.

"I wouldn't bother until we know—" Mandy began. She broke off as the plangent chords of the theme from the movie, *Gettysburg*, swelled from unseen speakers.

"Spooky," Bud Cross muttered.

Missy turned to him with a smile. "Guess that answers your question."

The music was like a Pied Piper. People left their cars and streamed toward us. Before long, a good-sized crowd of people and dogs, brought along by the Cross clan, had gathered. The music stopped as mysteriously as it had begun. In the silence I was aware of a faint noise. Chad was rubbing the plastic figure of a soldier against his palm.

An eerie cry pierced the stillness—the rebel yell from somewhere in the distance. The Cross dogs strained at their leashes and started barking. "Look, over there!" someone cried.

An arc of white light shimmered over the field—as beautiful and otherworldly as the music. "What's that?" people wondered aloud.

"This time, it's gotta be a special effect," Dylan muttered.

"No, it's… I think it's rainbow, but a white one," Missy said "Like I saw at the beach once. White rainbows are caused by the refraction of light in the fog."

As if on cue, a thin gray line emerged from the trees at the far end of the field and marched toward us, flags rippling in the breeze. They passed under the white rainbow. Then the mist lifted completely and the rainbow vanished, replaced by the dazzlingly spectacle of sunlight glittering on billions of blades of wet grass.

The soldiers came to a halt several yards away. One stepped forward. For a moment, I thought I glimpsed Beau. But my eyes had played a trick on me; it was Paul Newberger instead.

Missy went over to Paul and explained about her mother and Randall. I wondered how long they'd wait until it became obvious that Randall and Ginny weren't coming. Others must be wondering the same thing. Around me, people shifted restlessly and glanced over their shoulders.

"There she is!" Bud Cross shouted, as a figure all in black came streaking toward us. Ginny ran through the crowd of spectators into Paul's outstretched arms. When he released her, she turned to the rest of us and said breathlessly, "Sorry I'm late. Daddy wasn't feeling well, and I didn't want to leave him. I kept hoping that if he rested a few more minutes, he could come. Finally I just had to up and go. As I told Daddy, Wiley was everything to me. I wouldn't miss his Bang for the world."

Was this her way of saving face, or did she honestly not know about her father's imminent arrest? Either way, her declaration that Wiley was everything to her could only have hurt Randall deeply. He'd tried to keep Ginny from marrying Wiley; then after their elopement, he'd done everything in his power to tear them apart, ultimately resorting to murder. But now here was Ginny choosing Wiley over him yet again. It must have seemed like a final betrayal.

"If ever there was a man who believed in doing things his own way, it was Wiley," Ginny addressed the crowd. "Sometimes that made it hard for those close to him. I even used to joke that he was my 'cross' to bear. But I never stopped loving him." Ginny's voice quavered, her body swayed slightly. Paul extended a supporting hand.

Regaining her composure, Ginny continued, "As most of you know, reenacting was very important to Wiley. His role in the movie, *Gettysburg*, was a highpoint for him. He said that if he had died at that moment, he would've died happy. But he wasn't ready to leave us then. I don't think he was ready this time, either. At least he went out doing what he loved, reenacting Pickett's Charge.

"An individualist to the end, he didn't want an ordinary funeral, but the send-off we're about to give him. Dearest Wiley, we commit you not to the earth, which could never contain you, but to the ether. As Daddy used to say, the sky's the limit. May your spirit soar, free at last!"

Ginny nodded at Paul, who signaled to the other reenactors. As one, they swiveled sideways so that they were facing the direction in which Wiley had fallen during the reenactment of Pickett's Charge. They raised their rifles, the tips bristling against the sky.

"Ready. Aim. Fire!" Paul shouted. The guns boomed. Clouds of smoke erupted into the air. The explosion prompted a show of support from the Cross clan. "Atta, Boy!" "Go, Wile!" they yelled, tossing their hats into the air. The rest of us watched in silence. Dust to dust, ashes to ashes.

Images flashed through my mind. They weren't of Wiley, but of Randall—Randall as he had appeared to me that summer when I was nineteen. A small hard lump of loss formed in my throat. My vision blurred with tears. I wiped them away. The clouds of smoke dispersed, except for one gray smudge that lingered like an aerial postscript. Then it, too, vanished.

EPILOGUE

"The Civil War had many causes, and people had lives before the war began. Show not only the military side, but also the human side of the period."
　　　　　Reliving the Civil War, A Reenactor's Handbook

THE SHUTTLE WASN'T CROWDED. I had no bothersome seatmate, as on the flight to Washington for the Fourth of July weekend that, now, seemed like such a long time ago. I welcomed the solitude.

I'd left immediately after the funeral. The service had been high Episcopalian, with incense, beautiful flowers, and ethereal music provided by the organist and a boys' choir.

The priest had delivered a lengthy eulogy, and family and friends had offered many moving tributes to Randall. There had been no mention of his suicide by an overdose of heart medication. Or the fact that he had killed two people.

Mulinari and the local police had agreed with me to keep this last from Ginny for the time being. Having lost the two men dearest to her, she had, I felt, enough on her plate without finding out her father had murdered her husband.

Let Ginny and her daughters remember him as a good man rather than a manipulative murderer awhile longer. She'd been so distraught when, returning from the Bang, she'd found his room filled with medics and police and Randall lying there dead. He had left a note. He wrote that, foreseeing a protracted battle with heart disease, he had decided to end it all now. He didn't want Ginny to have to worry about him any more, didn't want to be a burden to her. I saw no reason to complicate Ginny's grief by revealing the cowardice that lay behind Randall's apparent selflessness just now.

My thoughts drifted from Randall to two others who'd figured prominently in the events of the past few weeks. From Mulinari I knew that Beau had been granted immunity from prosecution in exchange for testifying against his former associates in the gunrunning ring.

I also knew that Jake was out of the ICU and on the mend, though he faced a long and difficult recovery. I was glad for both of them.

A flight attendant brought me my complimentary beverage and snack, Sprite and a packet of peanuts. Right now, at Randall's house, they were drinking champagne, eating catered canapés, and sharing fond memories of him. I half wished I were there. But knowing what I did, how could I have joined in? Better to be here on this plane in transit between two cities, between the recent past and the immediate future.

Nate was meeting me at the airport. Beyond that, I didn't know what lay in store for me, wasn't even sure how I felt about seeing him again.

My mind circled back to Randall. Part of me still wanted to believe in the "old" Randall—the man I had known when I was nineteen. But how could I when this image clashed so violently with my current view of him? Was it possible to keep both without one canceling out the other? Maybe I could hold on to the old image if it remained blurry and vague as a barely remembered dream. Maybe…

"We'll be landing in Boston in ten minutes," the pilot announced over the PA system.

I fastened my seat belt, folded up my tray table, and secured my carry-on luggage. Then I leaned back in my seat, bracing myself for the moment when the wheels hit the tarmac and I would be thrust out of limbo into ordinary time.